Time at the Zenith

MAELYN BJORK

BOOKSIDE Press

Time at the Zenith © 2022 Maelyn Bjork

All rights reserved. No part of this publication may be reproduced, distributed, or transmitted in any form or by any means, including photocopying, recording, or other electronic or mechanical methods, without the prior written permission of the publisher, except in the case brief quotations embodied in critical reviews and other noncommercial uses permitted by copyright law.

ISBN:
Paperback   978-1-998784-26-4

The views expressed in this book are solely those of the author and do not necessarily reflect the views of the publisher, and the publisher hereby disclaims any responsibility for them.

BookSide Press
877-741-8091
www.booksidepress.com
orders@booksidepress.com

CONTENTS

DEDICATION 1
CHAPTER 1 2
CHAPTER 2 3
CHAPTER 3 7
CHAPTER 4 12
CHAPTER 5 17
CHAPTER 6 22
CHAPTER 7 28
CHAPTER 8 34
CHAPTER 9 39
CHAPTER 10 45
CHAPTER 11 51
CHAPTER 12 57
CHAPTER 13 63
CHAPTER 14 69
CHAPTER 15 74
CHAPTER 16 80
CHAPTER 17 86
CHAPTER 18 91
CHAPTER 19 96
CHAPTER 20 102
CHAPTER 21 108
CHAPTER 22 115
CHAPTER 23 121
CHAPTER 24 127
CHAPTER 25 133
CHAPTER 26 140
CHAPTER 27 145
CHAPTER 28 151
CHAPTER 29 157
CHAPTER 30 164

CHAPTER 31 170
CHAPTER 32 176
CHAPTER 33 183
CHAPTER 34 189
CHAPTER 35 195
CHAPTER 36 201
CHAPTER 37 207
CHAPTER 38 213
CHAPTER 39 219
CHAPTER 40 224

DEDICATION

This book is dedicated to two very special people in my life. First, to my son Chad West. He always seemed to have a sense of the paranormal. His life was cut short on August 13, 2012. He lived forty years. I also dedicate this book to my friend and special critique partner Doree Anderson.

CHAPTER 1

The merciless sun beat down on the city that mid-July day. No breeze stirred the leaves on the trees; nothing moved. All creatures now were waiting for the setting sun and the relative coolness that evening would bring.

The small house on Victor Street sat silent; no living thing stirred about the structure or yard. In the attic of the house, where the temperature registered above 140 degrees Fahrenheit, an entity flowed across the attic floor, sucking up the heat, taking vigil at the east window, watching and waiting. Could another tragedy take place in the house, another cause of death, another fatal accident? Yet to some, that same danger could be used for economic gain.

The entity flowed through the attic ceiling to the basement below. This was the where the danger could happen. At a precise time, the vortex would open. The innocent or uninformed would find despair. Here at the southeast corner, the entity spread its formless energy and waited.

The grandfather clock ticked and measured the time moving forward. Now the danger passed until the next time.

CHAPTER 2

Two hours later, a late-model midsize sedan slowly eased down a driveway to the rear of the house into a freestanding garage. A young woman exited the garage carrying a suitcase, a briefcase, and a large purse. Despite the heat, she was dressed in a business suit and, with quickness, hurried up the three steps to the south entrance of the house.

As Ana Lea Andreasen walked into the house, she realized the interior was stifling. Immediately, she dropped her burdens and went to the hallway and switched on the evaporative cooler.

Ana Lea was on a tight schedule, because in less than two hours, she was to host an important event that evening, a banquet scheduled in downtown Salt Lake City.

She dragged her heavy suitcase into the front bedroom and threw it on the bed. Immediately, she shed her clothes. Since she was hot and miserable, a cool shower was first on her agenda. After washing her hair and scrubbing off the travel grime, she stayed in the shower almost too long.

Wrapped in a towel, she went to the kitchen for a drink and found a can of soda. She poured it into a glass with ice and took it back into the bathroom. There, she worked on her hair and makeup, and soon, she stood viewing herself in her full-length mirror in the bedroom. She checked her image and carefully examined the red, off-one-shoulder, floor-length ball gown to be satisfactory. She had styled her long, dark hair up into a careless-looking twist. Next, she slipped her feet into matching red sandals, and her only accessories were a gold wristwatch and large gold dangle earrings. Now ready, she picked up a beaded bag and her briefcase and hurried to the south entrance of the house.

This time, she eased down her south porch steps and carefully stepped to the ground, for there had been times when she had caught a hem of long slacks or a long shirt with the heel of a shoe and had a minor mishap.

As Ana Lea drove away from her little house, she sighed with relief. It was so good to be home again, to return that evening, and to sleep in her own bed.

She had owned the house for three years and recently remodeled the front bedroom, bathroom, and kitchen. The house was located in Sugar House, one of the oldest suburbs of Salt Lake City, Utah.

Feeling slightly nervous yet confident, she practiced the speech she would give even while driving to her destination. Taking charge was one of Ana Lea's assets. It was time to let the Wright brothers know she was worth the salary they were paying her.

As she walked into the ballroom of the Marriott Hotel, she was greeted by Jacob Wright's wife, Joanna. "My, you look beautiful! I love the one-shoulder-bare-but-covered look. I knew how tight your schedule was, and here you are, lovely and ready to go. When did you finally get in?"

"About two thirty. I should have taken a taxi rather than parked my car in that outdoor 'oven' called long-term parking. It was a long, hot walk from the terminal."

Ana Lea studied Joanna. "You don't look too shabby yourself. That's a great color for your blond hair and blue eyes." She gave her friend a wide smile.

Joanna smoothed her long peach brocade dress. "I don't have your curves, but these long straight skirts with double slits are fun to wear. Here are some place cards." She handed Ana Lea a stack of large cards. "Put them on the tables on the south side of the room. It's the last of the cards, so I think we're about ready for our guests."

As Ana Lea placed the cards on the white cloth-covered tables, she took notice of the crystal goblets and fresh flowers on each round table. There were hundreds of guests expected. Those invited were the "movers" and "shakers" of the state.

A large banner hung behind the head table. It read "The Make It Wright Foundation." This organization was the brainchild of Joshua Wright, NFL quarterback for the Los Angeles Aces football team.

It took Jacob Wright, Joshua's brother, an ophthalmologist living in Columbus, Ohio, and his wife, Joanna, to set up the organization. The money raised would help abused and homeless women and their children who did not qualify for welfare, Medicaid, or certain types of job training.

Joshua Wright came striding across the ballroom, his strong, athletic body doing justice to his black tux and snowy white pleated shirt. "Well, are you ready to hostess this shindig?" he said to Ana Lea with a grin.

"Of course, if you're sure Nichole would rather sit this one out?" She laughed.

"Nichole does not enjoy standing on her feet so much anymore, too much weight out front." He gestured with his hand out front of his midsection. "The heat is bothering her too." He shrugged but smiled. "I suppose she'd rather sit than stand, at least until the baby is born. I just want her and the infant to be healthy."

Quietly, Nichole walked over to them. "Josh, we need a decision about the lectern. Oh, hi, Ana Lea. Wow, you are stunning in that dress. Aren't you glad we went shopping together?"

"And you are radiant. Is that what pregnancy does for a girl?" Ana Lea commented.

Nichole laughed. "I suppose that's all you can say to a woman who is beginning to resemble a beached whale. The sunny glow came from sitting by Joshua's pool while planning this charity party. Joanna and I had three lovely days in the sun. Oh, by the way, you have a place at the head table." Nichole turned, and her long sun-streaked hair swayed as she walked.

Soon, the ballroom began to fill with guests. Everyone had been invited from the governor to those in Congress, the mayor, coaches, and players from the athletic teams of the five major universities, as well as the NBA basketball team. There were also health professionals, those particularly sensitive to homeless women, children, and their plight.

Ana Lea stood at the lectern and invited everyone to stand while Jacob said grace. Dinner was served, and during the dessert course, Nichole was the first to speak. She spoke of dealing with and teaching children and students at a shelter school. She described the struggles of their families.

Joshua spoke next. He spoke of his experience with a friend he had known in graduate school.

"Years later, two days before Christmas, this girl knocked on the door of my house in Brentwood. She was bruised, beaten, and clinging to her were two small children. She and her children had left their home with just the clothes on their backs. Even though this woman had a law degree, she still had become a victim of spousal abuse."

He went on to tell how he helped her and her children have a Christmas. He realized then that even an intelligent, well-educated woman and her children could become victims of abuse.

"As I viewed how they had suffered, the germ of this foundation formed in my heart."

Across the room, Dr. Raymond Rossiter and his wife, Lorrie, sat listening to the speeches. Ray had brought along a first-year surgical resident, Clark Knowles, a medical school graduate from Boston University.

Clark had applied at University Medical Hospital for a residency in Salt Lake because of its medical reputation. But also high on his list were the fine numerous recreational activities available in the state of Utah. He enjoyed participating in several sports that Utah offered. Because he was single, Clark had also heard that the Intermountain West offered a great place to find pretty, well-educated girls to date.

After the speeches, Ana Lea announced to the audience that they were ready for the silent auction. Many generous sponsors had donated. There was a lineup of generous gifts and other attractions. She encouraged people in the audience to put in bids on the prizes laid on tables out in the hallway. "Please go out and take a look. There is everything from ski passes to weekend vacations, also some great sportswear."

CHAPTER 3

Soon, Ana Lea began circulating around the room, speaking to as many groups of people as she could, describing the foundation and the various ways guests could donate to the charity.

As she glided around the large hall, she noticed Joshua talking and laughing with a tall blond man she had not seen before. He seemed to be about Joshua's age, and the way he moved, he projected strength and athleticism. She decided to find out just who he was.

As she approached the two men, she noticed this blond man was also quite attractive. "Joshua, who is this long-lost friend of yours?"

Josh turned and grinned down at Ana Lea. "This guy taught me how to throw a football, at least he showed me and made worthwhile suggestions. They really helped me, a 'southpaw,' to throw straight. This is Mitch Kenyon. He quarterbacked the U team two years before I made the 'slot.'"

"I don't remember ..." Ana Lea said.

"You were probably in junior high when I played at the U." Mitch gazed at Ana Lea.

"This guy actually gave up football for baseball. Can you believe that?" Joshua laughed.

"What Josh here is trying to tell you is that I play baseball for a major league team in New Jersey." Mitch grinned.

"So you gave up football for baseball? Does your team play around here locally?" she asked.

"No. My team had a game in San Francisco yesterday. I heard about this party and flew in this morning. Besides, my wife and I own a condo in Deer Valley, and I decided to check on it before returning to New York."

"Yeah, this guy is putting me to shame. He met his lady, they got married, and now they have a baby girl. All this happened in the blink of an eye." Joshua laughed.

"Not quite that fast, but my life changed pretty quickly for the better. Look at you, Josh. You've been married how long?"

Joshua shrugged. "We got married Christmas week last year, and our baby is due in November."

"Seems to me both of you are 'novices' in the family-man department. But I believe you'll both do just fine." Ana Lea laughed and walked to another group she wanted to greet.

Clark Knowles turned to his mentor and asked. "Ray, do you know this Ana Lea Andreasen?"

"Yes, quite well," Ray answered.

"Tell me about her."

Ray sat back in his chair, and with a bland smile, he said, "What do you want to know?"

"Come on, Ray, the facts. Is she married, engaged, involved in a heavy relationship? How did she manage to land this upper management position?" Clark narrowed his eyes as he appraised her, and he felt his heart beat a little faster. "She moves and behaves with such confidence and sophistication. Yet she doesn't seem to be that old, and she *is* beautiful."

"Aren't beautiful women allowed to be confident and in charge?" Ray grinned. "She's a smart cookie. She was a stockbroker for a large firm. I was one of her clients, and she made me some money. When the mini-crash happened, she worked somewhere else. At any rate, the Wright brothers are fortunate to have found her."

"So what about her love life?"

"As far as her personal life is concerned, I cannot think of anyone she has been linked with for several years."

"Will you introduce me?"

Ray shrugged. "I suppose I could. Yes, I'll do that for a number of reasons. One, she's quite athletic, and, two, the both of you just might hit it off." Ray raised an eyebrow. Ray turned to his wife, Lorrie. "Babe, is there anything out there you'd like to buy for me or make a bid on for both of us?

As she stood, she touched his shoulder. "You seriously want me to go spend some of your money? I can do that—in fact, I'd love to." She kissed his cheek, patted her short blond bob, and walked out into the hallway. There at the tables, the items in the silent auction were displayed.

A half hour later, Ana Lea again took to the podium and announced the winners of some the various items in the auction. After the laughs and applause, most of the guests seemed to move into groups together for casual talk. She again walked around chatting with as many informal gatherings as possible.

She had seen Carlson Kittredge come into the room. He had brought his wife, Melanie. She knew he played for the Aces. He was the star running back, teaming up with the Joshua's superb quarterbacking. It had been so many years since she had seen him. The last time had been during the darkest period of her life. Now he and Joshua were strolling across the room straight toward her. Kitt was still impressive, at least six feet five, handsome, hair just as blond as it been when he was in college.

From another direction walked Ray and Clark. They were also working their way toward Ana Lea.

The man standing next to her had mentioned something to her, but her attention was on Kitt and Joshua. She had enough presence of mind to smile and nod her head at the man. Yet she had no idea what he had said to her.

They're only one table away. What will I say to Kitt? She could feel her heart beating a nervous tattoo. Automatically, she stepped back to make room for the two big men approaching her. As she moved, she caught the high heel of her red sandal on a corner of the linen tablecloth. Her narrow skirt did not allow enough movement of her leg near the slit in her dress, and she lost her balance. She slid down the cloth and smacked her head on the edge of the table.

Lying on the floor, she gazed up to see the two football men, but slowly, their faces faded away and became a dark blur, as did the rest of the room.

Kitt knelt down and reached to lift her up. "Keep her flat," Joshua ordered. "Remember our first aid training? She could have a head or neck injury."

"You're right. I'll be careful." He gently felt her neck for a pulse.

Ray and Clark reached her. "We're doctors," Ray said. "Let us take a look at her." While Clark knelt down to check her vital signs, Ray whipped out his cell phone and called for an ambulance. "She needs hospitalization. She could possibly have suffered a concussion."

Through half-open eyes, Ana Lea could see bright lights. *Head hurts.* She closed her eyes against the light. She seemed to be moving. *Dizzy. Where am I going?* Now she could feel the movement, and she gripped the sides of whatever she was lying on. *Narrow, like a bunk or cot.* The movement stopped, and she heard voices, words spoken in a clipped unemotional manner.

"More than likely a concussion. I don't like the fact that she has been unconscious for so long." She heard a male voice, deep and clear and somehow comforting.

The bed she lay on moved again but soon stopped. A drape or curtain brushed against her bare arm. She blinked, more lights, and she closed her eyes against the brightness. A cool cloth touched her forehead. "Ana Lea, can you hear me?"

"Um, yes … I can." She could think of words much faster than she could say them. A damp cloth moistened her face and neck. "Head hurts … Light hurts." She raised her hand, but it dropped against her face.

"Let's get her to radiology, an MRI. See Narrow, like a bunk or cot. the extent of her injury." His voice was masculine and familiar, but she couldn't put a name to it. She wanted to see who was talking, and she tried to push herself up.

"Stay down. We're taking you to X-ray." This voice was feminine.

The gurney began to move, and the dizziness subsided somewhat. She opened her eyes to see large gray elevator doors. After a short ride in the elevator, her rolling bed was pushed down a long hallway, and she could see wide double doors. *This must be radiology.*

She was helped out of her clothes and helped into a hospital gown.

Then she was thrust into a white tunnel, and after that, she was taken to a room. The lights were lowered, and the nurse left through a swinging door. The sounds outside the door caught her attention. She could hear movement on a hard floor and soft conversation. She settled into the bed, found a comfortable position, and slept.

CHAPTER 4

Early the next morning, she was helped to the bathroom by a medical aide, and soon, Ana Lea's breakfast arrived. Nothing looked very appetizing. She drank some decaffeinated coffee and nibbled on a slice of toasted white bread. She considered white bread not worth the calories it provided.

Through the swinging door came a young doctor. The name tag on his white coat read "C. Knowles, MD." "Good morning, Ms. Andreasen. How are you feeling this morning?"

He carried a chart. Obviously, he was in charge of her care. He introduced himself and seemed very professional. He looked familiar. Possibly she had met him at the banquet. When she was brought into the hospital, his voice was the one she had heard the night before.

"Other than suffering with a mean headache, I think I'm OK." She wiggled her fingers at him.

"I'd like to check your vision." He came close to her, and with a lighted instrument, he peered into her left eye and then the right one. When he moved back, he asked her to follow the light up and down and then sideways.

She executed the exercises well, and as she did, she noticed his eyes. They were an intense blue. No, on second perusal, they were blue green. His eyes were the most incredible shade of blue she had ever seen. They made her think of a sunlit ocean. Those eyes were set in a face of regular features. His skin, which could be fair in winter, was nicely tanned now. He had a fairly prominent straight nose and full mouth. His hair was dark, possibly curly, but cut very short. He was somewhat taller-than-average height, a few inches taller than she was. The physique under that white coat hinted strength, and his shoulders were broad.

He stepped back, smiling. "You did suffer a concussion. That fall last night gave your brain quite a bounce. The MRI showed some swelling, but it will subside in time. I'd like to come back later and check on how well you can walk, your balance, your short-term memory."

"You mean I can't go home?" She stared at him but then frowned.

Frowning hurt her tender head, and she placed her hand on it.

"That depends on your circumstances. Do you have someone who could stay with you tonight?" he asked.

"Hmmm." She tried to think and, at that moment, drew a blank. "Not anybody I can think of right now." She felt a deep frown and slid down into the bed.

"Then I think we'll keep you another day, just for observation." Did she see a slight smile?

"I'd like to take a shower and get some things from my house. I just can't walk out of here tomorrow in a red silk ball gown." She grumped.

"I believe Dr. Wright and his wife are taking care of that. They have permission to come visit you later this morning."

"Good. Joanna will know what I need."

Dr. Knowles moved to the swinging door of her room. "I'll check on you later. Oh, by the way, what's my name?"

"Why? Dr. C. Knowles. It says it on your nameplate."

"Drat. I wanted to test your short-term memory." He flashed a wicked grin.

"See you later." He swung out the door.

All morning, Ana Lea had visitors. First to come were Jacob and Joanna Wright. They brought a bag of clothes and cosmetics. Joanna had gone into her house and picked up what she needed and placed them in an overnight bag. "Here." Joanna set her overnight bag in the closet. She also handed Ana lea a small white sack. "I found your evening bag, and I left your briefcase in your house."

"Thank you so much for bringing me these things. How did you get in to see me? I know there are privacy laws now to restrict visitors."

"Doctors have their ways, and I also told them I was your employer." Jacob laughed. "We're just happy that your injuries are not more serious. We'll come and check you out tomorrow. We changed our return flight to Columbus tomorrow to one late afternoon. We need to get back to the kids and my practice."

"Since you're all settled in here for today, we've already made some appointments for this afternoon. We'll be seeing you tomorrow around eleven. Rest while you have a chance."

Jacob touched his wife's shoulder and guided her to the door with a gentle hand on her elbow. It was such a loving gesture it made Ana Lea inwardly wince. She had a pang of sadness for her own empty existence. Most of the time, living alone did not bother her, but now, because she was in a hospital, with no relative to visit her, she felt bereft. Her parents had moved to Tucson several years ago, but right now, she wished she could see her mother.

Her next visitors came as a shock to her. Joshua and Kitt walked into her room. Kitt still had the ability to raise her heart rate even though she had not been face-to-face with him for nearly ten years. The fact that he was married had not slipped her mind. He still possessed an infectious smile that lit up the room. His blond hair, tanned skin, and eyes of cornflower blue made him so sexy. He stood six feet five and had the physique of a star athlete, which he was.

"How did you get in here, Kitt? Did you tell them at the front desk that you were my brother?" She grinned back at him.

"No. I'm in the hospital for tests. Once you're in here, it isn't hard to move around and go where you choose."

"What kinds of tests?" She watched his face darken. "Oops, I suppose I shouldn't have asked."

"Hey, we didn't get a chance to talk last night. How are you doing anyway? Joshua mentioned that you are doing a great job with the foundation." He touched her leg lying under the blanket. A seemingly friendly gesture, but his hand lingered there too long. The warmth from his hand was pleasant but disturbing.

Ana Lea tried for a casualness she did not feel. "I'm going to be just fine, even better when they let me out of here tomorrow." She smiled up at the two big men. "Where are your wives?"

"Somewhere in the hospital. We're meeting them for lunch." Joshua gave her a friendly smile.

"So when do you two report for training camp?" She changed the subject. "We have to be there Saturday. Sad for us all, we must go back to work, earn our keep, support our wives, and soon, Josh will have a baby to worry about." Kitt shot a teasing glance at his friend.

"I know it will be a struggle on the paltry salaries you two earn, but we all must sacrifice," she said and laughed.

"Of course, he has house payments to make as well car payments and mortgages on his apartment buildings. His responsibilities are heavy." Kitt gave a sidelong glance at Joshua but then clapped him on his back.

"However, buddy, I think you'll manage to stay out of the welfare lines."

"I don't see you in the line for a free meal at the local mission either, Kitt." Joshua grinned.

Ana Lea smiled up at these two friendly giants and thoroughly enjoyed their repartee. She had become very fond of Joshua while working for him. At times, he could be as grumpy and ill-tempered as many man alive, yet since marrying Nichole, he seemed to be at a much more even keel. More often than not, he had become much more reasonable to have as a boss.

Ana Lea's relationship with Kitt was totally different. It started out as a college girl crush. Up until the evening before, she had nearly forgotten him. Seeing him again reminded her of a sad, bleak period in her life. Her tough, no-nonsense persona she knew was a thin veneer, easily cracked. The shy, uneasy, sometimes tormented girl lay just underneath.

The guys said their good-byes, and she was left alone for a time. Her head ached, and yet she was sleepy. She pressed the call button and asked for a pain pill.

A few minutes later, a nurse came bustling in. "I'm sorry, Ana Lea, but you are only allowed to take Tylenol. With a head injury like yours, the doctor would not recommend narcotics. However, I have two pills for you now." Ms. Miller handed her patient a small paper cup with two pills in it. She poured some water from the carafe by her bed.

Ana Lea frowned at the nurse but took the pills along with some water. "Thanks … anyway," she said as the nurse left the room. Snuggled into the bed, she managed a short nap. A soft knock on her door roused her.

In walked Melanie Kittredge and Nichole Wright. "Sorry we woke you. Melanie wanted to meet you before we left the hospital. We also wanted to thank you for the great event you put together last night."

Melanie came near the bed and put out her hand to Ana Lea. "I only know you by reputation, but you've done a marvelous job of forwarding the goals of the foundation. I'm impressed." Melanie had dark hair, fair skin, and a toned athletic body. Smiling, she dropped into one of the chairs near the bed.

"What have you two been up to?" Ana Lea asked.

Melanie glanced at Nichole uncertainly. "Kitt and I had medical appointments of our own. So did Nichole." The girl took a deep breath. "I've been to the infertility clinic. Kitt and I have been married four years, and we would really like to start a family. It doesn't seem to be happening—a pregnancy, I mean." The words came out in a rush.

"When I found out we were coming here to Salt Lake, I made appointments for Kitt and me. Amazingly, I managed to get him in for a physical. If the tests find something is really wrong, I think I'll be able to deal with the situation. But for Kitt, fathering a child is such a macho thing. So we came here to see the experts."

"I'm sure they'll find out everything is just fine. They'll probably tell you to take your temperature and the two of you to go somewhere romantic for a long weekend," Nichole said.

"Now, there sits Nichole, married to Josh seven months, and she is going on six months pregnant. I'm so envious." Melanie smiled, but Ana Lea detected pain in her eyes. "Of course, some of that could be because he wasn't playing football when he and Nichole married. She had *all* his attention."

Nichole's cheeks colored. "That too, and I'm not complaining."

CHAPTER 5

The door swung open, and in came a medical assistant carrying in Ana Lea's lunch.

"Here's your lunch, and since we've already eaten, we'd better go find the guys. We're flying back tomorrow. So we'll see you in a few weeks." Nichole came to Ana Lea's bed and pressed her cheek to her friend's. See you soon."

"I do thank you for coming to bid me adieu. I will be coming to Los Angeles to coordinate funding for the first educational center. I'll see you then." Ana Lea winced but smiled through a stab of pain in the back of her head.

"Of course, you'll see us because you'll be staying at our house. Now, is there anything we can do for you?" Nichole asked.

"No, I don't think so. Joanne and Jake came by earlier and brought me some necessities. I should be released tomorrow. Have a good flight. Thanks for stopping by."

As Ana Lea picked at her lunch, she chastised herself. *Get a grip, girl. You can't be wishing for a baby with no prospective man in your life. Now you have met Melanie, and you find she has her troubles too. Quit being jealous of Nichole. You know she'll be thirty-four when her baby comes. She had her share of lonely years before meeting Josh. Look at the bright side, girl.*

You have a great career, a car that is paid for, a house, and closetful of classy clothes. Stop feeling sorry for yourself.

The self-talk did not stop the tears from seeping from under her lashes or stop her nose from dripping. She hugged one of the pillows and cried a little. Crying made her eyes burn, so she fell asleep. She slept through her supper until a nurse came in and awakened her.

"Ana Lea, can you hear me?" She blinked open to see a different nurse.

"You've been asleep for quite a while. Let's get you up to the bathroom."

Ana Lea stared at her. "You're a different nurse. Did the shift change?" She stared at the young woman's ID. She read "T. Johansson."

"Yes." T. Johansson smiled. "I'm filling in for a friend. She had a wedding reception to attend."

"Where do you usually work?" Ana Lea asked.

"In the Pediatrics Department. I'll be here until eleven. I'll help you up." Ana Lea washed her face and hands, brushed her teeth, and changed into one of her own nightgowns. Now she felt more comfortable. As she readied for bed, she studied the young nurse. She was fairly tall, had auburn curly hair, and had blue eyes.

"Is there anything else I can help you with?" T. Johansson asked.

"I'd like some ice water and some more pain pills," Ana Lea said.

The nurse smiled and whisked out of the room.

Early the next morning, Dr. Knowles came in to give Ana Lea a final checkup. "If you pass the test, I'll let you go home." Checking her vital signs, he nodded in satisfaction. "Your heart rate and blood pressure are somewhat low for a female. You must work out." He lifted an eyebrow.

"I do. I start with warm-up exercises and then jog or swim if I get the chance. The plan is three or four times a week. I also ride a bike."

"That's great. Keep it up. You're all checked out. You can leave anytime after you've eaten breakfast. You may take two Tylenol three or four times a day. No more than that. Tylenol can be dangerous in large amounts. Call me if you have any negative symptoms."

He shook her hand. His hand was warm, and his grip was strong.

"You have a good tan too. Do you work out?" She couldn't help but smile and watch his green-blue eyes darken a little. She also noticed he was not wearing a wedding ring.

"Every chance I get. Sometime I'd like to tell you of some of my adventures since moving to Utah." He flashed a grin, waved, and was gone.

Midmorning, Jacob and Joanna came to pick up Ana Lea. An orderly brought her down to the front entrance of the University Hospital in a wheelchair. There she sat in the shade of the portico waiting for Jake to drive the car around the long circular entrance; Joanna waited with Ana Lea.

"While I was in that cool hospital, I forgot the city was in the grip of a heat wave. My house is going to be an oven inside."

"Not to worry. We went by your house this morning and turned on your cooler and fed your cat," Joanna said.

"What cat? I don't have a cat."

"Hmmm, well, she was there yesterday, so I bought a few cans of cat food and fed her. She's very sweet and friendly." Joanna sounded apologetic. "I'm sorry. I'm so used to animals. At home, there are two cats and a big dog. That's what I do first thing every morning—feed the animals."

"When I arrive home, I'll take a look at this cat. Is that Jake in a rented car?" Ana Lea pushed out of the chair, and Joanna grabbed her overnight bag.

Jake chose to park in front of Ana Lea's house; it faced north, and there was some shade from old trees there. "Let's get you into the house and settled." The house was cool and dim because she had not bothered to pull drapes or blinds when she came home from Ohio. The front bedroom she used was cool, and the blinds were closed.

"Look, girl, we don't want you going back to work until you are feeling better. Just give your head a few days' rest, and when the headaches subside and you get your energy back, then you may start working. One more thing— I had trouble getting your attic fan to work. It would turn on, but a few minutes later, it would make a clicking noise and shut off. Maybe you should call a repairman. Now behave yourself and plan on us checking up on you."

Ana Lea escorted them to her front door. After hugs and waves, she stood with the door open and watched them drive away. She could feel the waves of heat coming in from outside while standing there.

That attic fan again. I've had trouble with it from day one. Maybe I can find some repairman that can keep it running for at least an hour or two.

Though she felt headachy and edgy, she didn't want to go directly to bed. Instead, she went into her sunny kitchen and made a pitcher of iced tea. While the water boiled, she opened the south door, which was in her dining area leading outside to a covered porch. She found the cat in a shady spot in her flower bed on the west side of the concrete steps.

"Come here, cat. Let me take a look at you." The feline was rather small, a gray tabby with beautiful swirls of white fur mixed with the gray. What she noticed most were the cat's eyes. They were blue green, a bit lighter, but nearly the same shade as Dr. Knowles's eyes. "You and Dr. Knowles share the same eye color. Are you two related?"

The cat settled into Ana Lea's arms and snuggled. Soon, she began a soft purring sound. "It's pretty hot outside. I'll bet you're thirsty." She found an old plastic bowl and filled it with water. She set it down close to the french door, making sure she locked it. As she stood up, her head radiated with spasms of pain. *OK, head, I'm getting the message. It's time for more Tylenol and a nap. I'll forget about the idea of working on the Columbus project today. Maybe I will follow doctor's orders and give my head a rest.* Quickly, she made the tea and put the pitcher into the refrigerator.

Sunday evening, a cranky, exhausted Clark Knowles pulled into the driveway of the apartment he had rented. The building had been divided into four units, and there were four places to park at the rear of the house. Mercifully, it was on the east side, and he found a spot close to a tree, which leaned its branches from the backyard of the house to the east.

He had been on call all weekend and had gone into the hospital yesterday, midday. He had not eaten a real meal or slept in thirty-six hours.

It had been one emergency after another. Firecracker burns on three different kids and one adult. A two-year-old girl was brought in not breathing because she had tried to swallow a huge gumball. It had been necessary to do a tracheotomy to save her life. The next morning, when he had gone up to check on her, she was still unconscious and on oxygen. The plan was to transfer her over to the sister children's hospital.

There had been an older man who came in who had fallen while climbing a nearby mountain and broke his back. The break was severe, and Clark was surprised when the man showed no signs of paralysis. He could lift his legs and wiggle his toes. The guy couldn't understand why his wife couldn't take him home in a wheelchair and then bring him back the next day for X-ray work rather than going straight to radiology and the ICU.

When Clark entered his apartment, the sun still baked the front room and the upstairs bedroom in this west-facing house. He turned on the evaporative cooler and searched his refrigerator for something to eat or drink. All he found was a Pepsi, a bottle of orange juice, and a beer. The Pepsi won out.

As the apartment began to cool down, he climbed into the shower, which began to cool his exterior, while the soft drink cooled his insides. As he finally turned the water off, he heard his landline phone ringing.

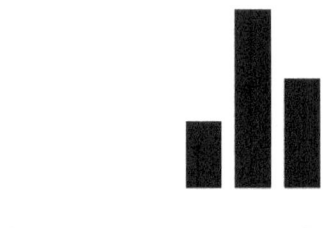

CHAPTER 6

"Great. I'm glad I caught you before you went out for dinner. I need an assist on a gunshot wound tomorrow morning."

"Why wait until tomorrow?" Clark asked.

"He's lost too much blood and needs to be stabilized. I'm up here watching him tonight. We're low on crossmatch."

"What's his blood type?" Clark asked.

"AB negative."

"Oh, boy, you've got your work cut out for you. What about a family member? Maybe someone has the same blood type and would donate."

"He became an orphan when the individual who dropped him off at emergency disappeared. No ID. Will you help me?"

"Sure. I need some food and about twelve hours of sleep."

"I'm not taking a scalpel to him until I have three pints of blood. Hopefully, I'll have enough by 6:00 a.m. tomorrow. Change of subject. How's Ana Lea Andreasen doing?"

"I haven't heard from her since she left the hospital," Clark said, suddenly feeling guilty.

"She's not the type to bother you with a call. Give a call or go by her house."

"What's her address? Maybe I will."

Ray rattled off the address and the coordinates to find her house.

"Good luck. See you tomorrow, early."

Clark went to a popular Mexican restaurant. Next stop was Ana Lea's house. He was ringing the front doorbell as the sun set. After the third ring, he saw a slight movement of the drape on the front window. Finally, the door opened. "Hi, I was in the neighborhood. Just your friendly physician checking up on his patient."

He tried for a casual smile, which he did not feel. Somehow, he felt as if he were seventeen again and calling on the prettiest girl in the neighborhood. He glanced around the deep white porch, and there he noticed a round navy-blue table flanked by two red canvas chairs.

"I … not really dressed to receive company." She hid behind the partially open door, and her thick, dark hair tumbled over her cheek.

"I'm not dressed as company, just making a house call on a hot July evening."

She stared at him for a long moment.

"I have dinner from Café Rio." He hopped from one foot to the other like a ten-year-old boy.

"Mexican food." She flashed a slight smile. "You said the magic word. Enter."

Clark retrieved the food from his car and bounded up the steps of the front porch. He walked through a navy-blue door. The house had a homey, pleasant feel.

Ana Lea wore a red sleeveless T-shirt and gray shorts. The outfit hugged her shapely body. She led him into the kitchen. "Set the food on the table. I'll be right back."

As a physician, Clark should not find one of his patients so blatantly female, but right now, he was thinking like a lonely man whose eyes had feasted on feminine perfection. He walked around her kitchen chastising himself for his nonprofessional reaction to his patient.

She returned a few minutes later; her face washed, hair combed and tied into a ponytail with a red ribbon. She had put on sandals.

From a cupboard, she took plates, and from drawer, she took forks, knives, and napkins. "What would you like to drink?" Opening her refrigerator, she took out a Coke, a Mountain Dew, and iced tea.

"The Dew will be fine." He watched as she set two sodas and glasses filled with ice on the table. He set out the food, and they sat down and began to eat. They were quiet, and he finally felt more comfortable.

"Did you work today?" she asked.

"Yes. I was on call all weekend." He gave her a brief description of his thirty hours in the Emergency Department.

"Whew, you really needed a break." She smiled. "I'm glad you came by." "I must not forget why I came here. How are you feeling? I know you must still have headaches. How severe and how often?"

"They're still with me but not as often or severe. The worst day was Friday, the day I came home from the hospital. I would sleep, wake up, take pills, and then sleep again. It was better Saturday morning."

"That sounds like the progression of healing for a concussion. "May I ask a question?" She nodded. "I know people celebrate with fireworks on the Fourth of July. Why are they still using the incendiary devices two weeks later on this weekend?"

Her laugh was musical, and she shook her head. "Didn't anyone tell you that we have Pioneer Day in Utah? It's in celebration of the arrival of the first Mormon Pioneers to the Salt Lake Valley. It happened on July 24, 1847. It's like Statehood Day, only we don't celebrate that day too much." She sat back and grinned at him. She reached for a container of salad and put more on her plate. "You want to finish this?"

"Sure." A few minutes later, the food was gone, and she began clearing the table. He jumped up to help her.

"There is a TV show I'd like to watch. Most of the time, I'm traveling and don't find myself able to view it. It starts in five minutes. Would you like to stay and watch it?"

Of course, he'd stay; just to be in the company of this beautiful girl. "I don't watch much TV either. Right now, I don't have a good set, but I plan to go shopping for one next weekend."

The words *Arrest and Prosecute* crossed the screen. The room she had led him had been a small bedroom. She had turned it into an office/den. A flat-screen TV was mounted on the wall to the south. A small sofa sat on the north wall. The east window was covered with a heavy cotton drape. There was also a corner unit near the TV with a computer and printer.

"Come sit here." She invited him to sit on the sofa, and she curled up in one corner of it.

Twenty minutes later, when a long commercial came on, she noticed he had fallen asleep.

Poor guy, I'll bet he's exhausted. I let him sleep for a while.

She turned off the TV and went into her bedroom, where she had a smaller TV. Kicking off her sandals and fluffing her pillows, she finished watching the program. She took two more pain pills and went back to bed and her TV. She pulled up a soft blanket and slid into a comfortable position, and soon, her eyes drifted closed. During a commercial, she fell asleep.

Sometime during the night, she awoke, turned off the television, and made a trip to the bathroom. On her way back, she glanced into her TV room and saw two bodies lying on the sofa. One was a man and the other a cat. *Oh, that's just Dr. Knowles asleep, next to my new cat.* She yawned, blinked, and stumbled back to her rumpled bed. She fell asleep instantly.

She was awakened by the sound of her front door opening and closing. A car engine revving up broke the early morning silence. She sat up with a start, waiting for the heavy fog of sleep to lift. Suddenly, she realized that her front door was unlocked. She hurried to the front door and locked it. There, she noticed her newspaper placed on the table near the door. Clark Knowles had just left and was kind enough to bring it in. *This is terrible. I allowed a strange man to sleep in my house! Doctor or not ... Ugh. You just broke all your safety rules, Lea.*

But later that morning, her head felt much better, but with less pain came restlessness. By noon, she was so bored with daytime TV she scrubbed her bathroom. She showered, put on makeup, but couldn't focus on the finances for the Columbus center.

She found a pair of linen slacks and a soft, loose-fitting purple knit shirt. She could use some fresh food and decided to go grocery shopping. Opening her garage at the rear of her property, she found it empty. *No car!* Where was her car? For a moment, she couldn't remember the last time she had driven it. Then she recalled she had driven it to the Marriott Hotel. Hurrying back to the house, she called the hotel. Finally, she was connected with the maintenance man working in the garage.

Several minutes later, he picked up the phone. He said, "Ma'am, I'm walking around the garage now. What type of car do you have?"

"It's a Subaru, four-door, late model, blue."

"Ms. Andreasen, I found your car. I suppose we should check our long-term parking tickets more closely. It looks to be OK, and the doors are all locked. You can come and pick it up anytime."

"Thank you. I'll pick it up today or tomorrow." Her plan to grocery shop evaporated. Now what? *I suppose I could take the bus downtown and walk over to the Marriott and pick up my car. I can't face moving around in the heat, not today.* Just thinking about waiting for a bus, riding it, and walking around downtown in one-hundred-plus-degree July heat, her headache returned. Thoughts of Clark Knowles invaded her mind. *Forget that idea. I don't know him that well.*

She made some lunch and sat there deciding if she should call him.

Meanwhile, she took off her slacks and purple top and flopped down on her bed. The ringing phone roused her from a light slumber. "Hello?"

"Hi, this is Clark. I want to apologize for invading your house and falling asleep last night. Very unprofessional," he mumbled.

"Don't be sorry. You must have been exhausted. I'm glad you awoke early enough to get back to the hospital in time. I should have at least gotten up and fixed you some coffee. Did the surgery you were to do this morning go OK?" "Yes, we saved the kid, but he's still critical. I should make it up to you.

What are you doing this weekend?" he asked. "Actually, I need a favor, tonight if possible." "I hope I can be of service. What do you need?"

"My car is still at the Marriott parking garage. I need it today, if possible," she said.

"Unless there is a major accident on one of the freeways or something similar, I could pick you up between six and seven this evening," he said.

"That would be so great. Call me when you're ready to leave the hospital, and I'll be ready when you arrive."

As they pulled into the parking garage next to her car, she touched his arm. "Are you interested in stopping for some dinner?"

He grinned at her, jumped out of this car, and ran around to open the passenger door. "Dinner? Where? I haven't lived here long enough to know a good restaurant .... What did you have in mind?"

"Close to my place is a Sizzler Restaurant. Not too expensive, and I love the salad bar."

"Sounds great. I'll follow you." As she walked to her car, he watched her trim figure, in soft gray slacks, slide into the driver's seat. How had he been so lucky to meet such a beautiful girl after being in this city less than two months? It must be his Irish luck.

CHAPTER 7

Clark, surprised at his hearty appetite, really enjoyed the salad bar and steak dinner. His companion made his evening even more enjoyable. He found conversation easy with her. She seemed interested in his work and asked thoughtful questions.

He then asked her about her work. "When you hosted the banquet, you seemed self-assured, in control, besides the fact you looked great. What else is in your job description?"

"I book hotels for banquets, and afterward, I am in charge of paying the bills, reconciling the books. Right now, Joanna Wright is searching for a building in Columbus, Ohio. It is to be used as a shelter for women and children. It must be large enough to house an educational wing. I'm planning a trip to Ohio at the end of next week and see what she has found. We'll then make a decision and, if possible, buy the building."

Soon, they were finished with their dinner and sat sipping iced tea. She checked her watch. "Wow, it's nearly nine. We'd better leave."

Clark walked her to her car. "Thank you for a great evening." Clark flexed his shoulders and wiped the back of his neck with a handkerchief.

"It's still so hot, unbelievable."

"It is July, usually the warmest month of the year in Utah. I will say, this year, it has been unusual for high temperatures. By the way, when do you have another evening off?"

"Thursday evening, unless we have a minor disaster that involves people pouring into the emergency room." His heart thumped in pleasant surprise at her question.

"It's my turn to fix dinner for you. Can you come by around seven?" She flashed a smile and touched his arm.

"Absolutely. I have surgery in the morning, but I'm off by six."

"Good. Thank you for your help picking up my car." Sliding into her car, she turned over the engine and switched on the AC. She waved as she drove out of the parking lot.

He seems like a good guy. Maybe he's the one to chase the bad memories away. Too bad just seeing Kitt dug them up again. Even though he's now married, it was exciting to see him. Turn a page in your book, Ana Lea, and forget him. You need fresh romance in your life, even sex. It only happened that one time. Yet that one night burned in her memory, and suddenly, she was cold. Perhaps a sweet, patient man could bring romance into her life. Possibly she could have sex and even enjoy it. Intellectually, she knew that. Emotionally, well, the old fears rose up to haunt her.

Just as Ana Lea slid a pan of biscuits into the oven, her doorbell rang, and she had invited Clark to come to dinner. As she glanced at the wall clock as she made her way to the door, it read 7:10. Anticipation of seeing him again had made her nervous. Hurrying to open the door, she found herself a little breathless.

He stood on her porch wearing pressed chinos and aqua shirt. As he passed her into the house, she picked up a whiff of soap and shaving lotion. "Come in, dinner's nearly ready." His tan slacks and soft shirt nearly the color of his eyes enhanced his good looks.

As she ushered him into her dining area, he handed her a tall bottle in a brown sack. "I didn't know what we were eating, so I picked up a bottle of a red."

Ordinarily, she didn't drink. "I'll chill it anyway."

He closed his eyes and shook his head. "Since being in Salt Lake, I never know who drinks alcohol and who doesn't. We don't have to open it if you prefer not to."

"It's OK." The oven timer went off. "Please sit down. I'll get the biscuits." The table was beautifully set with a linen cloth, crystal, and fine dinnerware. There was a small bouquet of real flowers as a centerpiece. He could see how hard she had worked to make this meal festive. She brought a large bowl filled with salad and a choice of two different dressings. She went back for a plate of steaming biscuits.

"Let's start with some salad." She went to the china cabinet and brought out two wineglasses and set them on the table. Next, she brought a bottle of nonalcoholic wine and handed it to him.

"Would you please open the wine?"

He did so and handed her a glass with a small amount in it. They dished up salad, and with his first bite of a hot biscuit, he nearly swooned. The rest of the meal, meatloaf, and baked potatoes were so good that, for a moment, he thought seriously of dropping to his knees and asking for her hand in marriage. However, when she served instant coffee with the dessert, he began to rethink the marriage proposal. First, he must teach her to make a decent cup of coffee. He was impressed with her cooking, and physically, she was in the top ten. Why wasn't she married? He planned to solve that little mystery soon.

Comfortable and relaxed, he asked. "How are your headaches?"

"They're less severe, and sometimes, I have no headaches at all. I worked a few hours yesterday. In effect, I've returned to work." She smiled. "Change of subject. Obviously you know I'm a Salt Lake area native. Where do you call home? Also, what is your background?" She leaned forward and refilled her glass with the wine.

"Home first. I was born in Holyoke, Mass. My family lived there until I was about fifteen. Then we moved to Boston because my father found a better job. I am the oldest child and have two younger sisters. They seemed to adjust to the move, but I was not a happy camper." He sat back and folded his arms across his chest.

"Moving when one is a teenager is very difficult. There are all kinds of sociological studies about how children react to such a move. How did you finally deal with your new situation?" She met his eyes and seemed to really be interested in his story.

"At first, it was tough going to a new high school, trying to fit in. I was too small to play football or basketball. I had played soccer at my school in Holyoke. I went out for soccer and made the team. The next year, I lettered in tennis. I always liked math and science, so my senior year, I became a tutor." "Being able to play sports is important to a guy, right?" she commented. "Yes, it gives you a place. It's either that or become a computer geek or gangbanger. My dad *banged* that idea right out of my head." He gave a hard laugh.

"Next would have been college, I suppose. Which one?" she asked.

"I went to Boston College on a tennis scholarship. Soon, I found that premed was more compelling than playing hours and hours of tennis. I had serious offers to go pro." He shrugged. "I had a couple of agents scouting me, wanting me to enter some tournaments. By then, I was too busy with my premed studies. However, when you don't play tennis and you have such a scholarship, you lose it." He shifted around in his chair, uncomfortable. He had said too much.

"You were that good? I mean to turn pro? Wow." She lifted her head and smiled.

"So how did you finance your medical education?" Her eyes locked on his. The kitchen phone jangled, ringing again. Her head turned in the direction of the sound. "I'd better get that." She jumped and ran to the phone.

A few minutes later, she returned to the table. "That was Joanna. She has booked me on a flight to Columbus next Friday."

"Do you think you'll be well enough to fly in a little more than a week?" His concern for her seemed genuine.

"Yes, I'll be fine. We need to nail down a building for our shelter in that city. Joanna has checked out several. She may have the last word on the funds we spend, but I manage them." She sat back in her chair. "Back to your story, please."

"This chapter is simple. I ran out of money, so I joined the army and became a medical corpsman. After basic training, I was sent to Iraq. Did three tours. That's why I'm here at U med doing a surgical residency at the age of thirty-four." He picked up his glass of wine and drained it.

"Why did you choose to come to Utah?" She leaned forward and finished her wine too.

"I'd never been west—I mean, besides California. I wanted to ski, play tennis, hike, and bike. Salt Lake offers all those things, and all within an hour of the city. I wanted to live somewhere different from the East Coast. And, boy, I found those differences here." He grinned and touched her hand resting on the table.

"Now what about you? Did you attend the university on the hill?" His teasing smile was friendly, and his beautiful blue-green eyes flashed.

She forgot the question. "Ah … what?" She blinked and shook her head. "The University of Utah is your alma mater?" He raised his eyebrows. "Yes. I started out in elementary education but ended up as a finance major. In some of the business classes, I was the only female."

"I'll bet every male in the class was on high alert when you walked into the room." Again, he flashed that easy, sexy smile.

Ana Lea glanced away. He was so distracting. She fairly jumped up and began to clear the table. He stood to help her. She began storing the leftover food in the refrigerator. She turned to him, wiping her hands on a towel. "Would you like a tour of my house? It was my grandmother's, and I bought and remodeled it a few years ago. She walked down a short hall to the room opposite the living room in front. "This is my bedroom. Next is the bathroom and, sadly, the only one on this floor. Next to that is a second bedroom, and I use it as a den."

He glanced in and smiled. "That's where I slept the other night." He grinned.

"Yes, you did." Suddenly, she was embarrassed about that. She continued to walk to a stairway. "Downstairs is the basement." He followed her down. "Here is another bedroom and the second bath. The furnace and laundry are located here." She touched a bricked area.

"You could have a family room down here." He walked over to the west wall. "Is this a roughed-in fireplace?"

"I believe so. Several members of my family have lived in this house at one time or another. Some of them remodeled here and there. Example"—she touched the wall on the east side in the corner—"there was a door to the outside here at one time. Somebody closed it up and covered it with this wood grain paneling. My garage is at the rear of the property. It would be convenient to have a door here to bring in skis, groceries, a bicycle, whatever. When someone added the side porch, they also built a 'cool' room down here." She went to a door in the middle of the south wall and opened it. Inside were shelves and room for a freezer.

"That would be a good idea, especially since your unattached garage is in the backyard. Many houses in Boston have the same setup. I've known many families that have dug out a basement door," he said.

They walked back upstairs. Clark glanced up at the ceiling in the hallway. "What's that, an entrance to the attic?"

"Yes, it truly is an attic, with a wood floor. There is a stair that you can pull down. Someday, I'll have to show you, but right now, it's too dark. No light fixture up there. One of those things I've planned to add."

He glanced at the gold trimmed clock on the living room wall. "It's getting late, and I'd better leave. I have an early morning assist." He took one last sip of his now cold coffee and walked to the door. He turned to her. "That's the best meal I've eaten since I left home. Thanks so much for inviting me."

She moved closer to him but seemed uneasy. Clark kissed her hand, and her heart thumped in a quicker rhythm. Her hand fluttered to her chest.

His hand rested on her cheek and slid up to her mouth, touching it. She opened it, and he kissed her tenderly. She sighed as he deepened the kiss, teasing her open mouth with his tongue. But then, he kissed her again and pulled away. "I'd better go now, or I won't want to go at all." His lips touched her forehead for a long moment.

She stepped back and blinked. Blindly, she reached for the front door and opened it. He stepped out, and she stood and watched him drive away. "Good night." Her words were lost in the warm, humid air.

Ana Lea closed and locked the door and, for a moment, stood with her back against it. *Wow, kissing him was amazing. He is an expert and has a lot of experience, more than me.* Her heart still pounded high in her throat, and her face felt unusually warm. *That man definitely pushed my buttons.*

CHAPTER 8

She walked into the bathroom, splashed her face with cool water, and smiled at her image in the mirror. She fairly danced through her bedtime ritual, wanting to hold on to the elation of being wanted and wanting back. It had been a long time since she felt even a sliver of passion, a possibility of romance. She couldn't wait to see him again.

Ana Lea scheduled a flight to Columbus for the following Sunday evening. Joanna had set up appointments for the two of them to check out commercial properties for the planned shelter. One of their priorities was that the building they decided upon must have the potential to not only house and feed but also have places for classrooms for training these women.

Each day, she felt better and had fewer headaches, and those were less severe. She did not need as much sleep than she had the first week after her accident. But as the days went by, she became frustrated—no, irritated— because she had not heard from Clark. He had not called or come by and had made no effort to contact her at all.

At first, she allowed that he was just too busy, working long hours at the hospital. However, as each day passed, she decided that he had not found her interesting enough to continue their budding relationship.

She had planned to ask him to feed her little cat while she was traveling. At the last minute, Sunday morning, she called a neighbor and hired her twelve-year-old daughter to come and care for her cat. Apparently, she was not as interesting as some other women he had met. Her self-esteem suffered.

When she reached the door of the Columbus airport, she was literally enfolded in the arms of Joanna Wright. As Joanna drove to the Wright home, she turned to Ana Lea. "Why are you so quiet? Are you still suffering with a headache?"

"No, my head is better."

"What is it? Why are you so down?" Joanna reached over and touched Ana Lea's arm.

"Oh, it's nothing … It's … actually, it's Clark Knowles. We had a date last week. Actually, I asked him to dinner. I thought that … we had clicked." She took a breath. "He even kissed me, but now nothing."

"What do you mean *nothing?*"

"No calls, no contact whatsoever. He just dropped me." She fought back tears and grabbed a tissue from her purse.

"How long had it been since you had this dinner with him?" Joanna asked.

"Ten days." Ana Lea slumped down in her seat.

"He's a medical resident, right? They are extremely busy. Maybe right now he has a heavy work schedule."

"I know that is a possibility, but couldn't he at least call me?" She sniffed. "You like him, then?"

"Yes. He's interesting, intelligent, and kind of sexy."

Joanna's mouth curved into a tiny smile. "Maybe we can find out how and what he's doing?'

"How, from here in Columbus?"

"Remember I'm married to an MD. They seem to have their own little club." Joanna steered up an off-ramp and took a narrow road. They soon drove down a residential lane, and houses became large on even larger lots. She slowed the car as they came upon a large country-style house with a wide porch and a three-car garage. Centered on the porch was a large blue front door with sidelights of leaded glass on both sides.

Ana Lea had visited the house before, and she always wanted to stop and stare. The structure was combination of white clapboard and gray brick. It radiated a friendly, welcoming atmosphere.

They walked into the house from the garage. Jacob?" Joanna called out. Several seconds later, Jacob Wright strolled into the family room. Even though he wore faded jeans and a soft cotton shirt, the clothes on his tall, lean frame radiated style and casual nobility. He admitted that he loved clothes, and the way he carried himself, even wearing old faded jeans, he looked elegant.

He once told Ana Lea that he, to pay for his medical school expenses, had modeled for a catalog company. At age thirty-nine, he could still turn feminine heads when he walked into a room. The dark curly hair and stone-gray eyes enhanced his chiseled features.

"Hi, darling, how was the traffic?" He kissed her lightly. He turned to his house guest. "How are you feeling? Are you still suffering with headaches?"

"No, my head is feeling better, and I'm ready to go to work tomorrow," Ana Lea said.

"I'll take your suitcase up." He disappeared up a wide flight of stairs.

"Come take a seat. I'll bet you could use some dessert." Joanna movedbehind a long kitchen bar, washed her hands, and opened the refrigerator. She took out a pie and a carton of milk. Just at that moment, the front door opened with a bang, and ten-year-old Kevin Wright charged into the kitchen area.

"Can I have some of that green pie now?" he asked and climbed up on a barstool next to Ana Lea.

"You may have a small piece, because it's time for bed, but, first, you must wash your hands," Joanna said.

The boy slid off the stool and turned to Ana Lea. "Hi, you staying with us?"

"Yes, for a few days." She noticed the dirt-smudged face, grimy knees, and tousled hair of the young boy. "What had you been doing outside?"

"Climbing trees and playing ball. Jason knocked a ball up into the tree in front of his house, and I climbed up to get it."

"You know what, if you need to wash your hands before dessert, why don't you wash all over and put on your pajamas? That way, you'll be all ready for bed," Ana Lea suggested.

"You mean like a shower?" His eyes widened.

"Exactly. I'll bet you can do all that in"—she checked her wristwatch—"ten minutes, maybe even eight. Shall I time you?"

For a moment, the boy looked uncertain, but then his face split into a grin, and he ran for the stairs. "OK, I'll yell down when to start timing me."

Jacob passed his son on the stairway. He grinned at Ana Lea. "Would you like to move in and become our official nanny?" He slid onto a barstool. "I've been standing up their listening to this conversation you've had with Kevin. Pretty crafty, lady." He turned to Joanna. "Callie and Zach are asleep."

"Good. It's so hard to get them in bed in the summertime," Joanna said. A voice called from upstairs. "Start timing me."

"OK." She glanced at her watch. "Meanwhile,"—she turned to her hostess —"I wouldn't mind some of that key lime pie."

For three days, Ana Lea and Joanna looked at several buildings for the shelter. Not only adequate size was of importance but also its location. They chose an older suburb adjacent to the city center.

When they returned to the Wrights' home, Ana Lea flopped down on the family room sofa and kicked off her shoes. "I'm exhausted. How do you manage to stay so unruffled?" She turned to Joanna, who had removed her shoes too.

"I'm tired too. I did the 'show property' for a living. I was a real estate agent in Provo. That's how I met Joshua."

"You showed him houses?" Ana Lea asked.

"An apartment building, actually. It was late afternoon, so he invited me to dinner. You know where he took me? Wendy's. Here's this multimillionaire football star, and he takes me out for fast food?"

Ana Lea widened her eyes. "How was the food?" She was silent for a beat. "But you did date him, didn't you?"

"Yes, for three or four months. When Joshua blew out his knee and couldn't play ball that season, Jacob came to town. That's how I met him. We double-dated, Josh and I, with Nichole and Jacob."

"How did you guys make the big switch?"

"Now that's another story, and fairly complicated. Right now, I need to drive the babysitter home. Would you take the package of chicken from the freezer? I think we'll barbecue some chicken."

The next evening, Ana Lea flew back to Salt Lake. West of Denver, the plane encountered a thunderstorm. It was forced to change altitude and divert to another flight path. Nevertheless, heavy turbulence occurred, which shook the plane. Her stomach did not like the shaking, and she developed nausea and a headache.

Once the plane landed, she was forced to take the shuttle out to the long-term parking area. Sloshing to her car in a heavy downpour, she found that the front tire was flat. *Great. How am I going to change a tire in a thunderstorm?* She trudged back and waited in the rain for the shuttle to take her back to the terminal.

She stood dripping wet at the Southwest Airlines desk, and, finally, the clerk gave Ana Lea a ticket to their in-town shuttle. Once on the shuttle, she decided at the best she was out of the rain. It was late at night, and only two people were passengers on the van. Its last stop was at Twenty-First South and Thirteenth East at a Chevron Station. It was over a mile from her house.

She just did not have the strength to walk that far dragging her suitcase and carrying her purse and briefcase.

The owner of the service station, Joe Franklin, came out and helped her into his small office. "Ms. Andreasen, I'll run you home, but I must stay open until ten thirty."

She sat in the air-conditioned office, wet and shivering.

CHAPTER 9

A few minutes later, a familiar Volvo station wagon pulled near a pump, and its owner began filling the tank. Clark glanced up and noticed a rather bedraggled Ana Lea sitting in the station office. He jogged inside. "What are doing sitting in Joe's office?"

"It's a long, miserable story, Clark." She felt cold, tired, and miserable.

"Well, come on, I'll drive you home." He picked up her suitcase and placed it in his car, and she followed him. When they reached her house, he helped her into the house and turned on her evaporative cooler.

He walked into her kitchen and began opening cupboards and the pantry.

He finally found the object of his search.

She stood in the entryway of her house, too befuddled to make a decision as to what she should do next. "What are you looking for?" She asked him as she shuffled into the kitchen.

"I'm making tea, While it steeps, go get into the shower," he ordered.

She automatically went into her bedroom, stripped off her clothes, and grabbed a terry cloth robe. A few minutes later, she emerged from the bathroom to the kitchen. At the dining table, she found a steaming mug of tea waiting. She sat, sipped, and closed her eyes in satisfaction.

"How and why did you end up at the Chevron Station dripping wet? Where's your car? Did it break down?" Clark asked. He tilted his head, and his mouth twitched.

"I suppose you would want to know. OK, I'll tell you the whole sordid, soggy story." And she did.

After she had finished, he sat back and said, "It seems that we need to make another trip to retrieve your car, as well as change the tire." He leaned back in a chair and sipped his tea.

She sighed .and nodded her head. "I'd really appreciate your help and service."

"OK. I'll be by around seven tomorrow evening."

"Since we'll be dressed casually, we could stop at the Subway on our way home. I'll make a salad, and we could eat back here. Does that meet with your approval?'

"Good plan." He stood and took another swallow of the tea. "I've an early surgery, so I'd better go." He marched to her front door.

She opened the door and stood holding it for him. He kissed her on her forehead and ran out into the rain. "Thank you again," she said as he jumped into his car.

The next evening turned out to be beautiful and twenty degrees cooler than the night before. The air was clear and fresh. Even the grass and the trees seemed cleaner and greener.

It took very little time for Clark to change the tire, and soon, they were on their way. He insisted that they stop at the Chevron and leave the car for Joe to check the tire. "I'm surprised at the change in the weather," he said. "I thought we would roll into October with temps still in the ninety-degree range."

"No, it's August, and the nights usually cool off from now on. You can open your bedroom window and let in cooler air," Ana Lea said.

"Is it safe to open windows here? I mean, what about break-ins?" Clark asked.

"It depends on where you live. This neighborhood is pretty safe. I would need to come visit your apartment and check it out." She gave him a wide-eyed innocent stare.

"It's not much, believe me."

They ate their sandwiches, salad, and chocolate chip cookies at her dining table. "Did you make these?" He waved a cookie in her direction before taking another bite.

She nodded and smiled.

"These cookies are grounds for a marriage proposal. Every guy should have a wife that can bake cookies like these." He laughed and swallowed the remains of the treat.

He stood and pulled her out of her chair, tilted her face up, and kissed her. "That's for making such good cookies."

She wrapped her arms around his neck and kissed him back. "That's for helping me with my car."

This kiss was deeper, teasing her mouth open, flicking his tongue inside. *She likes the kissing.* Her mouth was so soft, and the fit of her body against his heated his blood.

Yet she pulled away and laid her head on his shoulder. He grabbed her shoulders, pushed her away, and stared into her eyes. "You're sending me mixed messages, girl."

She dropped her head. "I'm sorry, it's just that …"

"When you decide what you want, please let me know." He stomped out the front door and stood near the porch rail, gripping it until his knuckles turned white.

She came outside and stood near him. "I'm sorry about my hang-ups. Perhaps when I know you a little better, when I feel I can share with you some of my sad and bad things in my life, I will."

"Look, Ana Lea, you're a beautiful, accomplished sexy girl of, what, thirty-one years. You sometimes behave as if you are an innocent, virginal college freshman. Do you want the truth? I'd like to take you to bed, and yet a no, also a yes. Why is that?"

She stared down at her hands gripping the railing, close to his. "Can I say that I'm not ready for sex right now? But I like you quite a bit. If you want to look for another more physically willing girl, I can understand that. Since I've known you, I'm much happier than I've been for a long time." She met his eyes in the nearly dark evening.

He enfolded her in his arms for a long moment. "It's hard to resist a girl with whiskey-colored eyes, who can bake chocolate chip cookies." He breathed in the scent of her hair and chuckled.

"I need a favor—actually, two." She backed away and sat down in one of the red chairs. "It seems that I'm constantly asking for your help." She dropped her head, but her mouth curved into a smile.

"And I'm in a position to grant you these favors?" he asked.

"Possibly, yes. First, I'd like to learn to play tennis, from a near pro." She waved her hand in his direction.

"OK, that's not difficult. What is the second favor?"

"I must go to Los Angeles at the end of the week. Would you mind feeding my cat while I'm gone?" Her eyes pleaded with him.

"You won't be my lover, but you expect me to feed your cat?" His voice was low. He wiped his face with his hand and began to laugh.

She stared at him. "I don't see what's so funny." She watched him throw back his head and laugh long and hard. As she watched him, she began to laugh too.

Soon, there were tears running down his face, and he clutched his stomach. "Girl, you are going to be the 'death' of me." He turned and sat down on a stair.

She knelt near him and touched his arm. She took a deep breath and asked, "Will you help me?"

He pushed up from the stair and took her hand. "When's a good time for a tennis lesson?"

When Clark walked into the hospital cafeteria for a quick lunch, he spotted Ray. It had been a few days since he'd seen him.

His friend waved him over to his table. "Sit down. How did that gall bladder go this morning?"

"Oh, fine," Clark said dismissively and frowned.

"Not in a pleasant mood today?" Ray asked with a twitch of his mouth.

"Oh, just tired, I guess." Clark ran a hand through his hair.

"Hmmm, and here I thought it had something to do with Ana Lea," Ray teased.

"If you must know, it does." Clark shifted uncomfortably in his chair. "She's a great girl, smart, pretty, but the relationship is in a holding pattern. When I get close, you know, try for a little … she, ah … likes being kissed but doesn't want anything to go further." Silence. "And I would."

"You mean sex?" Ray leaned back in his chair with a large grin.

"Yeah, I'll admit it. I want sex with her. Where I come from, with mature adults, it's the next step in the relationship, to build a strong physical relationship with her, and I really like her. I don't think she's a virgin but also have picked up some signals that there have not been very many men in her life either."

"I'm sure it is very difficult keeping a lid on your physical desires. I can't imagine not having a willing sex partner. I've been married seventeen years and have fathered four kids. Every now and then, my wife and I sneak off to a hotel and really get *it* together.

"My advice, for what it's worth, is to back off, do some activities with her. Get to know her better and then see how things develop. I didn't know her until about five years ago. There was some gossip about her having some problem with a guy," Ray said.

"Thanks, Ray, for listening." Clark gobbled down his lunch, for he had appointments all afternoon. He was now forced to focus on his chosen profession and put Ana Lea on his mental back burner.

To his surprise, she called him late Monday afternoon. She made small talk but finally asked another favor. "If you're going to help me with my tennis game and give me some instruction, we'll need to go shopping. I need a new racket. Would you help me pick one that is correct for me?" She seemed to be holding her breath, waiting, silent.

"So you really want to play tennis, eh? I suppose I could show you a few pointers."

"Could we meet tomorrow? I could go anytime, but it's better in the morning, because of the heat later in the day. Whatever your schedule, we could work around it." He could hear a bit of anxiety in her voice.

"OK, tomorrow. Is ten too early to go shopping?" Clark asked.

"No. Ten in the morning is perfect. Come by and we can go to the Sport's Authority. I'll see you then. Bye."

Clark put down the phone. *Good, she still wants my company. Maybe in a while, she'll be more interested in more of my body other than just my tennis arm.*

At the Sport's Authority, Clark found a good medium-priced racket for Ana Lea as well as one for himself. Since there were some interesting "end of summer" sales in the store, she went o4ff to shop, and he decided he could use some new tennis clothes too.

As they moved around the store, Clark was well aware of her long, shapely, lightly tanned legs in her white shorts. The pale orange sleeveless shirt she wore fit nicely across her breasts, and lovely they were. *Focus, Clark, keep your mind on your tennis moves, not more intimate ones.*

He checked out some bargain buys, and soon they left to find the court she had reserved.

Once there, they reviewed the basic swings, the footwork, and the forward and backhand ball returns. In a short time, they were playing a game, which became a set. Clark stopped to wipe the sweat from his face, and he caught a glance at his watch.

CHAPTER 10

"**H**ey, lady, do you know it's nearly one o'clock?" His throat felt like they were playing in the Sahara. He walked over to the folding bag she brought and grabbed a bottle of water. "I'll never get used to this dry climate."

"Sure, you will." She laughed. "About the time it turns fall, you'll love it. You know what, I'm hungry. Let's go over to the Training Table. It's just across Thirteenth East."

While eating hamburgers and drinking tall sodas, they discussed Ana Lea's lesson. "You know the basics. Now it's time to practice, to play regularly." He took a long swig of his soda.

"Today felt good. Exercise wrapped into a sport is more fun than just exercise unto itself. Thank you, Clark." She gazed into his eyes, and he found the golden ring around the brown irises in her eyes intriguing. Another aspect of her he found captivating.

He couldn't help but smile. "I had fun too. We'll have to do that more often, I'd say on a regular basis."

As they climbed into his car, she asked, "Say, you said you would show me your apartment sometime. I think now is a good time." She smiled sweetly.

He shrugged. "All right, but be prepared. I don't spend a huge amount of time on housekeeping details." He drove north, slowed in front of an aging tan brick duplex that now had been remodeled into four units. He drove around the back of the place and parked in the relative shade of the tree next door. He led her to the kitchen door, and they went in.

"This is the kitchen." She gazed at a small area, with its aging yellow-and-white tile countertop and an older drop in stove. No dishwasher and no disposer. When the floor tiles were new, they could have been yellow and cream squares but now were old, worn, and dirt colored. There was just enough room for a small table and two chairs. He led her down a short hall to the front of the apartment.

"This is the living room. At least it has a wood-burning fireplace." He gestured to a fireplace on the north wall. There was an old sofa of some indistinguishable color. The carpet in some ways matched the sofa, mud colored. A forty-two-inch TV rested on a stand against the one blank wall. He had pushed the sofa up against the large front window, covered with cheap beige drapes. "It's difficult watching TV in the afternoon because of the west exposure. But then, I'm not home much in the afternoon."

She gave him a thin smile and shook her head. "What about your bedroom. It is upstairs?"

"Yes, up here." He led her back into the hall and up some stairs.

The bedroom was large loft. As she looked around the space, she decided that it had been an attic like her house. It had a hardwood floor. She noticed a queen-size mattress, springs, and frame but no headboard. Also she saw one chest of drawers, a desk, and a chair. The closet was a walk- in built over the stairs. "You don't have a headboard?"

"No." He had stuffed his hand in his pockets and stared at his shoes. Ray and I went out one Saturday and bought that bed. The one that came with the apartment was pretty bad. This is a good bed." He sat on it and bounced up and down. "The bathroom is downstairs."

"How did you manage to rent this place?" Her eyes narrowed.

"I found a site for apartments online. The address showed it to be only four miles from the hospital."

"Did you sign a lease?" she asked.

"Yeah, for six months."

"Good. When your lease is up, I'll help you find something better." She turned and walked downstairs. "Thanks for showing the place to me."

Wordlessly, he walked to the door and followed her out to the car. He was irritated by her reaction when he knew he shouldn't be. "You don't think too much of my apartment, do you?"

"No, I'm afraid not, but the location is convenient to the hospital and shopping. You're not too far from my house either." She smiled and touched his arm.

He drove straight to her house and parked in front. They walked to her door, and he gave her a chaste kiss and backed away.

I think I've hurt his feelings, but I still have one more favor to ask.

"Before you go, did you decide you could come in and feed my cat?" She cleared her throat, which suddenly felt parched. "I'm going back to Los Angeles next Friday. I did ask you before, didn't I? It may be one of my examples of short-term memory loss." She gave a self-conscious laugh. "And also check on my attic fan? It is cooler at night now, but it does help cool the house during the day. I'll stock the refrigerator, and you can stay here at night if you choose."

"I can sleep in your bed?" He wiggled an eyebrow.

She pulled herself up, straightening her back, lifting her chin. "If you choose to? The sofa bed in the den is quite comfortable."

"I'll give it some thought." He walked to his car, opened the door, and then turned back to her. "I thought about it. I'll come over sometime Saturday."

"I'll hide a key to the back door."

He walked over and opened his palm. "Give me the key now." She obliged.

Clark's plan was to go to Ana Lea's house on Saturday to feed the cat. However, he received an invitation to go hiking up mountain trails at Snowbird, the ski resort. He had not been up there yet, so the decision was easy. Of course, he'd go.

It was late Monday afternoon by the time Clark returned to the little gray-and-white house on Victor Street. Clark had finished his shift at the hospital and stopped for takeout at Cafe Rio. He hoped the cat had not starved or died of thirst, but she strolled out, stretched, and yawned from a spot on the den sofa and whined at him. He gave her a large portion of food and water. Then he made a search of the refrigerator for a beverage.

There was perhaps an hour of daylight left, so he decided to check out the attic fan. He changed into some old shorts and a T-shirt before climbing up to what he knew would be a dusty area, full of spiderweb. He was correct in his assumption.

The attic had been constructed so it could be finished into a third level. The floor was of good oak and could be cleaned and finished. There were two sash windows, one on the east side of the north-south envelope roof and one on the west. He found the window on the east would open. He did that immediately, because he found the attic stuffy and hot.

It was evident that Ana Lea used the attic for storage. Shoved into the southwest corner were a Christmas tree box and several plastic storage bins full of decorations. There were other boxes there and a small three-legged stool.

He took the cover off the control box of the fan and checked the connections. The wiring seemed to be correct. As he examined the box, he felt a breeze blow against his neck and a strange whiff of something like newly turned earth. He jerked his head around, expecting to see someone or something, but found nothing. He went to the window and looked out and took a sniff. A slight fragrance of some flowers in the backyard wafted to him, yet not even a breeze ruffled the leaves on the trees.

One of the boxes toppled off a stack and fell over on its side. Clark jumped at the sound, his heart beating hard. He righted it and lifted the lid. It was an old apple box, and the first thing in it was a large cream-colored scrapbook. It was titled "All about Kitt." Clark pulled up the little stool, sat down, and opened the scrapbook across his lap and began to leaf through it. It held a loving account of Carlson Kittredge's career.

Page after page contained articles carefully clipped from newspapers and sports magazines. Neatly glued were strips of comments about the articles, the football games each article discussed, and the date it had occurred. They were in Ana Lea's printing.

There was a newspaper account of Kitt's marriage to Melanie. After that were articles of him playing with the Aces and he and Joshua Wright's winning offensive. The last picture was of Kitt and Joshua holding up their helmets in triumph, the day they won the Super Bowl.

Clark was stunned. He felt as if someone had punched him in the gut. Ana Lea had been in love with, or at least had a major crush on, Carlson Kittredge. No wonder she had never had a serious relationship with anyone for so many years. Had they been lovers? Had the guy moved on, leaving her with unfulfilled dreams? Could anyone ever compete with this dream man? Could he?

His own reaction surprised him. He was jealous, wildly envious of a person depicted in a scrapbook. He sat for a few minutes until he felt that same stirring of air and smelled the same earthy smell.

He decided he could never let her know he had seen the scrapbook. As he went to put the book in the box, it tipped over, and its contents spread across the dusty floor. A dark red book caught his eye. When he picked it up, he could see it was very old. It was smaller than the standard eight by ten inches, but it was thick. He could tell it was crafted of fine leather.

The light was fading. Clark picked up the contents of the box and put it back on the stack. He stood and stretched, for he had been sitting a long time. He closed the east window and, with the small journal in hand, went downstairs.

When he walked into the kitchen, he went to a drawer and found an old dishtowel. He carefully wiped off the dust and then, with a slightly damp corner of the cloth, cleaned off the little book as best he could, leaving it to dry on the kitchen bar while he showered.

After fixing a meal, he cleaned up and washed his hands carefully, as if he were to perform surgery. Clark sat down to examine the journal. Engraved in gold on the front right corner was the name Emily McBride. He carefully opened the journal, turned the yellowed pages, and read the first entry.

November 18, 1883

> I begin this journal on my seventeenth birthday. It is so beautiful, my favorite color. My father and mother bought it from Hyrum, the printer. He also prints scriptures and other church books. The leather is so soft, and it has my name engraved on it.

> I am soon to finish my schooling and will need to either marry or find a position to support myself. I dream of someday working in an office in the city. I could wear a white shirtwaist and a trim black skirt. I have seen other women dressed like that when I have gone downtown.
>
> November 29, 1883
>
> Charlotte and I were allowed to go to the Saturday evening dance at the recreation hall. I saw many young men and pretty young girls there. I danced with several boys from our church. Two asked Father's permission to call on me next Sunday evening. I will try to be a polite hostess and entertain them.

Clark skipped through a few entries. They seemed to be normal daily activities of Emily and her family. The next one that caught his interest was dated Christmas Day 1883.

He was about to read it when his beeper went off. He answered it. He was called to the hospital. He marked a place in the journal and closed and wrapped it. He slid the book onto a shelf in the den.

As he drove up the street, he realized he was curious and was eager to pull out that journal and read more about Miss Emily McBride.

CHAPTER 11

Nichole had invited Ana Lea to stay at Joshua's Brentwood house. He had set up an office of sorts for her in a spare bedroom. That's also where she slept.

From the time she arrived in Los Angeles, Sunday evening, she was very busy. She had many contributions from the Salt Lake function to organize. To those who had donated, she needed to send tax exempt information. Even with her own laptop, she needed a printer and a scanner, which Joshua provided for her. She worked long hours each day, until Nichole walked in her makeshift office on Thursday. "You did bring a swimsuit, didn't you?"

Ana Lea looked up from her stack of papers and smiled at her friend. "Yes, on your orders."

"Well, it's time you took a break. Get into that suit and come down to the pool, pronto," Nichole said. "I'll give you five minutes."

Being shut up in that bedroom, she had not paid much attention to the weather. Walking out to the pool deck, she found that the sky was a clear blue, the air warm, with a hint of a breeze. At one end of the pool, Nichole had moved a second chaise close to her own. A small table held iced tea in frosty glasses, a vegetable tray, and some cookies.

Ana Lea settled in and sipped the iced tea. "I could become accustomed to this quite easily. You have great tan, so you must spend some time out here." "Not as much as I would like," Nichole said. "I do have a household to run, shopping, laundry, and I cook most evenings. It was June when we first moved down here from Salt Lake. I believe you know that I finished out my teaching year. When Josh and I married, he was still nursing his knee injury, so we lived in my little house in Salt Lake. On the weekends, we went up to his condo in Park City. So I've been living here not quite three months. My gosh, it's three times the size of my house, and a swimming pool seemed such a luxury to me."

"Is that why you refer to this place as Josh's house, not your house?" Ana Lea asked.

"I suppose I still think of the little house in Utah as mine and this one his, but I'm settling in." She laughed. "Yet I still feel slightly guilty when I come out here and laze around for an afternoon. Besides now, being pregnant, my OB doesn't want me to sit too long in the heat of the sun. Bad for the baby. Right now, I'm going in the water to cool off." Nichole slid into the pool and began a smooth side stroke. "Join me."

"I'd love to." Ana Lea did a clean dive off the side. She came up, shaking the water from her face. "Ah, the water is heavenly."

Tuesday evening, Clark cooked a chicken pot pie and made a salad. Once he cleaned up the kitchen, he brought the journal out and began to read where he had put a book marker.

Christmas Day 1883

> Father brought home a sack of nuts, candy, and he even found two large oranges for the family to share. Charlotte, my next younger sister, and little Esther, who will go to school next year, were so excited to share the orange. Mother, Father, and little brother, David, had one to share also.

> We decorated the house with colorful ribbons, yarn, with fresh green boughs on the mantle.

Father would not let us bring a tree inside the house to decorate, mainly because they are still not very tall. He says that Christ Child should be the center of our Christmas, not a tree.

Amazing, thought Clark. Reading this journal was like a glimpse into the nineteenth century and the life of a seventeen-year-old girl; she writes with good grammar and has a nice way with the language.

The next entry that Clark viewed as significant was in January.

January 22, 1884

It has snowed steadily for two days now. The only place we can walk outside is to the barn to feed the horses and to milk the cow. It is so cold that even wrapped in my woolen coat, shawl, and bonnet, I become stiff and chilled while milking. One pleasant thing we tried was to leave the milk on the porch for a few hours. It is chilled and delicious to drink, but Mother says cold milk is bad for the stomach.

We have plenty of food, but it is tiring to not go to school and have new books to read. The two younger ones become bored and naughty. Mother told Charlotte and me that we must entertain them. We make up silly games.

Clark sat back and smiled. He wanted to share the entries in the book with Ana Lea. He wanted to know how Emily McBride fit into her family tree. *This book is a treasure, a glimpse into the lives of these people who settled in the west, especially this particular group who came here for religious freedom.* Clark read several entries about the winter of 1884. This time, he found the entry of significance.

TIME AT THE ZENITH

February 18, 1884

> Father brought home a young man to meet me, well, all the family, last evening. He already has a wife, but because he is a prosperous farmer and land owner, he has been called by the brethren to take another wife. He has a fine fruit orchard and farm in the Sugar House area. He can easily support another wife. Samuel Whitmur is his name, and he is quite handsome. He has dark blond hair and a sturdy build. Father spoke highly of him. After he left, Father said I should think on allowing him to court me. I must think and pray about this young man.

Just then, the phone rang. Clark carefully closed the book and went to answer it. "Hello?"

"Hi, Clark, how are you doing? How's Crystal?" Ana Lea asked. "I'm fine. Who's Crystal?"

"My cat. The reason why I called is that I'm going to stay here in Los Angeles until Monday morning. The Aces have their first preseason game Sunday, and Joshua has tickets for us to attend."

"Nichole and you? And why did you name your cat Crystal?"

"Because of the color of her eyes. Nichole, Melanie, and I have seats together." She sounded pleased. "I've never seen an NFL game before. It will be fun."

"So you are going to sit with Kitt's wife?"

"Yes, these are good seats. There aren't too many more games that Nichole can attend, she being seven months pregnant. So Melanie and I are there to take care of her. So is that OK with you to stay there and feed my cat?"

"Yes, of course. You know I'm sleeping in your bed." His laugh was deep. "I figured you would. Is it as comfortable as yours?"

"A little better, and there's plenty of room for you with me there too." He lowered his voice.

"Maybe, but then again, maybe not." She laughed and cleared her voice. "I should be home when you finish your shift. Perhaps we can eat out or fix something at the house. Oh, by the way, I put some of those chocolate chip cookies in the freezer. They're yours to eat and enjoy." She turned away and said something to Nichole and came back. "I'd better go. See ya Monday."

Clark now lost interest in the journal. So he closed it up, wrapped it, and put it back in the bookcase. He was thinking about Ana Lea and if she would see Kitt socially while in California. He wondered how the Kitt-Melanie marriage was progressing.

He flopped on the sofa in the den and turned on the TV. Nothing caught his attention. It was dark out now; he may as well go to bed in Ana Lea's bedroom.

The next evening, Clark, tired and yet bored, decided to pull out the journal. He found a fancy bookmark in the computer desk, so he put it in to mark the page where he had paused in his reading.

March 13, 1884

I went to a church social with Samuel, and he can dance quite well. The other girls studied him and nodded their approval. Samuel took me out on the steps of the hall, and we talked.

He said my eyes reminded him of the twilight sky. He said he was pleased with my gentle ways and complimented me on my thick, dark hair. I like him very much, because he is mature, not a boy. But what of his wife and little ones? How does she feel about him taking another wife? Will she accept me?

Easter Eve, 1884

Samuel came to our home and spoke to my father. He asked for my hand in marriage.

My father took me for a walk out to the barn. He told me of Samuel's request. I thought and prayed for several days. My answer, YES!

Late April 1884

My mother sent away, back east, for beautiful ivory-colored silk for my wedding dress. It is quite costly, but my sisters will be able to wear the dress when they marry. Also in the package was lace for a veil and for trim on the neckline. Samuel is building a room in his house for me. When it is ready, he will come for me. Where we live in Holiday, no family is in a polygamous marriage. One of Mother's friends warned against it. But I love Samuel, and I feel we will be happy.

June 3, 1884

The wedding is set for next Saturday. I asked Samuel to take me to meet his wife, Jerusha.

She is quite angry and opposes our marriage. The elders came to assure my family that Jerusha will adjust to me and the union. Samuel took me to his farm and showed me his fine stone house and the new room. His daughter Anna came out to greet me, but Jerusha would not speak with me. Another little girl, Rebecca, watched us through the window.

Clark could almost predict the problems poor, young Emily will encounter when she finally becomes Samuel's wife and he takes her home to live in the same house as Jerusha.

CHAPTER 12

Ana Lea drove into her garage, and as she walked toward the kitchen door, the marvelous smell of beef barbecuing assaulted her olfactory cells. Clark had found her barbecue and was grilling hamburgers. She dropped her belongings on the porch and ran to lift the lid and found fat beef patties grilling.

Clark bounced down the kitchen stairs wearing a chef's apron and waving a meat turner. "Oh, you've returned. How was your flight?" He kissed her lightly and moved over to the grill.

"You're cooking dinner?" Her eyes widened, and she smiled. "What can I do to help?"

"Bring me a platter to put the hamburgers on. Oh, and grab all the condiments you'd like with burgers."

"OK." She ran into the house. Soon, she returned carrying a tray with condiments, salad, buns, and pink lemonade. "You found the old picnic table." She set the tray on a red checkered plastic cloth. "Well, this looks wonderful." She began to toss the salad.

"The weather took a turn for the better, and when I found the table and grill in the garage, I decided that we could have a picnic in the backyard." He brought the meat to the table and began building a fat hamburger.

"Did your trip go well?" he asked after he took a bite from his burger.

"Yes, because I stayed a day longer, I finished most of the paperwork. I'll most likely need to go back in six to eight weeks, but only for a few days." She forked up a bite of salad.

"How did your week go?" she asked as she sipped her lemonade.

"The lemonade is a refreshing change. Thanks for fixing it."

"The usual, surgeries, postop work. I did get to assist an open heart transplant. That was exciting. You know if they had had that procedure when I was a kid, my grandfather may have … Well, that's in the past." He stared across the yard for a moment.

"Sometimes, I think back." He continued. "What would my life would be now if I had pursued a tennis career?"

"I would be seeing you in *GQ* in your underwear. Exposed would be those strong, shapely, hairy legs, well, the whole package. You would look out with those incredible eyes of yours and sell millions of Hanes briefs." She laughed, watching him blush.

"I don't think …" He cleared his throat. "That lifestyle didn't appeal to me. Too much of the Catholic altar boy left in me. So what about you? You said that the safe woman's major did nothing for you. Going for a business degree, was that a big decision for you?"

"Yes and no. The world of finance always appealed to me. My dad traded stocks for years, and I would look up stock quotes for him in the newspaper. So I became a stock broker. It was a real learning experience, let me tell you."

"All that time, no big, hunky guy tried to persuade you to turn in your broker's license for a marriage license?"

"I became afraid of guys for a while." She stopped and looked down at her hands. She had twisted them tightly together.

Clark could see the sudden tension in her body. He gently took her hand. "I cleaned off the glider over here under the grape arbor. Let's go sit over there and get comfortable."

She dropped into the glider, but she gripped the side of the swing.

"Are you sure you wouldn't like dessert," she asked in a strained voce.

Gently, he took her hand and pulled her next to him. "What is it? What's wrong? You're as stiff as a cardboard cutout."

"Old memories sometimes have a way of interfering with my thought processes." She cast her eyes downward, avoiding his.

"I feel you need to talk of these old memories. Give them the light of a new day, or evening since the sun is setting." He laughed. "Ole Doc Knowles, your friendly physician, is making a house call." He thumped his chest. "Tell ole doc your concerns and they will all vanish."

A tiny smile curved her mouth, and she put her hand in his. "You think coming clean with my nasty tale will make the memories, the nightmares, vanish? You're good, doc, but not that good." She took a deep breath but remained silent.

"OK, we'll have a fifty-minute session. You lie right down here in the swing, and I'll go find a notebook and pen. I might even try to fake a Viennese accent."

This time, she laughed and seemed to be more relaxed. Maybe his teasing had helped. Perhaps now he could get some answers of why she has these sexual hang-ups.

Sunset pink stretched across the western sky. As he gazed into her golden-hazel eyes, he could see in them the reflection of the sky. "Sometimes, by talking about those bad memories, it can be defused. One can gain a different perspective."

"Ah, you are now lying on my couch, Ms. Andreasen," he said in a poor imitation of Dr. Freund. "Good, now tell me what you are thinking. When did this experience happen?" Clark stroked his chin as if he had a goatee.

Ana Lea took a deep breath and glanced at the sky. *Maybe talking about the how and why it happened could help.* "The summer I turned twenty-one, my friend Cathy and I found jobs at Coulter Bay, Wyoming. It's part of the national park there near Jackson Hole. We were excited to have an adventure, getting away from our parents and living and working somewhere else for a while."

Suddenly, she stood up. "Let's go into the house. Maybe lying down is the way to confess my hang-ups." She grabbed some dishes, plates, tableware, and strode into the house.

"OK, we'll adjourn this session temporarily and move to the living room." He hurried after her.

Ana Lea slid onto her living room sofa and lay down. "Pull up a chair, Dr. Freund. I'm ready for our session."

Clark sat in the nearest chair, a wing chair in a floral pattern. "Yes, Ms. Andreasen, I believe when we were interrupted, you were recounting your summer in Wyoming."

"OK, I'll start there. I worked in the cafeteria. After about two weeks, I was assigned the cashier's position, because I seemed to be the only girl who could balance the books at night. Anyway, Cathy, my college friend, and I met these two guys from New York. One of them went to New York University. He was a cute guy, thin, dark haired, and had a quiet, sweet personality. His name was John. The other guy, his roommate, was big, blond, and hunky. He had an easy way about him most of the time. His name was Trace. He seemed to be interested in me, and John, the other guy, flirted with Cathy. The main problem for me concerning Trace was alcohol. Trace liked to drink—actually, they both did."

She took a deep breath, sat up, and seemed to be collecting her thoughts. "We hung with them most of the summer, doing casual stuff. A walk by the lake, lying in the sun, when there was a sunny day, taking a boat ride now and then. The last week in August, about ten days before the bay closed, we decided to drive down to Jackson for a cowboy band concert.

"I wanted to look nice, so I wore a skirt, light blue denim, and rather short, and a white western-style shirt. Cathy said I looked great. It's always chilly at night, so I did take a jacket.

"We went into this bar, and in the rear area, the band had set up for the concert. We found a table and sat down. The guys ordered drinks with alcohol. I had one, only one. The guys kept ordering more." She took a breath. "The band played for nearly an hour. Then they took a break. Cathy and John went out into the car. A while later, Trace and I went out to find them. Carly and John said they were going for a walk.

"Somehow, we ended up in the backseat. I guess I wasn't too sharp that night, but after a few kisses, his hands started roaming over me. Suddenly, he was on top of me, tearing my panties." She stopped and shook her head.

As she lifted her head, Clark could see a haunting fear in her eyes. As much as Clark hated to hear what she was going to tell him, he knew she needed to talk about her experience. He also knew he must listen. Already, he was silently cursing this Trace, who long ago took away something so precious to Ana Lea, her innocence.

"Oh, dear God, how can I?" she mumbled. She stopped and glanced at him. Her eyes were filled with tears. "I'll try to tell you everything. No one knows except my grandmother."

"If it's too painful for you, we can—"

"No, maybe if I tell you the rest … you'll understand. If I talk about it, maybe it will be better." She took another deep breath. "After, after he was finished, he reached on the floor of the car and found an old towel, picked it up, and cleaned up. Then he handed it to me. 'You'd better go inside. There's blood on your skirt. Oh, and comb your hair.' The way he said it, so matter-of-fact, as if I had smudged my makeup or ripped my shirt. I did as I was told. Though my body hurt, I was numb inside. I stood in the restroom staring in the mirror at the girl that once was me. The old me was gone.

"When I came out of the restroom, Trace stood waiting for me. He took my arm, and we went back to our table and sat down as if nothing had happened. There was a fresh drink waiting for me at my place. The jukebox was playing a country western song, and some people began to dance. At the rear, there was a dance floor. I sat there staring at the drink. My head was throbbing.

"John and Trace found something funny and were laughing. I felt a tap on my shoulder, and I looked up, and there stood Kitt. 'Would you like to dance?' He extended his hand. I guess I nodded, because he pulled me up and led me back to the dance floor. It was a slow dance, and I put my head near his shoulder. He looked down at me. 'Something is wrong, isn't it?'

"I burst into tears.

"He led me out into the chilly night. 'Stay here,' he ordered and darted back into the hall. He came back with my jacket, purse, and fistful of tissues. He took my arm and led me to his truck. 'Where are you staying?' he asked.

"I told him Coulter Bay, the girls' bunkhouse. He drove the forty miles back to where my things were.

"I cried for a long while but finally managed to get it together. I asked him why he was in Jackson Hole. He said, 'Football.' He'd been working out with the team at Boise State. He and some players all came down for the concert.

"'I'm going back to Salt Lake tomorrow,' he said. 'I could start the drive back now. Do you want to drive back with me?'

"I didn't have to think twice. Of course, I said yes."

CHAPTER 13

"After he had driven me back to the bunkhouse, we stopped for gas, snacks, and coffee. He drove until he got too tired, so we pulled into a gas station that was closed, and he slept for a while."

"'That guy, your date, he hurt you, didn't he?' Kitt asked.

"I said yes, but he didn't ask me any details. When we arrived in Salt Lake, it was dawn. He asked for my address. I couldn't go home. No way could I explain to my parents why I had come home so soon. I told him to bring me here, to my grandmother. I knew she would be up."

"I asked him if I could pay for his gas. He said, 'No. I believe in "what goes around comes around." Someday, you'll be in a position to help someone else, or perhaps even me.'"

"Why do you want to go to your grandmother's?" Clark asked.

"I told him I couldn't go home and that my grandmother would understand my situation."

"So what did you do, if you didn't want to call the police?" Clark asked.

"Kitt and I talked about the fact that I would never be able to prove rape.

He said that Trace would be 'taken care of.'"

"What about the worry of a pregnancy or an STD? Did those facts enter into your trauma?" Clark asked.

She suddenly stood up and began to pace. Ana Lea gripped the back of the wing chair. "Not at first, but when my period didn't come, I was frantic. My grandmother told me to go up to the campus clinic and get a checkup. I did, and the doctor said that my uterus didn't look like a pregnancy, but they gave me a test, and it came out positive."

Clark came out of the chair and put his arms around her. "God, I'm so sorry. What did you do?"

"About six weeks later, fall semester had started. One night, I began to have contractions. I was home living in my basement room, and I had my own full bath. I climbed into the bathtub and had a miscarriage. The next morning, I scrubbed it all away."

She gave a tiny shrug but then burst into tears. He held her and rocked her for a long time. Finally, she spoke against his shoulder. "It was the way I felt inside, as if I were a piece of meat that someone had taken out a chunk. My dreams of being an eager virgin on my wedding night were destroyed. I had always dreamed of having earth-shattering sex right off the bat with my husband. Later on, my fantasies took on a more mature theme—of meeting an older, experienced man who would teach me to have great sex. I never met that mature man."

She sat down on the sofa, and Clark sat next to her and took her into his arms. "Lea, I don't know what to say except that I hate it that this nasty experience happened to you. Especially to you, a virgin living in this culture of strict Christian values. Maybe now I can understand why you behave the way you do."

"Thanks for listening to my little tale of woe." She jumped up and stood looking down at him. "Maybe you can understand why I'm so freaky sometimes. I wouldn't blame you if you decided to look elsewhere for a more emancipated lady love. Maybe I'm not worth the trouble."

He stood and took both her hands in his. "This girl I see is beautiful, self-sufficient, sharp, and close to my age. As you well know, I am extremely attracted to you. If I can keep a lid on my sexual needs, and now I am more motivated to do so, we can still enjoy each other's company. Right now, however, I need to think about what you have told me." He stood and walked to the kitchen door. "Let's get the grill and picnic area cleaned up."

"No, I can do it." She called after him, but he had already gone outside. As they picked up and put away the remains of their dinner, neither of them said a word.

"Thanks for listening. I'm so glad that I could share my little story with someone." She watched as he set the plates and cups on the kitchen counter.

He moved like lightning across her living area, and she lost sight of him for an instant. The front door flew open, and he spoke as he opened her security door. "I really like it if you could have a sexual fantasy about me." He hesitated for a moment, and his smile seemed sad. "Let's give this a little time." He was out the door and down the porch steps before she could even reach to step outside.

She stepped out on the porch and watched the taillights of his car flash down the street. Her story was old and sad, but watching him leave made her even sadder.

Clark called twice, but Ana Lea did not see him for over a week. Labor Day week meant that many of the hospital staff were called in over the weekend. Clark was one of the young doctors doing double duty during the holiday. Finally, he called and asked if she could go jogging with him on Tuesday morning after Labor Day.

They met at Sugar House Park, and because all the schools had started, the park was nearly deserted. Ana Lea was a little late, so he drank some of the water he brought and paced around. Finally, she came jogging down the hill to the gravel track. "Sorry, I'm late. I overslept."

Clark watched her as she stretched out. But then she shot off in a steady run. He easily caught up with her, but she kept the steady pace. After once around the park, he picked up the pace. He was nothing short of amazed that she caught up and kept pace with him. She flashed an "I told you so" grin and started around the park perimeter again.

A quarter of the way around, she slowed the pace so she could speak to him. They both slowed and finished in a walk-jog. "Come to my house. I'll make you some breakfast." She took off and finished up at the parking area.

As he drove to Ana Lea's house, Clark mused about their relationship. He certainly enjoyed the time he spent with her. Could he actually fall in love with a girl without having a sexual relationship first? He wasn't sure.

Once she was home, she washed up, let him in, and started cooking. Over bacon, french toast, melon, and coffee, she began to talk. "I've had all week to think about me, about us. First, I believe that being as honest as I was with you is in the best interest for both of us. Telling you the reason about my sexual hang-up was important, but I think I should tell you about my goals. You should tell me about yours."

"My goal"—he smiled into those golden-hazel eyes—"believe it or not, is to finish my residency and find a slot with a medical group or with a hospital." He sat back and appraised her. Even with perspiration trailing down her cheeks and chest, her hair damp from the run, she was beautiful. "That's a long-term goal. A very short-term one would be to lie you on the living room floor, damp and sweaty, and make sweet love to you."

She blushed and wrinkled her nose. "Sounds rather … earthy … and primitive."

"Let me explain something to you. I'm not a womanizer. I've had experience with women, yes. Yet for me, there also has to be affection. I even loved a girl … once."

"You were in love?"

"A long time ago." He sighed.

"What happened?" She asked, her gaze steady on his face.

"I was in medical school. The poverty of a medical student and the amount of time I had to spend away from our little apartment were too much for her. She left. You know the rest. I joined the army as a medical corpsman. During my last tour in Iraq, my mother found she had breast cancer. She died four months after I came home."

"Oh, Clark, I'm so sorry." She reached for his hand across the table.

"It hit my dad pretty hard. I spent a fair amount of time dragging him out of bars, taking him home, and putting him to bed. I had applied for a residency in Southern California and had to turn it down."

"What did you do? Did you lose a whole year of study?"

"I worked as a bartender. It happened to be the bar my father liked to frequent. Besides, the tips were good." He shrugged.

"I'm impressed with your love and devotion for your family. I care about my family too," she said. "However, reaching the age of thirty-one and still being single, I am somewhat of a disappointment to my parents.

They come from the old school, where the girl may go to college but should marry soon after she is finished with her education."

"So they're upset because you're single? Is your family here in Salt Lake?" He shook his head in disbelief.

"No. My dad took a job in Tucson, Arizona, several years ago. He retired last year. Change of subject. My goals ... yes, I do like my career. Lately, I've yearned for a husband and baby. My old-fashioned upbringing tells me that a husband should come before baby. A good solid marriage is a goal too."

"So in an oblique manner, you're saying sex should wait until the wedding?"

"I'm programmed to think that, yes, but ... maybe not exactly the wedding night, but close. Maybe I shouldn't have said that." She dropped her head and blushed.

"So the wedding dress must be hanging on the closet door before the potential groom climbs in bed with you?" He gazed into her whiskey-colored eyes.

"Oh, Clark, I really care for you, and I don't want to lose you. It wouldn't feel right for me to just have an affair. Am I so really out of step with the social mores of today?"

"I need more coffee." He jumped up and took his mug into the kitchen. He walked back sloshing the hot liquid down the side of his cup and wiped it with a napkin. A grim smile curled his mouth. "You're not ready for a serious sexual relationship right now anyway. You couldn't handle it."

"Wait a minute!" She slammed her fork with a clink on her plate. "Me not ready, how can you say that?"

"Because of your lack of sexual experience, and only negative experience, I might add." He blue-green eyes seemed to bore into her soul.

"You think I'll hate sex because I was ... forced the first time?"

"Raped! You were raped. Turn that word over in your brain. Let it settle in there. Admit you were a victim of a sexual predator." He voice was harsh.

She turned away because she didn't want him to see the tears begin to crease tracks down her cheeks. She jumped up and went to the window, staring sightlessly at the trees across the street.

He walked to her, enfolding her in his arms. "Oh, lady, don't cry. No sense wasting tears on something so long in the past. Leave the pain, the guilt behind."

CHAPTER 14

She turned in his arms and tried for a watery smile. "I think I'll go shower. You can use the one in the basement bathroom. You left some clothes here last week, and I put them downstairs. Thanks for understanding."

He sighed. "OK. See you in a few minutes."

Clark found his clothes neatly laid out on the bed in the downstairs bedroom. Before he took them with him to shower, he wandered into the unfinished section of the basement. The night Ana Lea had given him a tour of her house, he remembered something strange about the unfinished area. Now, in the filtered daylight coming from an east window, he stared at the east wall. Drywall! That part of the area had been covered with wallboard, and the other two walls showed only the original cement. Why had someone put up a wallboard on the east wall?

As he studied it, he realized it had been several years since the wallboard had been taped. The tape was old, discolored, and beginning to pull away from the board.

He glanced around and noticed that a storage closet had been built on the backside of the furnace room. He looked into it and found a toolbox on the floor. He grabbed a hammer and began to pull the board away from the wall, working quickly, building up a sweat even though the basement was cool. What he found underneath the wallboard astonished him.

As he stood staring at his discovery, he felt a dry breeze across his back and the same earthy smell he had noticed when he was in the attic. The breeze felt almost like a touch, and he whirled around to find nothing. He shook his head. *My body has dried out from our jog, and I guess I felt a chill.*

Once Clark showered and changed clothes, he ran up the stairs and called to Ana Lea. "Hey, I need you to look at something. Can you come downstairs with me right now?"

The urgency in his voice made her scurry to the basement. "What is it?" "Come look at this." He took her hand and nearly dragged her into the southeast corner of the unfinished section. "I pulled off the drywall, and this is what I found. The stuff was old and came off easily." She stood near and stared at the wall. "What is it, a door?"

"You talked about digging out a basement door to the backyard. It looks like someone already has." He gestured to the outline of a door now filled with concrete.

"Amazing, an actual door. Hey, there's some writing on it too. It's hard to see." She turned to the toolbox in the closet and dug out a flashlight. She stood close and illuminated the door, studying the printing that angled down. It was written in red.

Clark traced the letters with his finger. There were nine large letters. "This is an *N*, and this may be an *E*. This letter is a crude *V*. Oh my gosh! It says 'never open.'"

"It isn't written in blood, is it?" She shrugged and smiled. "Just kidding." Clark gave her an incredulous gaze. "I'm glad you haven't lost you sense of humor, but what do you think it means? Have you heard anything, any rumors in the family about someone excavating an outside entrance and cementing it up again?"

"No, but I can ask around. Do you think it's because the house isn't structurally sound?" This area is directly underneath my kitchen cabinets and double sinks. It's not going to crash down into the basement if we dig out, is it? On second thought, maybe the ghost wrote the words. Perhaps that's why it's so hard to read."

"What ghost?" Clark rubbed his arms as if he were feeling a chill.

"Two of my cousins told me that my house is haunted. At least it was when they lived here."

"Why? Did they hear something go 'bump' in the night?" Clark laughed. "No. The report was that things go bump in the daytime."

"A midday ghost? Maybe he's a refugee from a cancelled soap opera, or at least they killed him off, and he resented it." Clark's mouth twitched.

"Oh, funny, now you're the one with the sense of humor, but yours is warped."

"Something's just occurred to me." She grabbed his arm. "Come outside with me. Humor me, because I'm curious." They walked outside, and she stood at the southeast corner of the house where the cemented up door was located.

"I'll get a shovel." He ran to the garage and brought back the tool. She picked up the shovel and began to dig up the flower bed at that spot. "Stop, you'll get dirt all over your white slacks. My clothes are old." He took the shovel and began to dig.

"Be careful with my petunias."

"You wanted me to dig. Besides, it's now September, and you'll need to plant them again next year. Aren't you curious about what we might find here?"

"True." She sighed. "OK, Sherlock, dig away. Just be careful." About ten inches down, the shovel banged against something solid. As Clark dug, he soon uncovered a stair. Then he dug out another and another. Soon, he came down to a concrete slab, flush with the original doorway.

"The doorway and stairs are already here. All that needs to be done is remove the concrete and hang a good metal door. Plus pull down the siding." Ana Lea felt a chill on the back of her neck, and the scent of newly turned earth assailed her nostrils. She shivered, even though she was standing in the warm, bright sunlight and the day was heating up. "Maybe we should leave it closed up."

His eyes narrowed. "Hey, did you feel a chill too? You're not superstitious, are you?"

"Suddenly, I had the strangest feeling about this door. I will, however, call my uncle Edward and some cousins and see if there was a rational explanation for someone to have dug out the door and sealed it up again. I'm sorry. Now you'll need another shower. Let's go in, and I'll stick your clothes in the washer."

"I think I have something to wear home before I change for my afternoon shift. I would be pleased if you washed a few things for me."

The entity watched as they walked back into the kitchen. It flowed down and covered the exposed cement door. *No. This is bad. They must be stopped. They'll open up the vortex. Danger, dangerous for them.*

Later in the week, Ana Lea called her cousin Jonas Riley. "Do you remember when we discussed cutting a door in the southeast corner of my basement? I've discovered it would be handy to use it when coming in from the garage, to take in skis, groceries, and to carry and store seasonal items, plants, stuff like that?" she asked.

"Yeah, I understand. Do you want to start on that project soon? I may have some time in a week or two. I'm working on an extensive renovation on a house above the boulevard. If the weather holds, I should be finished in ten days or so."

"There's something strange about my basement. My boy—er, friend noticed it and pulled off the drywall on the east wall. We found that a door had already been cut out and then cemented up. Outside, we found concrete stairs already excavated. Apparently, someone else thought it was the ideal place for an outside entrance."

"Whew, you actually found a door? I'll come over either this Sunday or the next and take a look at it," Jonas said.

"Could you ask around the family and find out who excavated it and later had it covered up?"

"I'll check with my dad. Maybe he knows something about this mysterious door. I'll call you when I have any updated info. Wow, this is really interesting," he said.

Ana Lea said good-bye. *Hmm, a mystery.* She always enjoyed learning about the unknown.

Later that evening, Clark called.

"Hi, lady, what's happening in your world today? Did you find out anything about your mysterious door?" he teased.

"No, but I've called and talked to a cousin. He's going to check with his dad and find out about the history of my house."

"I called to tell you I'm going biking in Moab this weekend. I should be back Monday night. Perhaps we can get together Tuesday."

"I'm leaving for Columbus Tuesday morning. Can you do the cat feeding chore for me?" She tried for a slightly pleading tone.

"Sure. I'll come over Tuesday evening. Can I bring over my coffee maker? I'm not crazy about the instant stuff. How long will you be gone?"

"I'll return Saturday. See you then?"

"Absolutely. We'll barbecue if the weather cooperates." She could imagine his teasing grin.

"Great! See you when you return."

CHAPTER 15

Monday evening, while Ana Lea was packing for her Columbus trip, Jonas Riley called.

"Hi, I checked on your inquiries concerning the basement door with my dad. His older cousin Dennis Riley lived in your house about thirty years ago. During that time, he was building his own house. He and his family lived in Grandmother's house about two years."

"Where were the grandparents? Were they living here too?"

"You wouldn't remember. Probably you hadn't been born yet. Grandpa had chronic bronchitis at that time. So he and Grandma bought a trailer and moved to Mesa, Arizona—you know, for the warmer climate."

"How long did they stay in Arizona?" she asked.

"Dad thinks about three years. It was during that period that our cousin Dennis excavated the outside entrance. At that time, it became part of the city building code that a basement had to have an outside entrance or deep windows for quick evacuation."

"Did *he* cement it up again?"

"I don't think so, but I'm not sure. When Dennis's family moved out, I believe the door was still there. OK, this is the interesting part." Jonas dropped his voice in a conspiratorial manner. "During the time Dennis's family lived there, their youngest daughter lived with them. She was, I believe, about sixteen years old. Her name was Denise, named after him. Anyway, Uncle Dennis finished the basement bedroom for her and the bathroom downstairs. At that time, she attended Sugar House High. She cut more classes than she attended, coming and going out of the house through that basement door as she pleased. In the neighborhood, she was known as the 'wild child.'

"At any rate, she turned up missing. The police put out a missing persons report on her. During that time, kids ran away from home, used drugs, got into all kinds of trouble." He laughed. "The search for her was not high priority. Lots of kids ran away from home. Nothing was heard about her for a year. The exact date, a year later after she had gone missing, her mother's car was stolen right out of the driveway."

"Who stole the car? Was it a friend of the daughter's?" Ana Lea asked.

"They put out a stolen car alert. They didn't find out anything, until they located it. Denise was never seen again—alive, that is." Jonas sounded subdued.

"You mean they found her dead?" Ana Lea was horrified.

"The highway patrol in California found her body at a rest stop on Interstate 10 about two weeks after her mother's car was stolen. She had delivered a baby in her mother's car, bled out, and had gone into the restroom and died."

"Oh, the poor girl! How did she manage to steal her mother's car a year after she went missing? What happened to the baby?" Ana Lea felt a shiver of dread.

"The police searched the trash cans, the restroom, and the surrounding area. Never found the baby. She either delivered in the car and went into the restroom to clean up, or delivered in the restroom. They dusted the car for fingerprints and found a strange set in the car, but there was no match in any of the fingerprint databases."

"Why no match for the fingerprints?"

"If someone has never been fingerprinted for one reason or another, the individual won't be in any database. From the autopsy, the California ME determined that the baby was full term, large, from the vaginal tearing. They think someone could have helped her and taken the baby. Or because she was bleeding out, they panicked and left her there and took the baby and fled. That's the theory anyway."

"This is a heartrending but a very intriguing story. The big mystery is— how did she manage to get her mother's car, at eight or whatever months pregnant, and end up in the desert in California? Obviously, she was driving to some destination, went into labor, delivered, and died," Ana Lea said.

"Either that or a friend, or potential father, stole the car, drove to California, and met up with her, and who knows? Dennis and his wife had already moved out of the house, so it was vacant when they brought her body back and had the funeral. Grandma and Grandpa came up from Mesa for the viewing, and I believe they moved back in the house that spring. Grandpa died a few years after that, but Grandma lived there until she was in her late eighties."

"Did Grandma know about the door?"

"I'm sure she did. Did she ever say anything to you when you visited her in the summertime?" he asked.

"No, but she didn't like the basement. She seldom went down there. She once told me that bad spirits were down there. As I grew older, I decided that she was just telling me stories. She did plant flowers where we found the stairway. I'd forgotten about that. Has someone written all this history down?"

"Maybe my mom has. She's the official journal keeper of the family," Jonas said. "So do you still want me to open up the mysterious door? Or are you superstitious and want to leave it closed?"

"Let me think about your offer. Also, can you give me an estimate? Thanks for relating the family mystery. I can't wait to tell my boy—er … friend."

Ana Lea couldn't reach Clark that evening because he was doing emergency surgery. Her plane left early the next morning for Columbus, so she left him a message that she would call later in the week.

Clark had forgotten to feed Ana Lea's cat until late Wednesday evening. It was dark when he finally arrived at the house. He managed to feed Crystal, grab some milk and cookies, and drag his exhausted body into the TV room. He crashed and woke only when the cat roused him the next morning by licking his face.

On Friday morning, Clark sat in Ana Lea's kitchen drinking coffee he had made with his coffee maker. He watched dark clouds gather outside the large east kitchen window. He felt comfortable as if he were at home his home. He liked sitting in the normally sunny kitchen and wanted to live here and share it with the girl he now knew he loved. He'd even share it with a cat named Crystal.

It was Thursday evening, after Joanna and Ana Lea had been to the shelter building checking on the finishing touches of paint and some trim. It was late afternoon when they left. The dedication of the building was Friday, the next evening.

Even though it was mid-September, the days were hot, and the building was stifling. The electricians were due to turn on the AC later that afternoon. When they walked to the car, Joanna held her head and handed the keys to Ana Lea.

"You drive. I don't feel up to it."

"What's the matter? Are you coming down with something?" Her friend gave Joanna a concerned gaze.

"I'm not sure, well, not exactly. Just drive west on this street. When you come to Eighteenth Avenue, turn right. There's a Target in the next block." She leaned back against the seat and closed her eyes.

Once Ana Lea brought the big SUV to a stop in the Target parking lot, she turned to Joanna. "Are you feeling well enough to go into the store? There has to be a snack bar near the entrance."

Joanna eased from the car and went straight to the snack bar, with Ana Lea trailing behind. She turned to her friend. "You still drink diet cola?" A nod from Ana Lea told her what to order. She returned with two drinks in paper cups and a pretzel.

"Are you drinking lemon-lime soda now? I thought you didn't like it." Ana Lea sipped her iced cola.

"I needed something cold and laced with sugar." Joanna set a plate with a large pretzel on the table. She broke off a chunk and munched. "Have some of it. It's cinnamon sugar, and it's good." She pushed the plate across the table.

Ana Lea watched as the food revived her friend. "Do you feel better? Are you are now ready to shop?"

Joanna nodded. "Then let's do it."

Later in the evening, as they sat eating takeout chicken and side dishes, Joanna seemed just fine. Jake had come in late, fixed a plate of food, and took it into his den.

While the two women cleaned up, Joanna turned to Ana Lea. "Could you do me a favor?"

"Absolutely. What do you need?"

"Could you read Callie a bedtime story, while I scoot the boys upstairs for homework and showers?"

Callie came downstairs carrying a book. "I want this one, Aunt Lea, OK?" "Sure. Let's go upstairs and I'll tuck you in after the story."

Much later that evening, there was a knock on the door of the guest bedroom where Ana Lea was staying. It was Joanna. "Hi, may I come in?"

"Of course. Are you feeling better?"

"Oh, much better. In fact, I'm brimming with good news."

"I like good news. So tell me." Ana Lea patted the place on the bed, where she sat propped up, with a book in her hand.

"I don't know if you know much about my background, where I grew up, went to school?"

"I know you have a master's of business degree from Brigham Young, and you grew up in Phoenix and joined the majority religion when you were in Provo."

"That's the part that goes on a résumé, true. But I was a sexually abused child, and it went on into my teen years. I was victimized by my father." She looked away, and her hands were clenched in her lap.

"Oh, Joanna, I'm so sorry!" Ana Lea gripped her friend's shoulder.

"I dated very little in high school and college. When I met Joshua, I was twenty-eight years old. He was so kind to me, never coming on to me, but I did like kissing him. The year Josh was healing from his knee injury, I met Jake. He was suffering too. He had just lost his wife, the love of his life, six months before.

"We just sort of fell in love over the telephone. When we married last December, having sex with him was my duty, and because I loved him, I could do that. I wanted so much to please him."

"Just to please him?" Ana Lea's eyes narrowed her eyes, but watching Joanna's face, she smiled.

"After we'd been married for a few months, I realized that even though I had married a whole family, I wanted at least one child of my own. A a few months later, I went to see an OB-GYN specialist. He checked me over. I had suffered some female problems, but the doctor said physically I was OK and could have a child." She smiled, but her cheeks colored in a blush.

"We talked about intimate positions, and he gave me this 'how dumb are you' reaction. He reached into a drawer and handed me a little booklet. He said, 'Look this over.' It gave me some definite suggestions.

"I thought about this piece of advice, and so one night, I sort of seduced Jake, and I tried some of the booklet's suggestions. Jake said, 'Are you sure you want to this?'

"And I answered yes. From then on, that was our way. It must have worked, because I'm pregnant." Joanna grinned.

"How far along do you think?" Ana Lea asked.

"About a month, maybe more. A baby due in June. Can you believe it?"

She put her hand on her chest.

CHAPTER 16

Friday evening, Clark picked up some dinner and took it to Ana Lea's house. He planned to eat there and feed the cat. Once he had finished eating, he thought about Emily's journal and went to find it.

He had stopped at the place describing Emily's marriage to Samuel.

> June 17, 1884
>
> My heart is full. So many glorious things are in my mind as I write. Samuel and I were married yesterday at my aunt Millicent's home. Since this is a second plural marriage for Samuel, it must be done quietly. Already, there is pressure on the brethren of the church from Washington to condemn polygamy. How can they do this when it is the Lord's will and his commandment?
>
> My dress is so beautiful. Samuel said that I looked like a sweet young angel. We had a special dinner at my aunt's. I was so nervous that I did not taste much of the food.

Samuel took me to his house and helped me unpack my belongings in the room that he had built for me. He also bought a fine brass bed for me, for us when we are together to sleep in.

To leave us alone, Jerusha and their two girls had gone to visit her parents' farm for a few days. I was so nervous and frightened about the wedding night. Somehow, it was upsetting to me to spend it in the house of another woman. It was kind of Jerusha to leave.

Still I was scared and shy. Samuel came and kissed me. I stood stiff, I could not relax.

Samuel laughed, and he left me to spend my first night in my new room alone. He left and walked into the room he shares with his first wife. As I lay there in that big bed, I thought of all the things my mother had told me. That it was my duty to submit to my husband so that I may have children. She promised that sometime later, I would come to enjoy marital relations with my husband.

Clark couldn't stop a grin as he read that entry. Good old Samuel was a smart guy. He did not force his bride into sex before she had time to think about being married and what it would really mean. He read on. The next entry was a few days later.

June 22, 1884

I pondered whether to write the details of what went between Samuel and me at our first night together. The day after our wedding, I awoke to tea and cooked oats for breakfast.

He had even found wild strawberries to have with the cereal. He took me into his orchard, and we seemed to walk for miles. There were fruit trees of every kind: apples, peaches, apricots, with a garden of vegetables close to the house. There were other trees in the orchard, not fruit but old ones, some with twisted branches and thick trunks. They had provided shade for many years before the fruit trees grew larger.

After supper, Samuel found me reading in my new room. We opened the windows, and the summer breeze ruffled the white curtains.

Now, what I write is very personal, however, I do this for a daughter I might have who would someday read this many years from now. I will tell any reader how sweet Samuel was to me. He was kind and gentle, stroked and kissed me and so patient with me. A woman couldn't ask for a better husband than the one I now have.

Afterward, we lay close together, and Samuel explained that man without a woman is incomplete. That our joining was God's way of making two people one. My Samuel is a sweet, tender lover. No woman could ask for more.

Late June 1884

Jerusha and her girls returned to the farm. I truly expected to be an equal sister-wife, but she treats me like a servant girl. She gives me difficult, messy chores to do and then scolds me if I am not finished when she decides I should be.

Clark was pulled away from his reading when the phone rang. It was Ray. "I thought you'd be at Ana Lea's, and I was correct." He laughed. "Hey, I have two tonsillectomies tomorrow morning. Two girls, both with infected throats. How about your help?"

"Sounds good. What time are you planning to start? Taking out tonsils will be a new one for me," Clark said.

"We'll need to meet the kids about seven thirty. See ya then."

Clark put the journal away for another day. The last entry did not surprise him at all. If he were a betting man, he could have predicted Jerusha's animosity and won the lottery.

Ana Lea came home late Saturday and found Clark had been sleeping in the den and leaving rumpled sheets and clothes thrown on a chair. There was a note pinned to the bathroom door: "Got called in, multiple gunshot victims, gang related."

She settled down in front of the TV. Maybe there would be a report about the gang shooting on the late evening news.

Sunday afternoon, Ana Lea's doorbell rang. She was anticipating Clark's arrival, because she had suggested he come for dinner when his Sunday shift was over. When she opened the door, she found Jonas Riley standing there.

"Hi, cousin." He offered her his hand. "I came to take a look at your 'mysterious' basement door." He laughed.

"I'd appreciate it that you came. Follow me." She turned and led him to the basement stairs.

She found the flashlight and showed him the door with the scrawled letters on it.

He studied it, stepped back, and then examined it up close. "As far as drilling out the concrete, that's no problem. I have no idea why anyone would write such a warning on it. I can build in extra support, if that appears to be necessary. Let's go look at it from the backyard." He walked quickly to the stairs.

While they were both outside, Clark drove his car into the narrow drive behind the house. He jumped out and walked over to Ana Lea and Jonas. "Hi, I'm Clark Knowles." He put out his hand.

Jonas turned and grinned. "You must be the 'er' friend this girl keeps referring to." He stuck out his hand and introduced himself.

"So do you think drilling out the door is going to be too much of a job? Also, is it going to be expensive?" Clark asked.

"Not too difficult. The labor will probably be a little more than the cost of a good metal door. I definitely recommend one of the strong steel models because of the weather around here in the winter. You could wake up one January morning and find the door entrance completely covered with snow, right up to ground level," Jonas warned.

"It snows that much here, at this elevation?" Clark narrowed his eyes. Jonas turned to Ana Lea. "Your boy—'er' friend hasn't been here through a winter yet, has he?"

"No, I've been here since early June, and all I've seen is heat, lots of *dry* heat. Of course, now the weather has moderated somewhat."

"Come on, Clark, you have to admit it's nice today." She put her hands on her hips.

He squeezed her shoulder. "You're right, it is pleasant out here today." He turned to Jonas. "Let's go inside and talk about your costs."

Once Jonas had left, Ana Lea went into the kitchen to finish preparing dinner. Clark walked behind her and wrapped his arms around her. "I haven't seen you for several days. You need a 'welcome home' kiss."

Her lips were soft, warm, and they tasted of cheese. "Is there cheese in this casserole you're baking?"

"Yes, cheddar, sour cream, and broccoli. Are any of those on your 'don't care for' list?"

"No. It all sounds quite edible." He watched her place the flower-decorated ceramic dish in the oven. "What else are we eating? Is there something I can do to help?"

"You can find some dishes, silverware, and set the table."

"Yes, ma'am." He was so familiar with her kitchen that it was easy for him to do something simple to help her.

Soon, the chicken dish was ready, and they sat down. "How was your trip?" he asked between mouthfuls.

"Good. We dedicated the building we are going to use for the shelter and educational area. The one in Los Angeles will be ready in less than a month." "How was your week, especially the gunshot victims you needed to help last night?"

"It's a good thing most of these dumb kids are such bad shots. Otherwise, we'd be burying them rather than patching them up. Say, let me ask you something. When you told me about your experience in Wyoming, I wondered how you knew Kitt."

She frowned, finished chewing, and took a large sip of water. "I met Kitt at a fraternity party, probably two years before. It was during the summer between my freshman and sophomore college year. My best friend Cathy and I went up the canyon, with the plan of just meeting lots of guys but not getting involved with any of them. It was fun, a barbecue in the mountains, with maybe forty or fifty kids in attendance. We hiked to the top of Storm Mountain."

"Storm Mountain, where's that?" Clark asked.

"It's up Big Cottonwood Canyon. Anyway, there was beer and probably 'grass,' but we didn't get into that. Somehow, we found an empty picnic table, and Kitt sat down next to Cathy. She saw someone else she wanted meet, so she jumped up and left, leaving me alone with Kitt. We talked for hours, and, finally, he walked both of us to our car, and he kissed me. No big romance, just a kiss. So when I went to the first fall football game, I watched for him on the field." She shrugged.

"You never dated him?" Although Clark wanted to hear the truth, part of him didn't want to know if she had an undying love for Kitt.

"No. However, I did date one of his fraternity brothers. And later that year, I went to a party where he had been invited. By then, he had graduated and had been drafted by a team in Cincinnati. We danced a couple of times. That was it."

Clark felt his breathing return to normal, and he relaxed his hold on the coffee cup he had been gripping. All he could think of to say was "Hmmm, interesting. Change of subject. This Jonas Riley, how are you related to him?"

"Jonas is my cousin. His father is my mother's older brother. He's probably about forty, or did you notice that? Speaking of Uncle Martin, Jonas checked with him. You won't believe the story he told me about this house, when my other uncle Dennis, his wife, and his daughter had lived here." She stood up and cleared the table. "Do you want dessert while I tell you this amazing story, or do you want to pie and ice cream later?"

"By all means, I'll refill my coffee cup, and you can weave your tale right now, Miss Scheherazade." He took his cup to the kitchen, refilled it, and sat down again.

"OK, this all happened about thirty years ago …"

CHAPTER 17

The Salt Lake shelter occupied Ana Lea's time for the next few days. Clark had been assigned the night shift for the next two weeks, so she only spent time with him on Sunday. For those two weeks or so, they didn't see much of each other. They chatted on the phone from time to time, but both of them were heavily involved with their careers.

The first Tuesday in October, Ana Lea was awakened by a horrendous sound of a drill. It sounded as if someone was drilling away the foundation of the house. She hurried into a robe and went out the kitchen door. It was Jonas using what seemed like a cement jackhammer.

"Hi." She sounded over the din.

"Hi, Ana Lea." The drilling stopped. "I thought I'd get as much done this morning as possible. Look at those clouds forming over the mountains. We're in for a big storm."

She squinted up at the eastern mountains. The clouds had moved in, and there was a stiff south wind. "You're right. We're in for a change in the weather." She hurried back into the house. *Time to dig out some warmer clothes.*

That afternoon, while Ana Lea worked on the finances for the Salt Lake shelter, the phone rang. "Hello?" she answered.

"Oh, Lea, I glad I caught you home. The opening of the Torrance shelter has been moved up to Saturday, and that evening, there is a formal dinner, black tie. You need to get down here ASAP. I called Delta, and they have a flight out of SLC at 3:00 p.m. tomorrow. Can you be on it?" Nichole Wright said.

"Oh, boy, that soon? I have nothing formal that is for the fall and winter season. I'll have to go shopping."

"You can shop down here with me. I know some great discount stores. Just bring your credit card and black shoes."

"OK, Nichole, I'll put my fashion needs in your capable hands. See ya tomorrow."

It was late afternoon when the Delta flight landed. Nichole was waiting for her in the terminal, near the door. "Come on, grab your luggage, I'm parked in a fifteen-minute zone outside the door."

Nichole drove into the spacious garage and opened the back of her SUV.

She began to tug out Ana Lea's suitcase.

"Don't you dare lift that beast—it will send you in premature labor."

"If truth be told, I wouldn't mind having this baby soon, as in the next three hours." She sighed.

Ana Lea lugged and dragged her suitcase into the family room. Rex, the family dog, met them with barks and brushes against both Nichole and her guest. Ana Lea gave the dog a scratch behind the ears, and he seemed to be content with her ministrations.

"Rex!" Nichole shouted. "Go lie down. That dog, sometimes he really thinks he's king around here. Right now, I must hit the ladies' room. I'll be back shortly." Nichole lumbered down the hall to the guest bathroom.

Soon, she returned and began a search of the refrigerator. She found sacks of fresh vegetables and a frozen spaghetti dish. "Would you mind standing here and chopping vegetables for a salad, while I pop this dish into the oven?"

Ana Lea walked over the sink to wash her hands. "How long will the main course take?"

"About an hour, but I'll make up some garlic bread and iced tea. While the salad chills, we can gab."

The next day, Nichole drove to the shopping destination, and while driving, she explained the banquet they were to attend. "This is a big deal because Josh's team, the Aces, has become involved. Important. We have to look glamorous. Oh, and your date is Kitt."

"Kitt!" Ana Lea's heart rate jumped into triple time. She managed to take a breath and gain some control. "Whose idea was that?"

"Joshua's, or maybe they both came up with the plan. Why, are you opposed to attending this shindig with a married man?" Nichole teased.

"What about Melanie? Why isn't she coming with Kitt?"

"She's supervising a big book tour because some of the heavy mystery writers are going on tour together. You know the book industry is in a spin over e-publishing. Those big guys want to stay in print, hard cover."

Ana Lea took a calming breath. "Of course, I'll accompany Kitt. After all, I know how to behave as a professional."

"Oh, here we are." Driving west on Sunset Boulevard, Nichole took a sharp turn up a narrow street and turned into a gravel-covered parking lot. There were only three other cars parked there. The original blacktop had worn away, the parking area looked rutted, and scraggly weeds were struggling to survive here and there.

"What is this place?" Ana Lea asked. Across the back of the building, she read, "Saul's Dresses and Suits." The paint was old and missing in places.

"Again, tell me. What is this place?" Ana Lea asked.

"A hidden treasure. I'm still such a tightwad, and so is Joshua for the most part. Even living in his Brentwood house hasn't turned me into a spendthrift. It's ingrained in me to go cheap, I guess." Nichole laughed.

"Hmmm, maybe I've had the wrong idea about clothes shopping. We'll just have to see." Ana Lea shrugged as they walked down a rather steep, cracked concrete walk to reach the front door of the store. They entered a poorly lit, low-ceilinged building.

Ana Lea took a sniff. It even had an old, slightly musty smell. She glanced around. Everywhere, there were racks of clothes. Once inside, it seemed much larger than it appeared from the outside. Toward the rear, there was a wide stairway leading to a loft floor, and it too was loaded with merchandise. A small sign pointed to the rear of the main floor, Formal Wear. She ambled in that direction, gazing at all the racks as she passed.

Ana lea began searching through an area of formal gowns in her size. She found the merchandise to be of superior quality, and the prices were even better. She turned to Nichole. "Some of this stuff is designer quality. Why is it here?"

Nichole shrugged. "Why spend a thousand bucks on a dress when I can pick one up here for a quarter of the price?" She pulled a beaded knit dress off the rack and waved it at her friend.

"The maternity dresses are upstairs. I'll see you in a while." Nichol huffed up the wide stairway.

Ana Lea found several ball gowns and some funky party dresses to try on. Finally, she found one that favored her coloring and figure type. It was royal blue, a soft silky fabric, with a boat-shaped front neckline, three-quarter sleeves, and a plunging wide V in the back. It was trimmed with small paste diamonds around the sleeves and the front neckline. The skirt flared out below the knees gracefully to the floor.

As she moved back and forth in front of three-way mirror, a voice spoke behind her. . "Is there anything I can help you with, deary?"

She whirled around to see a tiny woman in a shapeless green dress, with tightly curled carrot-red hair. Gazing down, Ana Lea looked into a wrinkled face. Around the woman's eyes were gobs of black eyeliner and bright green eye shadow. "Excuse me?" she said.

"I'm here to help you. My, you look lovely in that blue number. Not many women have the body to put into that dress, but you do." She smiled, showing a few missing teeth.

"You're the saleslady?" Ana Lea asked.

Just then, a voice came from the stairs. "Hey, girlfriend, what do you think of this dress?" Nichole came down the stairs wearing deep emerald-green gown in a crepe fabric with heavy matching satin trim. The neckline had a wide oval shape showing some cleavage, and Nichole, in her present condition, had plenty to see. A green ribbon threaded under the bust and tied in the back. The skirt fell in soft pleats that opened up as she walked.

"Whoa, a sexy maternity dress." Ana Lea laughed.

"Mrs. Wright, how are you?" The tiny woman practically skipped over and took Nichole's hand to help her down the last few stairs. "My goodness, you've really blossomed out."

"Hi, Myrna. This is my friend Ana Lea from Utah."

"What do think of your friend in our royal-blue silk?" Myrna asked.

"Gosh, girl, turn around," Nichole ordered.

Ana Lea turned and picked up the long skirt and let it drop gracefully from her hand.

Nichole gasped. "That is very feminine, wow, beautiful—no, it's downright sexy. You're going to need … a"—she cleared her throat—"a special bra with that one."

Myrna touched Ana Lea's arm. "We have just what you need." The little clerk hurried to the front of the store and called out over her shoulder. "What cup size are you, deary, a C or a D?"

The formal dinner was held in a ballroom of a large hotel on Wilshire Boulevard. Ana Lea, slightly nervous to wear the back-revealing dress, borrowed a shawl from Nichole. Most of her anxiety stemmed from having Kitt as her date.

Joshua always looked marvelous in a tux, but Kitt was overwhelming. Those wide shoulders, trim waist and hips, and his height commanded attention. Many feminine heads turned as the four of them found their table, and this room had several NFL players, coaches, their beautiful wives and girlfriends in attendance.

After the dinner speeches, the band took center stage and began playing some popular older rock songs. Kitt escorted Ana Lea to the floor. When he went to put his hand on her back and found bare skin, he grinned.

"Where would you suggest I put my hand?" he teased.

"When I bought this dress, I didn't think about dancing." She blushed.

"I have an idea." He wrapped his hand around her back and rested tightly on her side. "This is quite a dress, or the lack of some of it. It has my stamp of approval." He chuckled.

What have I done? I wanted to impress Kitt. In the future, I better be careful what I wish for.

CHAPTER 18

Ana Lea was relieved when the next song changed to one upbeat and they could dance an '80s swing. The next song was slower, and Kitt held her too close. Rather than enjoying being close to him, he just made her nervous.

Later on, they changed partners. Kitt danced with Nichole, and Josh with Ana Lea. Josh had no problem with her dress. He rested his hand lightly on her back and held her easily.

"You look beautiful. When we hired you, your good looks didn't really enter into the equation. However, I think you being attractive as you are is a plus to our organization," Joshua commented.

After another dance, Nichole sat down and took a deep breath.

"Sorry, I'm dancing for two here, and I'm tired. Can we leave soon?" She touched her husband's arm.

"We can. Kitt and I will circulate the room, while you and Lea take a breather."

Once they reached the Wright home, Joshua helped Nichole out of the car. She slowly climbed the three front stairs carrying her green high-heeled sandals. She turned to her two guests. "I'm tired, so I'll be a poor hostess and leave you two to your own devices. Lea, you know where I keep the drinks and snacks, so eat or drink anything you choose."

Joshua came in from the garage. "I'd better see to the comforts of my 'lady fair.' It looks like I'll need to lug her upstairs and help her out of her clothes." "Tough duty, buddy, but I think you're up for it." Kitt cleared his throat and winked. "I mean, you can handle it. Good night, you two."

"It's a beautiful night. Let's go, you and I sit by the pool." Without waiting for a reply from Ana Lea, Kitt began opening cupboards and the fridge. He found sodas and ice for the glasses and carried them out through the patio door to the pool area.

She found crackers, cheese, and fresh carrot sticks, and carried a plate of the snacks and followed him out. Kitt had already pulled two lounge chairs close together. She wrapped the cream-colored fringed stole firmly around her back and sat down. If they were going to chat, she decided on a neutral topic, the NFL season.

As Nichole and Josh entered their bedroom, Nichole gave a tired sigh. "You really are tired, aren't you? I thought it was all a ploy to help a rather uncomfortable Lea. I could see how nervous she was dancing with Kitt, having all his undivided attention. And that dress, any man under the age of eighty would say, 'Wow!' I always suspected she was a beautiful girl, but tonight, I'm a believer."

"Poor Josh, stuck with the pregnant blimp." Nichole called from the closet, reaching for a shoe box on a high shelf for her green sandals. Josh reached over her and pulled down the box.

"Thank you. Would you mind helping me with the zipper on my dress?" "It would be my pleasure." He slid the zipper down and held the dress as she stepped out of it. He hung up the dress and rubbed Nichole's shoulders and back, while she stood in the closet.

"Mm, that's so nice," she murmured.

She lumbered over to the big bed. Josh shed his tux and came to her. "You need help with those support pantyhose?" He slid them off her legs and began to massage her feet. Her head fell back, and she sighed in pleasure.

"I need a nightgown." She slid off the bed, padded over to the dresser, and found one of white cotton.

He followed her back to the bed and snapped open her bra. As she slid out of it, he cupped her full breasts. She leaned back against him with her eyes closed. He took the nightgown from her hand and pulled it over her head. It floated easily over her swollen body.

"Open the curtains a wee bit?" Nichole asked.

He shed the remainder of his clothes and opened the sheers. He stood for a moment looking out. Kitt glanced up and smiled, giving no other indication of seeing Josh standing there naked.

"Did Kitt or Lea see you standing there au naturel?" Nichole asked.

"Just Kitt, and he sees me like this every day in the locker room. Lea was facing the other way."

Nichole was so happy to be here in this bed, in this house with Josh. She felt as if the world came tumbling down, he would dig her out and save her. Perhaps it was being pregnant and how vulnerable she felt now. She worried about her baby, wanted to keep him safe too. She had always been so self-reliant, but now she could lean on Josh and not worry. Perhaps it was because she was so comfortable and happy to live with him, but in her heart, she knew it was her love for him and his for her. She opened her arms to him, and he came and filled her with pleasure.

Kitt's mouth twitched, and with a slight shake of his head, he sipped his drink.

As he drank, he seemed to stare at Ana Lea. Sitting out here alone with him, she seemed even more uneasy than before. Finally, she brought up the subject of Kitt's wife, Melanie. "Where is Melanie this weekend?" even though she remembered Nichole told her about Melanie's travels.

"She's in Boston right now, I believe. From there, they go to Atlanta and then back to New York. She's scheduled to come home on Thursday. It's the busy time of year for her because her publishing house is gearing up for Christmas."

"You're right, we must start thinking about Christmas, since it's October." She was making dumb small talk and glanced away from him. She checked the folds of her dress and wrapped the shawl more tightly around her shoulders.

"Going to the banquet with you was … nice." *Couldn't she say something more interesting or clever?* Her voice died away.

"I'm quite happy you were here to accompany me." Now the grin was larger.

It was time to leave. She reached for her shoes, but Kitt swiftly snagged them and slid off the chaise and stood up. As she moved to the sliding glass doors, he blocked her path, placing his big body very close to her.

"You want to go in now? It's much too early." The smile widened, and he gave a slight shake of his head.

"I have some work to finish up. I should—"

He took her hand and tucked the straps of her shoes in it. His big hand splayed across her back; the shawl slid down to the concrete. He gazed into her face, his eyes boring into hers. "You have mighty soft skin. You feel and look so good to me." Kitt nuzzled her hair. "You really are beautiful tonight, and so desirable."

She did enjoy the compliment, especially coming from him. Still, he made her so uncomfortable. She took a step back. "I really should be—"

"Not yet." His mouth descended on hers. The kiss began soft and gentle.

He teased the corners of her mouth with his tongue. She opened her mouth to him. She was more curious about him and what her reaction would be to kissing him. He explored her mouth, deepening the kiss, tasting her. He moved to her earlobe, neck, nipping as he went.

She gasped. *This man is an expert. But do I want what he is offering?* She managed to back away from him. It took her a moment to find a voice. "It was pleasant kissing you, but inappropriate. You're a married man, and I'm seeing someone."

"Ah, but my wife is far away, and so is your … someone. We could enjoy each other and have a great time." He looked into her eyes. "Are you aware of what you do to men, to me? Just one night, Lea. I'm a good lover. I'll give you a night to remember. What do you say?"

A lecture on conventional morality rested on the tip of her tongue. But what good would it do? For a moment, she was silent. She finally managed to gain some control when she was shaking inside. "I can't forget the kindness you showed me so many years ago. You were so kind, wonderful, and unselfish. But I'll not repay you by becoming another notch on your mental bedpost. Now I must go in."

She managed to swing away, snatch up the shawl from the ground, and scramble to the sliding door leading into the house. "Good night,

Kitt. It was an enlightening evening." She just barely slid through the half-open door, shut with a bang, and locked it.

He stood close, with his hand on the door, a half smile on his face. Then he shook his head and walked away.

A few minutes later, having changed into her cat-decorated nightshirt, she stood in the bathroom and stared into the mirror. She had brushed her teeth but could not seem to move away from the mirror, from her reflection. *What was it I felt while kissing Kitt? Passion, yes, but no real affection, no real caring. It was gut-level marvelous to feel desired by a big important man, but I want everything, not just a fling.* She thought of Clark, of kissing him. She closed her eyes and could imagine his arms around her, his mouth on hers. A feeling of warmth spread through her. She missed his body close to hers, his touch. In short, she missed Clark!

CHAPTER 19

When Ana Lea opened her eyes, the room was filled with light. What time was it? She glanced at the clock radio. Nine? She scrambled out of bed and searched for clothes to throw on.

As she descended the wide curved stairway, she heard Nichole call from the kitchen. "Lea, what do you want for breakfast? If you want more than a tea, you'd better get down here now."

Ana Lea found her friend in a chilly kitchen. The source of the chill came from the wide-open sliding door. Visible fog was rolling in from the backyard. "May I close this door? It's cold in here." She stood for a moment staring out at the fog-shrouded pool and the trees that lined the brick wall.

"Oh, sorry. I grew too warm while was fixing breakfast. But then I'm always too hot. I have my own 'internal combustion engine' in here." She patted her large belly.

"You're wearing a sweatshirt, maybe that's why you're warm." Nichole was enveloped in the familiar teal of an Aces shirt, with its black-and-gold playing card logo on the front. Under that, she wore a pair of baggy gray shorts, with fuzzy white slippers on her feet.

She put her hand to the back of her head and tilted it, model style.

"Don't you like my morning attire? The shirt and shorts are Josh's, and they actually cover me. While you're standing around, would you mind taking this doggy dish to the laundry room for Rex?"

A large dog door had been cut out of the utility room entrance leading outside. Rex must have smelled his breakfast, for he banged through the swinging entrance and headed for his food. Back in the kitchen, Ana Lea found a tea bag, mug, and the hot water tap to make some tea. "I really like this 'steaming water on demand' tap you installed."

"'One of the perks of being married to rich man." Nichole reached into the refrigerator for a plate of chilled fresh fruit and set it on the table.

Ana Lea made herself a bowl of cereal and spooned some fruit on it.

"Where's Josh?" she asked between spoonfuls of her breakfast.

"He's out jogging. He'll be back soon. We're actually going to church this morning. During the NFL season, that doesn't happen very often. But this is a bye week, and we're going to the noon service. You're welcome to come along."

Ana Lea shook her head. "I didn't bring anything to wear. You go ahead. I'll start on the receipts from the banquet."

Nichole shrugged. "Another question. How did you and Kitt get along last night?" She tilted her head, and a little smile curved her mouth.

Ana Lea dropped the spoon in the cereal bowl with a clink. "If you'd really like to know, he propositioned me."

"What! The rat." She tilted her head and shrugged. "Why am I not so surprised? I probably could have predicted that behavior from him."

"Does Melanie know how he chases women? She has to, and I presume she does," Ana Lea said.

"I think she went into the marriage with her eyes wide open, but she loves him. And I think he loves her—his version of marital love, that is. So how did you react to his offer?"

"I, of course, turned him down. What really happened is that I found out I prefer kissing Clark." She took a deep breath. "When I'm with him, the attraction is much more genuine. There's real affection."

"I'm surprised that you and Clark haven't yet 'gotten it on' as it were," Nichole teased.

"Am I hearing this from the virgin-on-her-wedding night, Nichole?" she teased back.

"Wait a minute, where did you hear that tale?"

"Oh, I heard that from someone in the know." Ana Lea's smile was superior. "I always dreamed of the big night, but it won't happen." She dropped her eyes. "To keep Clark happy, I think I may jump in the sack with him sooner than later."

"Hmmm, sounds like love to me. You are in love with him, aren't you?" Nichole nodded.

Ana Lea swallowed and took a deep breath. "Yes." Until that moment, the idea of loving him had just flitted around the edges of her mind and had not settled in her heart. Now it was lodged there along with its steady beat in her chest.

That same Sunday morning, Clark sat in the den watching a football game.

The teams playing were not of any great interest to him, so at halftime, he went for some lunch. When he returned, he spied the red journal and decided to check on Emily's life as a sister-wife.

He read the next entry.

Late August 1884

> Nothing I do is pleasing to Jerusha. I try my best, but she is never satisfied. She won't let me cook any of the dishes my mother taught me to make. My day is brightened only when I care for the little girls, Anna and Rebecca. We play games and run in the orchard. We even make a game of washing their clothes, and they like to help me. One night at dinner, Jerusha complained to Samuel that I run and play like a child, not a married woman.
>
> Samuel does not know how to deal with her cross demeanor. When it is suppertime and we are all around the table, usually, she is careful not to be cross with me. But last night, she slipped and showed her irritation and dislike of me.
>
> Every night, I pray that I will find a way to please her, that her heart will be softened and she will learn to treat me as an equal. True, I am not yet eighteen, and she

is near the age of thirty. She is a plain woman, spare, with thin pale brown hair. Yet she is good with her girls. Young Anna likes to help me with the milking and butter churning. We laugh together.

The next entry Clark found interesting was in the only August entry.

Early September 1884

My mother and my sister Charlotte came for a visit with me. They brought a picnic, so we walked deep into the orchard, for it was a hot day. We found good shade and spread our quilt close to the split willow tree. After many questions from my mother and sister, I told them about Jerusha's dislike of me and her behavior toward me.

My mother shook her head, and her expression was one of disappointment of my situation. "I'm not surprised," she said. "I'm afraid this is a common problem of being the second wife in a polygamous union. I thank the Lord I never had to deal with such a situation. This woman, Jerusha, is jealous of you, your youth, your pretty face, long dark hair, and soft feminine body."

Then my sister, Charlotte, mentioned that she met Jerusha's brother. "He has returned from his mission to England, and I met him at a social. He mentioned that his father gave some land to Samuel as a dowry for Jerusha. She was nearing age twenty-four and had no suitors. No wonder Samuel wanted to marry you. Every man needs true love in his life."

At that moment, I felt sorry for my sister-wife. Until then, I had no thought of her and her jealousy of me. I vowed to be more kind and thoughtful to her.

Clark pondered the Jerusha, Emily, and Samuel triangle. Not so different from the present. Was he in a similar three-way with Lea and Kitt? He certainly hoped he would be the winner.

Clark had a shift at the hospital at three that afternoon. He mentally switched gears to become the doctor, the surgeon that he must be, when it came time to walk through those sliding glass doors of the hospital.

The flight from LAX to Salt Lake International was taking too long. Ana Lea mentally urged the 737 jet liner to fly fast and straight to its destination.

Once she reached her house, evidence of Clark was everywhere: a coffee cup in the sink and clothes in the dryer waiting to be folded. She found one of his jackets in her front hall closet.

The sofa bed in the den was open, the bedding rumpled. She picked up a pillow on which he had been sleeping and sniffed it. There was the subtle scent of his aftershave. Holding the pillow to her face reminded her of having Clark close to her. Damn it, she *had* fallen for him.

The thought of loving Clark was at first not only visceral but also emotional. As she unpacked, she thought of the concept of being in love. The idea settled in her mind, intellectual, rational, and it definitely felt right. It was a peaceful yet overwhelming feeling. It felt as if she had wrapped herself in a warm, soft blanket.

She had been single, separate emotionally for so many years, existing as alone individual. Could she truly be half of a couple? Another thought slid in her head. Did Clark love her? He wanted her sexually, but love? Though she was attractive, she was flawed inside; could he truly love more than just the outside cover?

The weather had changed dramatically. After the blistering heat of summer, sunshine and cool autumn temperatures were pleasant. But the beautiful October weather had given way to wind and dark gray clouds blowing in from the north. One cold morning, Ana Lea changed over to heat on the thermostat. The next change was searching her closet for a sweater or sweatshirt rather than a lightweight cotton blouse she had first pulled from her closet. After dressing in a sweatshirt and jeans, she decided to make a pot of chili.

Now she needed the ingredients and began to make a shopping list.

It was after seven that evening when Clark finally pulled into the driveway. Ana Lea had been forced to make a quick trip to the post office, and Clark found the house empty, but a wonderful smell wafted from the kitchen. He found a pot on the stove and lifted the lid. "Mmmm, chili." He searched for a spoon to taste the steaming stew.

Soon, he heard her car pull into the drive behind his and her familiar footfalls on the side porch steps.

She burst into the kitchen, trying to hold on to her bag of groceries and keep the door from blowing off its hinges. "It's getting bad out there. Hi." She set the food sack down and went to him and gave him a light kiss. He pulled her closer to him and deepened the kiss.

"Wow, if I always get a greeting like that, I'll go back out and come in again." She laughed. "Sorry, had to make a fast trip to mail a packet and went again to the grocery store."

"What did you need from the market?" he asked. He began to empty the sack. "Great, salad and bread. How about cheese melted on warm french bread?"

Working together, they soon had their supper ready. "I think a fire would be nice. I'm going out for wood before this storm really hits." Clark grabbed his jacket and tromped out to the garage for the fuel. When he came back, the door banged open as he came in, and Ana Lea ran to hold it open.

While he started the fire, she set the food on the table. "Oh, Jonas came over to work on the door," Clark informed her. "He has ordered a metal door, and it should be in by the end of the week. Right now, he's closed it up with plywood."

"I'll need to give him a check for his labor," she said.

"I've already paid for the door," he said.

"Did we agree to that?" She gave him a questioning gaze. He shrugged. After dinner, they sat by the fire with their dessert, and she noticed the dark circles under Clark's eyes. "Do you want more coffee?" she asked.

"I don't think I could drink another cup of coffee if my life depended on it. I'll drink this milk"—he lifted the glass—"even though it's skim." He chuckled.

CHAPTER 20

"While living in this house, when you've been gone, feeding the cat and overseeing the installation of the basement door, I'm afraid I've really settled in." He stopped for a moment and took a deep breath. "I'm comfortable here with you. I want to be here with you, now and forever."

She knelt close to him. "I've been thinking along those lines too." She stopped, breathed in, and breathed out. "I want you here with me too. So if inviting you to share my bed will be an incentive, then you're welcome to stay."

His expression was one of genuine surprise. A wide grin creased his face. He slid over and took her face in his hands. "If you're not ready for our situation to go any further …" He knelt in front of her. "I can be noble and wait." He kissed her again but then pulled away and noticed a dark place on her throat. "What's that mark on your neck?"

She touched her throat. Damn, when she'd changed into this low-necked sweater, she forgot about the "love bite," compliments of Kitt, on her neck. Her hand flew to the spot. "Oh, I sort of, ah, picked that up in California."

Clark yanked her to her feet and dragged her into good light of the kitchen. "That's a hickey. What did you do while you were there?" Have a little snuggle time with Kitt? He kissed you, didn't he, and gave you this?" His finger prodded her neck. "Did you jump in the sack with him?" His teal eyes darkened with anger, and a blood vessel pulsed in his neck. In short, he was furious.

He's so angry, so jealous. Will he hurt me? She felt a shiver of fear. She had never seen him angry before, and she was frightened. Yet his accusing words filled her with righteous anger. She stepped closer to him and, with her right hand, smacked his cheek. The sound of her blow startled even her. "Oh, how can you say that?" she screamed. "I told him *no!* A big, fat *no.*"

"You let him kiss you. You stood or lay still long enough for him to chew on your neck. You say you care enough for me to move in with you. Who do you want, Ana Lea? You'd better make up your mind." He stomped into the den, where he had changed out of his doctor attire and grabbed up his car keys from the desk. Barefoot, dressed only in a T-shirt and a pair of plaid shorts, he marched to the south door, threw it open, and dashed down the stairs.

Just as he stepped off the porch, a bolt of lightning flashed the sky, followed by an earth-shattering clap of thunder. She was amazed at the amount of effort it took to slam the french door closed.

She stood and watched as he gaped at her car. The rain poured down as if the sky had opened up. Suddenly, she could see why he just stood there. Her car was behind his in the narrow driveway. As she saw his predicament, her anger evaporated. She found the whole situation funny.

Another clap of thunder, and Clark jumped back onto the porch, threw the door open, and stumbled into the house. He needed to throw his weight against the door to close it. He stood there, dripping puddles on the hardwood floor. He flipped back his wet hair from his eyes and crossed his arms upon his chest. "Your car is behind mine. I need you to come move it so I can leave."

As Ana Lea gazed at him, she could not hide a wide grin. Hands on her hips, she tilted her head in his direction. "I'm not going out there. It's blowing, thundering, lightning, and raining like crazy. You'll have to wait until the storm is over." She couldn't stop the smile tugging at the corners of her mouth. A choking sound from her throat bubbled into laughter.

Clark looked down at the growing puddle underneath his feet, soaking the wood floor, and also began to laugh. From both of them, hysterical laughter erupted. He slumped down and leaned against the wall. She dropped and knelt in front of him and grabbed his shoulders as she continued to convulse with laughter.

"Come here," he choked. She wrapped her arms around him and pressed her lips on his. The kissing spread to his cheek, neck, and damp shoulder. He managed to stand, pulling her up with him. "Once, I told you that I wanted to make sweet love to you on the floor. Well, how about right now?"

"It's warmer on the carpet." She turned and moved near the fireplace. She took the soft green blanket throw and spread it on the carpet. She sat on the blanket and took off her shoes.

He ran down the hall into the hall bathroom. While he was out of sight, she took off the blue sweater and tossed it on the sofa. Another bolt of lightning shook the house, and thunder was massive and earsplitting. The lights flickered and went out. The only light remaining was from the fireplace.

He returned from the bathroom wearing only his boxer shorts, a lighted candle in his hands. He set the candle on the small table by the sofa. "Quite a storm." He knelt near her and took her into his arms, cradling her and rocking her. He kissed her shoulders, neck, and somehow, he pulled off the tank top. He rolled her over and snapped off her bra and tugged off her jeans.

She lifted her head. "What are you doing?" She could feel his hands on her legs, stroking and caressing her. A shiver ran through her.

"Just relax. Pretend we're lost and found a cabin with only a fireplace for light and warmth. Now, we must keep each other warm."

"Hmm, good, ah, yes." He was working relaxing and stimulating her all at the same time. She lost the sense of everything else but where his hands were, the crackle of the fire, and the rain pounding on the living room window. She felt something strange and wonderful: desire. An urge to join her body with his, and the fear was gone.

She closed her eyes and let the lovemaking happen. She realized that he kissed her long, deep, and all consuming. Tension built in her body, and breathing was difficult. Somehow, a deep release came, and she was limp. She lay there wrapped in his arms. What she had done with him was more amazing than she could have dreamed.

He collapsed on her, and she held him for what seemed like hours, but it had to be much less. She became aware of the rain crashing down outside and drops spitting into the fire.

"Are you feeling OK? I tried not to hurt you." His face was close to her, and he rolled to her side.

"Mmm, I think . . ah, I'm feeling amazing." She closed her eyes and thought about pushing up to a sitting position. She had not the will or the energy.

"The reason why I … Do you want me to help you up?" he asked.

"Yes, lets' just take this … us to my bed." He helped her up and pushed her toward her bedroom. She watched him pull down the bedspread covers. She slid into bed and found the sheets cold. "Here, come in with me." She grabbed his hand. "Warm me."

"If that is what my lady wants." He pulled her into his arms and rubbed her back. She closed her eyes and fell into a deep sleep.

The light coming from the east window near her bed woke her. She touched the side of the bed where Clark had been and found it warm but empty. She glanced at the clock, nearly nine. Wow, she had slept the long night, dreamless, so comfortable. She curled up and slept again. The cat came and jumped up on the bed.

Ana Lea eased out of bed and walked into the kitchen and fed the cat. As she walked to the bathroom, she decided a hot shower would ease the stiffness she felt. Once out of the shower, she went to the kitchen and found the chili pot soaking in the sink. She also noticed some coffee in Clark's carafe. She poured a cup, laced it with cream and sugar, and warmed it in the microwave.

It was just what she needed to bring her back to reality. As she cleaned up the remaining dishes and pot, she thought about her first ever positive experience with sex. She decided being pressed into the floor by Clark was worth an incredible orgasm, if that is what it had been. She decided that was what she had experienced. Just thinking about it brought a warm tingle settle deep in her belly. Was this what she had missed all these years?

She knew it was good, because it had been with Clark, and he certainly knew what he was doing. She couldn't wait until they spent another night together.

She worked on the Los Angeles accounts until about two. Then she set to work to make a special treat for Clark: sour cream pumpkin cake. Once it was out of the oven, she threw on a raincoat and went to Costco.

When he was ready to leave the hospital, he called. "Hi, Ana Lea. I left some of my clothes at your place. Do you mind if I come and get them?"

"Yes, come and have some dinner. I have enough for two, so plan to eat with me."

When he walked into the warm kitchen, he picked up the aroma of roast chicken and some kind of pumpkin dish. He was tired, hungry, but happy. Now he must find out what Ana Lea thought about the sex between them. She was an amazing girl, a great cook, and she had allowed him to make love to her. Yet he still wasn't sure how it had been for her, but he needed to know, to talk with her about it.

She served him the chicken and rice, and they ate quietly. She would glance at him from time to time with a strange little smile teasing her mouth.

When it was time for dessert, she asked if he wanted coffee with the cake.

"It's from this morning. I can make you a cup of instant, but you taste it and see."

The first bite of the cake was so delicious; he decided to marry this girl as soon as possible. But after they ate, he set down his fork and said, "Let's go sit in the living room, because we need to discuss some things."

She tilted her head and gave him a quizzical smile. "OK." She took another sip of tea and followed him to the sofa.

"I'm a doctor, and from that standpoint, I would like you to tell me how you felt after our lovemaking last night. You were really tight, like a virgin. I had to guess since I've never made love with one. I want to know if I hurt you and if you were OK with it."

She cleared her throat. "It was … and I …" She blinked and smiled down at her hands folded in her lap. "It was good, and I'm fine. I was a little stiff and sore this morning, but it's better now. I don't know what you did—well, I do know. Anyway, I realized that for a long time, I've been missing a part of life that you, last night, showed, opened up for me. Thank you." She kissed him, a kiss of genuine love. She sat back and smiled. "Can we do it again?"

He blinked. Did he hear her correctly? She wants to have sex again? "When?" he asked.

"Maybe later tonight. I'd like my food to digest a while longer, and there's a program I'd like to watch on TV. She stood, and with a sidelong glance and a little smile, she went to kitchen and began cleaning up.

CHAPTER 21

The violent storm of the night before, which had continued into the next day, now had become softly falling snow. The power had been restored to Ana Lea's neighborhood. She stood holding a cup of tea and staring out the kitchen window at the flakes drifting down. She was reliving every second of that stormy night: her silly fight with Clark and then becoming his intimate partner when they had made love. Continuing the experience last night, in his arms was beyond what she could have imagined. To be and have a lover, the whole idea was amazingly satisfying. She began to think of ways to show her love for Clark.

Yesterday, she had bought chicken and rice. What could she fix for dinner tonight? She had leftover chicken, but was there enough for a casserole? She needed broccoli, sour cream, and bread, so that meant\ another trip to the supermarket.

"Wow, the first snowstorm of the season. You warned me." He hung up his coat in the hall closet, walked into the kitchen, and grabbed her in a tight embrace. "How's my fair lady this evening?"

"Fine," and she kissed him back. "Dinner's ready."

Over coffee, Clark reached his hand across the table, took hers, and said. "OK, when do you want to get married?"

She sucked in a breath and frowned. "What, no bended knee, no promises, and then begging for my hand?" she teased. "I thought that we should tie the knot soon, but how soon, I haven't been able to think that far yet."

"How about the first week in December? I can take five days off." He seemed to want to legalize their relationship, and quickly.

"That's only six weeks away." She began clearing the table. She stuck her head around the archway from the kitchen. "OK, I think we can make plans that quickly. After all, your family is across the country, and mine is scattered here and there, so it won't be a big wedding."

She came back to sit on the sofa. "You make a list of whom you would like to invite, and I'll do the same."

He grinned and shook his head. "I didn't realize a casual remark about marriage would become a list-making undertaking." He rubbed his eyes. "Let's clean up, and then I must retire to my less-than-satisfactory apartment." He raised an eyebrow.

"You don't want to stay here?" she asked.

"I was here with you last night—at least we were in your bed. The night before … well, being on the floor wasn't too uncomfortable. I suppose I could stay here. Sometimes, I do much better thinking on my back. I'll just lie in my bed and stare up at the ceiling and decide on tuxes, flowers, bridesmaids …"

"Oh, stop it. I'll do all that planning. Think about it, I am a professional planner. All you must do is contact your family. Number-one item is choosing a date."

He kissed her mouth, full and deeply. He stepped back and sighed.

"Six weeks is a long time to wait to move in here. I enjoy your lovely …" He cleared his throat. "I'd better go. I've at least two hours to review for surgery tomorrow." He walked to the door and planted a kiss on her forehead.

She glanced at the clock. "Great, I'll be able to watch my favorite nine o'clock show."

"When we get married, I'll order Netflix for you. Then you can watch all your favorite shows while I'm at the hospital. I'll have you in bed with me early." He waved as he opened the south kitchen door.

The next day, Ana Lea called Nichole. "Hi, lady, how's that bundle of joy you're still carrying around?"

"Still inside. Lazy kid doesn't want to come out and meet his parents. My due date is one week away, but I have a doctor's appointment later today, so I hope he says go to the hospital."

"Well, the reason I called was to ask a favor. How would you like to be my matron of honor?"

"Married? You're getting married. Where? When?" "Maybe the first week in December."

"Why don't you make it legal down here? I can see you walking down my beautiful curved stairway. The weather is much more dependable here than in Salt Lake in December. Since your parents live in Tucson, it's just as easy for them to fly over here."

"You want a wedding ceremony at your house? You're having a baby! There's too much work for a new mommy."

"I can see you coming down my beautiful stairway in some white slinky thing with a little veil. Besides, the baby will be a month old by then. I've plenty of loose-fitting clothes that are dressy that I'll be able to wear. I'm not going to scrub the foyer myself. I'll hire someone to clean the whole house. You forget, I married a millionaire."

"What about a dinner? You won't want to use your house for that," Ana Lea asked.

"We can find a hotel. In fact, everyone who is invited from out of town can book a room at that establishment. There's an advantage to having Melanie Kittredge as a friend. She has all kinds of connections. I'll give her a call and get some ideas."

"You sound mighty enthusiastic about *my* wedding. I'm pleased for the help, but why is that?"

"You may not have heard about the day Josh and I, and Joanna and Jake got married, have you?"

"No, but I'd love to." Ana Lea laughed.

"Suffice to say, we threw a double wedding together, with flowers and food, and bought dresses in a little more than two days."

"Hmmm, that sounds like quite a tale," Ana Lea said.

"Someday, when you and I have a whole afternoon to hang together, I'll let you in on the craziest week in the history of the Wright brothers and their brides. Getting back to your wedding, I'll check around and give you a call," Nichole said.

"I'll talk to Clark and see what he thinks. Thanks so much for the offer. Keep me posted on the baby's arrival. Bye."

That evening, Ana Lea told Clark about Nichole's generous offer.

"Hmmm, the only people from Salt Lake I would consider inviting would be Ray Rossiter and his wife. Of course, I'd like my father and my two sisters to come. They could just as easily fly from Boston to Los Angeles, as to Salt Lake. I'll talk to Ray and call my dad. What about you?"

"My two best girlfriends from college are both married and live out of state. As far as my extended family here locally, there isn't anyone that I'm close to. I'm better friends with Nichole and Joanna than anyone else. Of course, I'd need to invite my brother."

"I didn't know you had a brother. I suppose there are many things we don't know about each other, and as time goes by, we'll learn more and more." He took her hand. "OK, Los Angeles it is."

The next evening, Clark showed up with another armload of his belongings. He had sports equipment and the clothes needed for those activities. Ana Lea surveyed the items in his arms. "Let's take those downstairs. Maybe we can move some stuff out of the closet in the little bedroom. As far as the skis, I have a storage place in the extra closet down there. I think we can fit them in."

"I'd like to call your cousin Jonas again. We need him to take a look at the unfinished part of the basement and plan some strategic storage areas. A good example are all those books in boxes you have on the floor of this closet. Let's go downstairs and take a look."

"A bookshelf, and I'd love one built right here." She tapped the wall next to the basement bedroom door. "I'll call him tomorrow."

"Good idea. Now let's go out and get a hamburger." He escorted her upstairs.

A week later, Ana Lea received a call from Josh. "Hi, Josh, how is Nichole?" She knew he would tell her about a new baby.

"She had a boy. He was large, over nine pounds." He was silent for a moment, and then she heard him clear his throat. "She had a rough time."

"Is she OK?" Ana Lea felt a ripple of fear for her friend. "She's going to be fine, just has to take it easy for a while."

"Going to be fine?" Ana Lea was concerned for both Josh and Nichole.

"It was bad. I was terrified I was going to lose her." Josh's voice dropped low, raspy, and she knew he was crying.

"Oh, Josh, do you need me to come down? What about the baby?"

"My boy is fine, beautiful, and she's in good spirits, but the doctors had to do a C-section. She was not allowed to raise her head off the pillow for two days. You can imagine how she complained about that." His voice sounded stronger.

"Tell Nichole to take it easy, stay down as much as she can."

"I'll tie her to the bed if I have to." She heard a low chuckle.

"My mother is here, and I'm hiring a nanny. As far as your wedding is concerned, call Melanie Kittredge. She seems to have things under control."

"I am suggesting we ask the pastor of our church to officiate at the ceremony. Does that meet with your approval?" he asked.

"Let me run this by Clark. Thanks for your help, and my congratulations on adding a baby to your family. I'll talk to you soon." Ana Lea sat at the kitchen table thinking and staring out into the dark yard.

Would Clark, raised as a Catholic, object to an evangelical pastor marrying them? She hadn't even given a thought to the type of clergy they would use. She would need to talk to Clark, but not tonight. She knew how tired he would be when he arrived at her house after a night shift.

She had a trip lined up to fly to Columbus because of another dedication of the new wing of the building. This part was to house a training area, part of the program of their shelter. There would be the usual dignitaries and officials at the ribbon-cutting ceremony. The media would be there, and they would expect a sound bite from Joanna, and maybe even her.

Joanna had done all the planning, and Ana Lea marveled at her friend's expertise with the media and other officials. Thinking about that caused her to drag out her cosmetic case and begin packing essentials for her trip in two days.

Tomorrow, she would tell Clark about the Wrights' new baby boy and discuss with him whom he would like to marry them.

After supper the next evening, they discussed Nichole and Josh's baby and her complications during childbirth. Next, she asked him whom he would prefer to marry them. "You mean which preacher or priest or Mormon bishop should have the privilege of legalizing our relationship?" He stared with a serious face and narrowed his eyes. But then he wiggled his eyebrows.

She burst out laughing. "Precisely."

"Well, a priest won't do it, unless you join the Catholic Church. A Mormon bishop might do it, if he thought he might get some new converts. So I guess we're down to the preacher."

"Glad you approve, because that's whom Josh suggested." She flashed an innocent smile.

Joanna and Ana Lea left from Jacob Wright's home, and upon arriving there, they were whisked into the shelter school. The press was ready to snap pictures as they emerged from the car. "It must be a slow news day," Joanna cracked but handled things beautifully.

"Let us get to the ribbon cutting, guys. Then when we're up on the platform, you press people can snap all the pictures you'd like," she said.

Luckily, the ceremony was short, and the speech by a city manager, brief.

When they were ready to leave, Jacob came up to them. "Ladies, I have a consult at the hospital in about twenty minutes, so I'll miss lunch. Jo, make sure you eat something nutritious, not just a salad."

She reached up and kissed her tall husband on the cheek. "Yes, doctor, I'll follow your orders." She waved at his retreating figure. Turning to Ana Lea, "Let's go in for the luncheon and, afterward, do some shopping."

Driving to the restaurant, Joanna asked her friend. "So what's your wedding dress like?"

"I haven't had time to look for a dress yet. We've spent the past week moving Clark's sports equipment into my house, and anything we don't really need, out."

"Ah, welcome to taking care of a man. And it gets more complicated when there are children involved." She laughed ruefully.

"How are you doing being pregnant, along with everything else you must do to keep the household running?" Ana Lea asked.

"It gets crazy at times, but believe it or not, my training in business has helped me. I am accustomed to making lists and organizing household chores. I keep a calendar on the fridge. On my list is a search for your wedding dress."

CHAPTER 22

Joanna drove to a large group of outlets on the western edge of Columbus. Of the 127 retail stores, there was a bridal party dress outlet called Joanna's Party Pretties and Bridal Shop.

"And do you have stock in this place?" Ana Lea teased. "No, but I wish I did, because they do carry great dresses."

This shop reminded Ana Lea of the discount store where she and Nichole had shopped in Los Angeles. As she gazed at the rows and rows of merchandise in the establishment, she turned to Joanna. "How do you find these places? Nichole knows where to find stores like this too."

"We're both, I suppose, dedicated shoppers set on finding the best merchandise at the lowest possible prices. I love good clothes, and I have a fairly large wardrobe, but I refuse to pay retail." Joanna tilted her head.

"This way to the bridal section."

"You always managed to look classy, well turned out. Are shopping places like this the key?" Ana Lea asked.

"To a degree, yes. Come on, let's start searching for that special dress for you."

After trying thirteen different dresses, Ana Lea, with Joanna's encouragement, finally decided on a winter white strapless gown of silk brocade with a short train. It had a rather narrow but draped skirt, pulled up to the back, echoing the dresses women wore in 1890s. "Since its winter, I think it needs a stole or jacket," Ana Lea said.

The tall, severe saleswoman had said little, allowing them to discuss each dress.

"I believe I have just have the thing to complete that dress." She quickly returned with a little three-quarter sleeve bolero jacket in sheer lace. The color matched the dress, and Ana Lea slipped it on.

"Yes, that's it. Perfect." Joanna picked up the price tag. "Great, you'd pay over a thousand bucks for this dress retail. Now you need shoes. Hurry and change. There's a good store across the parking lot."

Once they had locked up Ana Lea's purchases in the trunk of Joanna's car, she steered Ana Lea into a snack and candy store. "I need an afternoon break. Even though I'm pregnant, I allow myself one Diet Coke per day, and I need my fix now."

"I am so happy and relieved to find a wedding dress. It's taken a load off my mind. Lately, I worry about everything."

"Such as?" Joanna asked.

"What my mother will think of Clark. I know she'll be relieved to have me marry *somebody*. But to a Catholic boy for Boston? But I do love him."

"That's the only important thing," Joanna said.

"Did you find that shop when you were looking for a wedding dress?" Ana Lea asked.

"No. Nichole and I went to the mall and hit the after-Christmas sales. It took us about three hours to decide on dresses, shoes, the works. We married the Wright brothers the next day."

"Amazing, I had no idea you two put the weddings together so fast."

"It was all pretty whirlwind, but I'd do it again in a heartbeat to marry Jake." Joanna stared out the large window by their table. "See that pizza place over there? I think we should whirl over there and pick up some dinner."

Clark eased his old Volvo station wagon down the hill from University Hospital onto the expressway through slashing rain. Since it turned from October to November, the weather in the Salt Lake Valley had turned from a pleasant Indian summer to freezing rain, nonstop—rain that turned to sleet and after dark became wet snow. All this made driving up to the hospital truly a challenge.

The hospital complex was located up against a mountain behind the sprawling University of Utah campus. The university owned the land, and a group of medical facilities had been constructed there. The setting was breathtaking, allowing one to stand and stare out a large wall of windows and see across the whole valley to the Great Salt Lake. The higher elevation than the valley below also made for heavier precipitation and cooler temperatures.

Ana Lea was again out of town. He wondered if she would continue to travel this much after they were married. Once he reached her house, he fed the cat and pulled out a frozen entree she had prepared for him. He had also made trips to bring his remaining belongings into her, which would soon be *their*, house. One of the pluses living in Lea's house was the furnace. It was fairly new and put out comfortable warmth. The one in his apartment was temperamental, which reminded him of his last dwelling while living in Boston. Even though the little house on Victor Street was older, it was a mere adolescent compared to some houses in that New England City.

Friday afternoon, just about the time Clark was leaving to go to the hospital, Jonas showed up with a truckful of drywall and lumber, ready to work on the basement room.

Although the day was cold, the cat had wanted to go outside, and Clark had let her out. She came back in with Jonas and the building materials.

"I'm going to the hospital, so let yourself out the basement door when you're ready to leave." Jonas nodded in understanding and went back to his work.

A bus rollover on the I-80 freeway kept Clark working nearly all night. As part of a surgical team, he removed a ruptured spleen from a twenty-year-old male with extensive blood loss. He volunteered to stay and keep watch on the young man until he stabilized and began to improve. It was well after midnight when Clark decided he could leave his patient in the hands of the nursing staff. "I'm going home and to bed. If an emergency arises—"

"We know, Dr. Knowles. You need some rest, so if all goes well, we'll see you tomorrow afternoon. Have a good morning's sleep." Ms. Wilson laughed.

Clark drove back to Lea's house on autopilot and fell into bed, not waking until nearly eleven that morning. Crystal, the cat, woke him by brushing her fur against Clark's shoulder. He was further roused by a rough cat tongue grazing his chin. "OK, cat, you want food and I want coffee."

Once she had been fed, he let her out the kitchen door. He stood gazing out the large kitchen window watching dark clouds gather over the mountains. Another storm was approaching.

After showering and more caffeine, he went downstairs to move items from the area where Jonas was working. The chore was time consuming but needed to be done, for the builder would be there sometime during the afternoon to work for a few hours. Clark could hear the piteous cries of the cat outside the basement door and went to let her in.

It was exactly high noon when Clark opened the door. The animal hesitated rather than scooting in and took off across the yard and scampered up the apricot tree. "Go ahead, run away, cat." He slammed and locked the door. "Now you'll have to sit out there until Jonas comes!" He yelled at the door in disgust. *Why did she run away like that? What we need around here is a dog. Then Crystal would really have a reason to run.*

The entity relaxed its vigil. The time of danger had passed. The cat had understood the warning to not come into the house at that precise moment. The man, Clark, had been saved too. The entity drifted back upstairs to the attic to drain any heat from that area of the house. There was less and less on this cold November day.

Once Clark returned to Ana Lea's house, he called to check on his patients and found all were stable. He made breakfast and tried to watch a repeat college football game but lost interest. *It's time I found the journal to see how Emily's life is progressing.*

He opened it to an entry she had written in October.

October 20, 1884

> Jerusha is with child again and quite ill. She lies in bed most of the day. It is up to me to walk little Anna to school and see to the chores. This I do not mind, because I can cook the way my mother has taught me. We have much dried fruit from the orchard. Samuel went into

the city and bought these wonderful glass jars. They keep the fruit and some vegetables from spoiling. We have meat, potatoes, and carrots in the root cellar. We have plenty of food to last through the winter.

Samuel and I have more time together now that the crops are in and put up. We sit over a cup of tea in the evenings and read from great literature books. There is a library wagon that comes every few weeks, and we can borrow a book to read. Sometimes, we play games with the girls before their bedtime.

When he was in the city, he bought cotton cloth called calico. He bought it for my eighteenth birthday. Yet he also bought some for Jerusha. There is enough of my cloth to make a dress for me and each of the girls. It has little flowers on a blue background. I will try to have the dresses ready by Christmas.

Christmas 1884

It is very cold, and darkness falls late in the afternoon. Perhaps it is because we are living in an orchard. The big fireplace keeps us warm, and the coal truck came and brought us a great pile of coal. There are mines of this black rock found in the eastern area of the state only three days away. We are blessed to live here in Deseret.
We all went to church, but we were told to say that I am Jerusha's niece living with them to help her during her confinement. The government in Washington hates the idea of polygamy. Those men in power don't understand that it is a choice. We are not forced, but it is also a commandment from our Lord.

My family came with gifts, and this Christmas, Samuel helped me find a tree to bring into the house. The girls and I made decorations, and we even put a large candle on top. It snowed the day after Christmas and became terribly cold. Again, the feeding of the animals and milking became most difficult.

Clark was fascinated reading about the lifestyle these people lived and the sheer amount of work there was to do to maintain and prosper. He decided he must research Mormon history and read about the fight between the U.S. government and the polygamists. Something visceral about polygamy appealed to him, or perhaps it was just testosterone. Right now, between his job and keeping Ana Lea happy, he had all he could handle with one woman.

Ana Lea returned from Columbus, excited about their coming wedding. She hid the wedding dress she had purchased in the closet downstairs because Clark should not see it until the ceremony. She spent hours on the phone with Melanie to fine-tune the plans.

"I've booked a room for the bridal suite and suggested that if some of the guests wanted to stay at the hotel, they would give them a special rate. I'm e-mailing you three styles of decorating, with possible cake decorations to coordinate with the table themes," Melanie said.

"The hotel can do all that?" Ana Lea was surprised.

"Oh, yes, they do lots of weddings, large and small. A picture of your wedding dress would help to tie the theme together."

"I'll contact the shop where I purchased it. Perhaps they will have a picture from the place they ordered it."

"It would help if you flew down and day or two early to see if you want to make any little changes." Melanie sounded very professional.

"I can manage that. In a few days, I'll be able also give you the number of guests we are expecting. Thanks so much for your help." She dropped the phone back into its cradle. Even small weddings took more planning than she had expected.

CHAPTER 23

Clark and Ana Lea were invited to the Rossiters' for Thanksgiving dinner. Ray and Lorrie had been married for eighteen years and had four children. The first two were identical twin boys, now sixteen years old. As Lorrie and Ana Lea set food out on the bar in the large kitchen, the hostess told her guest the story of the birth of the twins.

"We didn't know there were two of them inside me. At the time, we lived in a basement apartment. Ray and I were so poor that all we could afford was a one-bedroom apartment in an old house. It had a tiny kitchen and, of all things, a dining room. The living room being larger, Ray had set up part of it as his study area, putting in his desk and filing cabinet. The lone bedroom was so small that all we could cram into it was our king-size mattress and springs close to the small closet. By the door, we found room for a small chest. We had to sit down on the bed to open the closet door. We didn't even own a crib."

"Wow, it sounds like a typical college apartment. I was fortunate because I lived at home when I went to the university. But I did have a number of friends that had pads like the one you describe," Ana Lea said.

Lorrie went on with her story. "'My mom came up with a crib she had found at the garage sale. She took it home, scrubbed it down, and painted it white. The next day, two weeks early, I went into labor. While driving me to the hospital, Ray stopped because he spied a garage sale. I'm sitting in the car having contractions, and he's out there shopping. He galloped down this sloping lawn back to the car and told me he found a chest with a changing table built on top for ten dollars. Between contractions, he helps me up on the lawn to take a look at the chest. I pull seven dollars out of my purse and hand it to him. He digs in his pockets and comes up with three more, and we bought the change table baby furniture. The man who sold us the chest helped us put it in the trunk. He said, 'I don't think your wife looks too good. Maybe you should take her to the doctor.'

"Ray answers back, 'It's OK, I'm a doctor, and we're going to the hospital.'"

Ana Lea shook her head in amazement. "I can't believe you were shopping for baby furniture while in labor. Weren't you afraid you'd have the babies on the lawn? So did you end up putting both babies in one crib?"

"I knew I had more time before they would be born. When we finally reached the hospital and I was wheeled into a labor room, a nurse came in with a stethoscope to listen to the baby's heartbeat. She listened for a while and then turned on her heel and quickly left the room. She came back in with a resident, and he listened.

"He gave me a big smile and said, 'I'm picking up two heartbeats. I believe there are two of them in there. I gotta find Ray and tell him he's going to have twins.'

"I yelled back at him. 'Hey, I'm the one having them. He just put 'em there!'

"To answer your question, yes, both babies fit in one crib for several months. In fact, some psychologists suggest that twins should be put together because they comfort each other.

"The dining room became the nursery. The neighbors gave me a shower after the babies were born. I received several little matching outfits and enough money to buy a double stroller.

"It was tough back then, but we were so much in love, and we lucked out. Both boys weighed in at a little over six pounds and were healthy. Now look at them, Jason and Jeremy are already taller than Ray. If you work to make the early years of your marriage good, Ana Lea, the later years seem to take care of themselves. We waited four years for the next baby, Candace. Stephanie came along three years after that." Lorrie tucked a strand of blond hair behind her ear and yelled, "Come on, guys, dinner is served!"

Later on, when Ana Lea and Clark returned home, she related Lorrie's story to him.

"I knew that Ray and Lorrie married young. I suppose everyone has their struggles to get started and have to work hard to reach their goals." Clark smiled at his fiancée and pulled her into his arms for a kiss.

"We're pretty lucky, you and me. Because we are marrying now when we're somewhat older, we are better established. We'll need to watch the expenditures, but if we're careful, finances won't be too much of a problem. I wonder what our struggles will be?"

The first Monday in December came, and with it a heavy snowstorm. Ana Lea was to fly to Los Angeles on Wednesday, and the wedding was on Friday. Tuesday, she sat at her computer to work but accomplished very little. Her thoughts were scattered in many directions. She worried about the weather, the guests who were flying in from various parts of the country, and the wedding itself.

Clark seemed oblivious to the stress of the upcoming wedding. He seemed consumed with his work, as usual. She knew he seldom lost his focus on his work. Would this passion he had for his profession be a problem for them?

The night before she left for Los Angeles, she asked him about his strong focus on his work. He stood, put an arm around her, and stared down at her. "Do you really think my profession is going to come between us?"

"I don't know, but it is something I have thought about." As she watched him slide into bed next to her, she fluffed the soft pillows and leaned against them.

"Right now, being a resident, I'm under lots of pressure to do things right, be thorough. However, when I can work into a practice or secure a place on the surgical team in the hospital, my life will become less hectic. You are so important to me, the most important person in my life, and I love you." He leaned down and kissed her, sweet at first, and the kiss deepened.

"I believe you, and I love you too. But—" Another kiss warmed her. She smiled and pulled him over for yet another kiss;, she was feeling desire for him. "Only a few more days and we'll be married, and we'll have more time for this." She snuggled down with his hand on her breast.

"Wake me up when you leave, 'cause I have more packing to do."

"Right now, you have my full attention." He hugged her and began the now familiar foreplay they both enjoyed.

"I think you have my full focus too." She snapped off the lamp near her bed. "After tonight, I won't see you again until you arrive in Los Angeles."

By the time Clark checked in his luggage, the plane had already begun to load, and he was forced to run all the way to the very end of the Delta gates. As he finally settled into his seat, he realized that this had been the first time he had been on a flight since April of that year.

As he stared out into the darkness, the fact that he was going to be married in less than twenty-four hours slammed into him. Marriage! He had been "footloose and fancy-free," to quote an old axiom, for thirty-four years. Was this really what he wanted?! He took a deep breath and settled back into his uncomfortable coach seat.

He knew he wanted to be a surgeon, the best possible. He knew he desired Ana Lea more than any woman he had ever known. He enjoyed living with her for several reasons. He liked coming home to her. She was a good cook, and she took care of him in ways his previous bachelor existence could not compare. He was amazingly attracted to her, and she had lost her fear of sex and become a great partner. For that alone, he would stay with her, but even with all that, he did love her. He smiled, closed his eyes, and dozed until the flight attendant asked if he wanted a drink.

The flight was a little over an hour, and to his surprise, Joshua met him. "I figured I could help you with the baggage better than Lea. I'm taking you to the hotel because you're the last arrival in the wedding party."

They walked out of LAX and into a chilly, foggy night. Wisps of fog wrapped around Clark as he walked to the parking slot. "I've never been in Southern California in the winter before. I guess I expected it to be warmer." Joshua laughed. "We have our winters just like Utah, just a milder version."

Clark walked into an informal dinner finding nearly everyone involved in the wedding waiting for him. Ana Lea hurried over, brushed her lips over his, and took his hand. "Glad you could make it," she teased. "Come and eat now, but after that, we'll get you settled into your room for tonight."

"My room for . . . ?"

Patrick Knowles walked over and slapped his son on the back. "Good to see you, boy." He wrapped Clark in a bone-crushing hug. "Come with me. We're sharing a room. I couldn't see paying for a single room when, for a little more coin, we could share one tonight." His lined face crinkled in a grin, and Ana Lea suddenly noticed that Patrick's eyes were a nearly the same blue-green color as Clark's.

Clark turned to his prospective bride. "I thought that we ... ?" He glanced around the room. He gave her a slight nod. "OK, I'll room with Dad."

Patrick led him into a pleasant room on the sixth floor. There were two queen beds and the usual desk, TV, and good-sized closet. "Put your things in the closet. You can unpack later. We should go back down so you can have a bite to eat and visit a bit longer. I've been a chattin' with the Andreasens. Nice fellow, pretty wife. I can see where your girl got her pretty face."

Once they reached the room where they had dined, Clark was introduced to Ana Lea's parents, her brother, Bradley, and his wife, Josie. They had brought their three children for a visit to Disneyland for a few days after the wedding. Clark's two sisters, Megan and Eileen, had come but without her husband. Jake and Joanna had taken a cottage on the hotel property, and so had the Rossiters.

It took several minutes for Clark to get Ana Lea away from the group. "Where are you staying tonight?"

She smiled up into his face. "I'm staying with Josh and Nichole tonight, but I'll move into the bridal suite tomorrow, with you, if that suits you fancy." She gave him a sidelong glance and a wink.

"Whose idea was it for me to stay with Dad? Much as I like him, I think he snores."

"His. He wanted our relationship to at least look more traditional. This way, you can better anticipate the wedding night." She smiled and shrugged.

"I was hoping for a pre- and a postwedding night." His sigh was audible. "Hang in there for one more day. After that, our fun will be legal." She kissed him but then dragged him over to meet all the guests.

Early the next morning, Ana Lea stood staring out the sliding glass door, watching the mist and drizzle curl around the swimming pool and deck of Nichole's house. She had hoped for a sunny wedding day, not one reminding her that even in Southern California, the weather could be damp and chilly.

She had put on the kettle for a cup of tea and stood waiting for the water to boil. Then she remembered that Nichole's kitchen had an instant hot water tap. She turned at the sound of a fussing infant. Nichole came down the stairs, her long hair tousled, wearing one of Joshua's terry robes. She uncerimoniously handed the squalling infant to Ana Lea and went to the refrigerator for a tall glass of ice water.

"Feeding this child is my first priority when he's in a screaming mode." She took the baby from her friend and plopped down into a big leather rocker and began to breastfeed him. The child began his suckling with great gusto.

Lea turned to make her tea. "What do you like to eat for breakfast? You certainly must replenish what that boy is taking out of you. I'll fix whatever you want."

"I eat a high-protein breakfast. I've found it keeps both mother and child nourished and helps my energy level. And, of course, liquid, because I find I am constantly thirsty."

After searching the refrigerator, Ana Lea made bagels with melted cheese, along with sliced apples and oranges and tea for both of them. She nibbled at her breakfast as she cleaned up the kitchen. "Is there anything I can do for you?"

"Not for a while. My morning routine is that when he naps, I nap. I will need my dress pressed to wear to the ceremony. We need to leave for the hotel at around two. The wedding is scheduled at four."

Ana Lea paced around the kitchen. "I'm a little edgy right now. I think I'll go for a run. You take a nap while I jog around Brentwood."

CHAPTER 24

After her run, Ana Lea felt much calmer yet invigorated. She showered, washed her hair, and threw on a robe while pressing Nichole's dress. Her wedding gown was being professionally done at the hotel. She dressed in a jacket and slacks and held Josh Junior while Nichole did her own grooming. By early afternoon, she borrowed Nichole's car and drove to the hotel.

Joanna was there to help her into the wedding ensemble. "Did you take a look at the room Melanie has decorated? It's beautiful, a bower of greenery and flowers. There are tables set up for the banquet. I'm amazed at how well she planned this party."

"I helped her yesterday. If she ever tires of her publishing duties, she should take up wedding planning," Ana Lea said.

"I think she has really enjoyed doing this." Joanna pinned the veil on Ana Lea's dark hair.

She stood and studied her reflection in the full-length mirror. *The veil works well with this dress. You know, girl, you don't look half bad!*

"You are a beautiful bride. Clark will be absolutely speechless when he sees you." She gave her friend a careful hug. "It makes me wish that I had been married … What's done is done, and I'm happy to have Jake for my husband. I'll tell them you're ready."

All the guests were assembled. A talented keyboardist played the wedding march. Clark stood in a gray tux, with Ray Rossiter in a similar suit at his side. Ana Lea walked in with a bouquet of lilies in her hands. She came into the room from the rear and slowly walked up the side to the bower in front and came to stand beside Clark.

He was stunned by her beauty and could do nothing more than grin at this vision of womanhood that soon would be his. Her whiskey-colored eyes glowed, and her dark hair gleamed under the gauzy veil.

Pastor Wells stood in his dark suit smiling and began a little talk.

"Ladies and Gentlemen, we are gathered here this afternoon to seal in marriage this man, Clark, and this woman, Ana Lea, each willing to …"

Clark heard little but now knew that this most important decision of his life was the right one. Soon, it was his turn to say, "I will." It happened all so quickly, and as he took the ring from Ray and slipped it on Lea's finger, and she took one from Nichole, and he spread his left hand to receive his from her, his love for her knew no bounds.

The guests came to congratulate and offer words of praise for the girl he had picked for his wife. They decided to cut the cake after the banquet. Now pictures were taken by both a professional and anyone else who held a camera.

Clark found that he had an appetite and then remembered that all he had eaten that day was a bagel and several cups of coffee. Wine was served and some of a nonalcoholic variety to those who did not drink alcohol. He found that now the gathering really became a party. People were moving around the room chatting with one another. His father-in-law came to congratulate and have a fatherly chat with him.

"So how did you meet Lea?" Walter Andreasen stood tall, broad shouldered, but with middle-age thickening of his waist.

"Lea had an accident at the July banquet for the Make It Wright Foundation. I was there and became her physician." Clark smiled and hoped his anxiety at meeting Lea's father didn't show.

"Well, I've head of other ways to meet a potential mate, but that's way up there as unusual." He clapped his new son-in-law on the shoulder. "Just take good care of her."

Bradley and his wife left because they needed to pick up their children. They had left them with a cousin. The wedding party moved to the side entrance of the hotel nearest the parking garage. Though the entrance was sheltered from the busy parkway by greenery and a curved driveway, the sounds of traffic were only slightly muffled.

As the group stood talking, the sounds of squealing brakes and grinding of metal against metal of several vehicles crashing were deafening.

"God, what was that?" Kitt immediately took off at a dead run down the curved driveway. For a moment, the others turned and stared at his disappearing back.

"It's bad!" Kitt yelled as he jogged back to the group. "Multiple car pileup. Maybe we can help." He shrugged out of his jacket and pulled off his tie. He handed them to Melanie. "Call 911!"

Josh followed his friend's example. He set down the baby carrier, pulled off his tux coat, and handed it to Nichole. He glanced at his wife and pointed to Kitt's path.

"I know. Go!" Nichole watched her husband run down the drive.

The three doctors were quick to follow Josh, all handing their jackets to their wives. Clark gently touched Ana Lea's cheek. "I need to see what I can do," he spoke as he backed away and broke into a run to the street.

Melanie gave directions on her cell phone, reporting the accident. Other people from the hotel heard the crash and walked down the path. For a moment, the five women stood around looking at each other. Ana Lea was the first to make a move. "It's too chilly out here for JJ. Let's go back inside." She picked her skirt in one hand and the infant in his carrier in the other. She was surprised how heavy it was. Nichole grabbed Clark's tux coat from the new bride and followed her into the hotel.

Joanna took Lorrie's hand and touched Melanie's shoulder. "Let's move into the hotel." For a moment, Melanie stood transfixed but then reluctantly followed the other two women. By then, screaming sirens cut the damp night air, and the shouts of men could be heard.

Baby JJ began to fuss. Nichole stopped. "He's probably hungry." She picked him from the carrier and patted him.

Ana Lea whirled around and spoke to the others. "We're going up to the bridal suite so the baby can have a meal."

Joanna touched Melanie's shoulder because she could see the worry on her face. "That's a good idea. We booked a cottage. We can relax and wait there." She gestured to Lorrie. "Come."

Once Nichole and Ana Lea walked into the bridal suite, Nichole asked her friend to help her take off the dress she wore. She slipped out of the black brocade jacket and black knit dress she had chosen for the wedding. "This isn't nursing wear, but it was the only outfit that would accommodate these oversized breasts." She sat down in the curved upholstered chair and began to feed her infant.

"I'll get you a glass of water." Ana Lea brought the water from the bar located in the living area of the room. Then she began to pace around the spacious area, pausing to look out the wall of windows. They, however, looked down on the inner courtyard, not the street. *Just like Clark to run off and play doctor on his wedding night. OK, Lea, this is what you married, so buck up.*

JJ finished his evening meal, and Nichole went into the bathroom to change his diaper. She set the sleeping child back into his carrier and flopped down on the cream brocade sofa. "This has been quite a day, and it's catching up with me." She looked up at the new bride. "You're pissed, aren't you? I mean, you have every right to be upset."

"Yes, but I think tonight is a sample of what I have legally bound myself to. Change of subject, may I ask a question?"

"Ask away." Nichole tilted her head and smiled.

"The nursing business is amazing. You have milk ready to feed him anytime he wants it?"

"Whenever he hungry, it's there ready to feed him." Nichole found a pillow and pushed it behind her head and tried to stifle a yawn.

'You're exhausted, and I believe that sofa makes up into a bed. Let me open it, and you can take a little nap. It may be hours before the guys get back. In the meantime, we should get comfortable."

"If you're going to start moving furniture, you'd better get out of that dress. Come over here and I'll pull down that zipper," Nichole said.

She checked the closet and found two terry cloth robes hanging on the rod. "Here, you put on this one, and I'll wear the larger version," Nichole said.

She watched as Lea opened the sofa and found pillows and a blanket in the closet.

"Oh, this is nice." Nichole lay down and closed her eyes. Soon, she curled up on her side, and to Ana Lea, she seemed to fall asleep instantly.

Continuing to pace, Ana Lea found that her eyes were gritty, her head felt heavy, and her neck muscles were stiff. *I may as well get comfortable.* She searched for one of the nightgowns she had brought. Carefully removing all traces of her wedding accessories, she scrubbed off her makeup. She took the rose from the middle of the king-size bed and found a vase and put it in water. The small box of chocolates she set on the bar, and she slipped into bed. She said a little prayer for Clark and the other men who so quickly acted to help others. *Some wedding night!* She fluffed a pillow, plopped down on the bed, and closed her eyes.

A soft knock at the door brought Ana Lea out of a sound sleep. She jumped up, suddenly realizing that it wouldn't be Clark because he had a key. She grabbed the terry cloth robe and wrapped it around her sheer lacy nightgown.

Looking through the peephole, she saw Josh and opened the door.

"Come in. Nichole and the baby are asleep."

"Good. She's still not quite recovered from his birth. She needs lots of rest."

Snapping on a bedside lamp, she took a good look at Josh. She sucked in a breath at his appearance.

"I know, the tux is probably ruined." He stared down at the grease and bloodstains on his shirt and pants. We all ended up like this." He sniffed the shirt. He took Ana Lea's hands in his, his eyes dark and serious. "Kitt was injured. One of the poles that the larger truck crashed into snapped. Kitt was working to free a woman from the passenger side. The pole crashed into him. He was also taken to the hospital." Pain darkened his gray eyes. "We're not exactly sure what his injuries are."

"Kitt, oh my god!" She was stunned, but a terrible pain grabbed at her, and she fought back tears. "Does Melanie know?" The anguish she felt was just as much for her friend as it was for her husband.

"Jake came back and took her to the hospital. I believe Joanna went with them too."

"What about Clark? Is he coming back soon?"

"Everyone else is fine. When I left, Clark and Ray had been drafted into a couple of surgical teams. They should be back soon."

Nichole stirred and opened her eyes. "Oh, Josh, you're here." She eased up into a sitting position. He bent and kissed her on the cheek.

"Come, lady, let's go home."

Ana Lea clicked on the TV, searching for any news about the crash, but all she found were old movies and infomercials. She lay back down and drifted into a fitful sleep. Sometime later, the sound of water running woke her. Someone was in the shower. Clark!

She slipped out of bed and walked into the bathroom. The only light on was the one recessed inside the shower stall. It gave off a diffused glow through the steamy glass walls. Yet she could easily see the outline of Clark's physique, the wide shoulders, trim hips, his short, dark, wet hair. A sense of relief coursed through her, but something else, pure love, with a little lust thrown in.

CHAPTER 25

She slipped off the nightgown and tossed in on the bed. Could she do this? Initiate lovemaking with Clark? Now he was her husband. Of course, she could. She could do anything that would please them both. For a moment, she stood just outside the shower but then took a deep breath and opened the door. He turned his head and smiled. She picked up the soap and stepped behind him. "You want your back scrubbed, meester?" she whispered into his ear.

"Is this a service that comes with the bridal suite?" He bent his head and nuzzled her neck.

"It does tonight." She began washing and stoking him. It didn't take much before he was aroused and pushing her up against the glass wall of the shower box. Soon, she found this position a great advantage to them because of their similar height. The joining of their bodies was easy and a whole new experience for the bride.

Once out of the shower, Clark wrapped in a towel, padded to the door, and dropped the night lock. "Time to go to bed." He rubbed her dry, slid her across the big soft bed, and crawled in next to her. "This wedding night could last all day tomorrow."

It was late afternoon when the ringing of the phone awoke Clark. In the darkened room, he blindly groped to stop its insistent jangle. He found nothing as he touched bedside table, but Ana Lea tapped him on his shoulder and handed him the phone.

"Hello?" His voice was raspy and low.

"Clark? I wanted to catch you two before you went off sightseeing or … whatever." He immediately recognized Ray's low chuckle.

"Good morning, Ray." Clark stopped to yawn. "How's your day been so far?"

"Pretty good. Lorrie and I are leaving in the morning. We're going to stop and visit her sister in Vegas on the way home. Just wanted to congratulate both of you again. We really enjoyed your wedding. Even the unplanned events afterward made for an interesting experience. Thanks for picking me as your best man."

"Thank you, Ray. I value your friendship. We both do."

"You're planning to be back bright and early on Monday morning?" Ray asked.

"We're going to see an Aces game on Sunday, and we have a flight out that evening."

"To let you know, I called the hospital not long ago for an update on Kitt's condition. He suffered a skull fracture and a broken shoulder. His back doesn't show any trauma. He's still in a coma, so a visit now would be futile."

"Thanks for the info. Have a safe trip home. Bye."

While Clark was on the phone, Ana Lea moved to the bathroom.

"That was Ray?"

Clark nodded and sat up but could not see his bride.

"Hey, I finally figured what a bidet is for, and I just used it," she called from the bathroom and giggled.

Clark stood and stretched, did a few arm swings, knee bends, and toe touches, but when he tried to go into the bathroom, she had shut the door.

"Stay out, I'm getting dressed. No more sex for a while 'cause I'm faint from hunger." He heard her laugh.

"I suppose we can take a break from our honeymoon frolic to eat." He chuckled. "'Must keep up our strength for later."

She came out of the bathroom carrying her makeup case. "Hurry, I seem to remember that we are to meet the families tonight for dinner. Take a look at the clock—the dinner hour is fast approaching."

"Ugh, I remember. I'll hurry."

On the way downstairs to meet with Clark's dad and sisters, Clark told Ana Lea about Kitt.

She shook her head and sniffed but then reached for Clark's arm. "I'm feeling sadder for Melanie than Kitt right now. There's really nothing we can do for either one of them except pray."

An evening meal with Clark's father and two sisters, plus her parents, was more positive and low key than Ana Lea had expected. They all met at an Italian restaurant down the street from the hotel. Walter Andreasen was surprisingly pleasant, which was out of character for him. Usually, he tried to dominate the conversation: more or less take control. He brought in the evening newspaper. The front page showed the multiple car pileups and the heroics of the three doctors and two Aces football players. There was a side article about Carlson Kittredge, star running back for the Aces football team.

"You two know this Aces football star?" he asked his daughter and her new husband.

"Yes, Dad. Kitt went to the university while I was there. He played for the football team."

"So how did he get invited to your wedding?" her father asked. "His wife, Melanie, helped plan the wedding."

Walter nodded his head. "Makes sense now," he said and went back to eating.

Ana Lea's experiences with her father in the past few years had been, for the most part, negative. He lectured long and relentlessly about how she should behave, what she *could* be doing with her life. She was forced to answer his questions with long explanations defending her job and her lifestyle.

Mrs. Andreasen had her own ideas. "Daughter, I am so pleased that you've found a fine man to marry. Oh, especially a doctor!"

Patrick Knowles, Clark's father, said, "Well, Clark's done very well. He's found not only a pretty girl but also one that is smart and has a good profession." He grinned. "She seems to come from good family stock." He nodded at the Andreasens. "And looks like a good, strong girl who can carry and give birth to several children."

"Dad!" Megan scolded her father. "Let them get through the honeymoon before you expect them to start a family."

After the dinner group broke up, Patrick took Ana Lea aside. "I was more serious than not about grandchildren. So far, Eileen has just one child, a sweet little girl. Megan shows no sign of marrying very soon. Give me some grandchildren to enjoy in my declining years."

Clark walked up. "Declining years! Dad, you're only, what, sixty-two? You'll live at least twenty more. You've lots of time, while we need time to adjust to each other and for me to go on with my professional goals."

"Nevertheless, you're both in your thirties. No time to waste. Make me happy in my old age and give me some grandchildren, and soon."

Megan stepped over and touched Ana Lea's shoulder. "I suppose you've already found out that behind the quiet, studious intellect"—he glanced at Clark—"probably lurks a real passionate stud." She poked her brother in the ribs. Clark blushed at his sister's comment.

"Not to worry. I'm capable of handling the quiet student and the passionate stud, but he already knows that." Ana Lea snuggled against Clark's shoulder.

"OK, Dad, Lea and I will take your request under advisement." He gave a forced laugh.

Ana Lea led him over to her parents. They said their good-byes and began their stroll back to the hotel in companionable silence. Swirls of fog had moved in off the Pacific Ocean, wrapping around trees, bushes, and cars. Once they reached their hotel room, Clark turned to his bride.

"What are your feelings about giving the in-laws a grandchild fairly soon?" Clark spoke as he loosened his tie, took off his jacket, and hung it in the closet.

"Mmm … I really haven't thought too much about it. I suppose it would be better if we waited a year or so. I wouldn't mind a baby then." She plopped down in a chair and kicked off her high heels.

"A beginning embryo or a finished fetus?" he asked.

"My goodness, Dr. Knowles, using terminology like that makes me wonder if I should brush up on my biology." She stood and ran her hands down his chest and slowly unbuttoned the soft green shirt. "I had in mind a seven- or eight-pound finished product."

He kissed the palm of her hand and touched the tip of each finger with his tongue. "When would you like to begin work on this project?"

"I think we've already started." Sliding her hands under his open shirt, she moved close to him. Wrapping her arms around him, she already felt comfortable and very married.

During the night, Ana Lea stirred, and when she touched her husband, he squeezed her hand.

"You're awake. Did I disturb you?"

"No, I guess I'm not used to having so much sleep in one day." "The time spent in bed hasn't been *all* sleep." She laughed.

"Since last night, and we began our *marital relationship*, have you thought using any birth control?" he asked.

"No. I figured if I became pregnant, it would not be a problem." She came up on one elbow. "Why, do you want me to go back on the pill or use some other form of birth control?"

"No, I … well, I thought perhaps Dad is correct in saying that we should work on trying for a child soon."

"Well, I do travel some, and you are always so busy and are always somewhat sleep deprived. Maybe it will take us a while to hit it just right. I looked it up on the Internet. It takes the average couple, not using birth control, eleven months to conceive. So we have quite a while before worrying about it."

"Maybe being in our thirties, we're less fertile, or for a shorter period in the monthly cycle," he said.

"OK, if you're concerned, when we get back home, we can both go get a checkup, but in the meantime,"—she stroked his chest, bent, kissed him, and nuzzled his neck—"we should take advantage of this big … comfortable … bed." She became a little breathless. "Enjoy it to the fullest."

The next afternoon, the newlyweds went to the hospital to see Kitt. A floor nurse came up to Clark. "Dr. Knowles, how are you? We found out it was your wedding night when you were in surgery with Mr. Castelano. We were really grateful to you that evening, you and Dr. Rossiter and Dr. Wright."

Ana Lea was pleased and proud that the hospital personnel recognized Clark. She stuck out her hand to the nurse; "A. Whitney," her name tag read. "I'm Mrs. Knowles, Ana Lea Knowles. We came to see Mr. Kittredge."

"Oh, yes. He's in room 427. I believe his wife and Dr. Wright are here too."

When they reached the room, Melanie was just walking out. "Melanie, how are you doing?" Ana Lea reached for her hand. She looked so drained, deep circles under her eyes. Her usually immaculate dress and grooming had given way to wrinkled clothes. Her hair hung down, lank and neglected.

"I'm hanging in there. Kitt is better this afternoon. The coma is lighter. He's become restless. Jake and Joanna are in there now. They sent me to the cafeteria for some lunch. I may go home and change clothes, clean up a little." She tried for a wan smile.

"That's a good idea. If you can clean up, change clothes, you'll feel better." Ana Lea gave her a little hug. "We'll hang around for a while."

"You two are on your honeymoon. It was thoughtful for you to come." She rubbed her eyes. "I think I will go home, maybe take a nap." She backed away, shoulders hunched, head down. She looked so sad, depressed; Ana Lea's heart went out to her.

Clark and Lea eased into the darkened hospital room. Jake looked up. "Hi, guys, you two managed to get vertical again." He grinned.

"Hi, Jake." Clark walked over and carefully perused Kitt. "What's the prognosis?"

"They set his shoulder, and the procedure went well. The coma is lighter. From the X-rays, the skull fracture doesn't seem major. His primary physician isn't quite sure why he hasn't awakened."

"Where's Joanna?" Ana Lea asked.

"Joanna suffers from afternoon sleepiness. Being nearly three months pregnant, she still needs to sleep more than normal. I sent her back to the hotel."

"Josh was kind enough to get us some tickets for the game tomorrow morning. Are you and Joanna going?"

"Of course. I don't get a chance to see my little brother play his favorite game very often. I talked to him this morning. He's working with another running back for the game. He's frustrated and saddened because he's lost Kitt as pass receiver, as well as he's concerned about his friend. They go way back."

Ana Lea stood at the foot of Kitt's bed. Her thoughts went back to his rescue of her, when she so desperately needed one. Kitt is a womanizer, yes, but a decent man, no question. She said a quiet little prayer for him and for Melanie.

He deserved a chance to change his behavior, to become the husband that Melanie really needed.

CHAPTER 26

The Aces-Titans football game began the next morning at ten thirty, Pacific time. Nichole managed to get them into the VIP box. There was an elaborate buffet lunch set out for anyone invited in the weatherproof area.

They all became aware of the signs and banners throughout the stadium wishing Kitt a speedy recovery. At halftime, the CEO, Jack Douglas, of the Aces organization, gave a statement about how valuable a player he was, and as Kitt's boss was sure he would recover to play again.

The Aces trailed until well into the fourth quarter. With four minutes left on the clock, Josh's passes suddenly became more accurate, or at least the running back's timing became better. They pulled the game out with a last-minute field goal winning by two points.

The press was all over Joshua and the coach, Koslophsky. Josh spoke about his long friendship with Kitt and his fine athletic skills. There were many questions about the crash. Was it true that Kitt was a hero and he was first on the scene to help? That he had asked the other men attending the wedding party for their help? Both coach and quarterback gave truthful accounts of what they found and what everyone did until the police and ambulances arrived.

After they left the stadium, Clark, Ana Lea and, Nichole went back to the Wrights' home to pick up Ana Lea's clothing she had left there. While she packed, Clark sat and talked with Nichole. "Lea and I are so appreciative of all your help, the use of your house, and offering your home for our wedding."

"I'm just sorry we couldn't have had the wedding here, but baby JJ threw the plans for a loop. However, may I offer you some dinner? How about some wedding cake? There's some of it left."

"No, we've a plane to catch, and it leaves in about two hours. But before Lea comes down, may I ask you a question?"

"Fire away."

"When Lea came home from here in October, she mentioned this date with Kitt." He looked down." She came home with a bite on her neck. I wondered if she said anything about the incident to you."

"Don't worry about that. I noticed it the next morning. Lea was disgusted with Kitt, not enamored. She told me she only cared about you, and she married you, didn't she?"

The conversation trailed off when they heard Lea come down the stairs carrying a suitcase. Nichole dropped her voice. "Oh, here she comes." She cleared her throat and turned in Lea's direction. "Did you find all your belongings?"

"Yes. I'd left my blue scarf and some makeup in the bathroom." She turned to Clark. "I guess we're ready to go." She hugged Nichole. "Thanks, friend. Thank you for everything." She shrugged into her coat that Clark held for her.

"Yes, thank you, Nichole, and tell Josh of our appreciation. Keep us updated on Kitt's condition." Clark walked across the marble floor of the foyer. "Destination LAX."

The lively rock music coming from the clock radio jolted Ana Lea from a deep sleep. She opened one eye and looked at the clock, 5:40 a.m. Clark jumped from the bed and hurried to the bathroom. She slammed off the alarm and rolled over, muffling the sounds of the shower with the comforter over her head.

She settled down in a somnambulant state. Her prior resolve mentally bit her. *Remember, you planned on making some coffee and even breakfast for Clark and kissing him good-bye each morning.*

Ana Lea moaned and settled deeper in the bed. The angel on her right shoulder spoke to her. *Get up, it will become easier each time you do it.* The devil on her left shoulder whispered, *Not this morning, maybe tomorrow.*

She sat up and fished with her toe for a slipper near the bed. Locating one, she searched for its mate. This action forced her to slide out of bed and stand. She reached blindly at the foot of the bed for a robe.

Even though drinking coffee was not her habit, Clark had taught her to make coffee the way he liked it. Watching the dark liquid bubble, she decided that perhaps a cup would perk her up. She needed serious help to stay on her feet and not retreat to the welcoming warmth of the bed.

She took half a cup and liberally laced it with milk and sugar. After a sip or two, she decided that it was not too bad, and she knew the calorie content was not a serious breach of her daily diet.

The bathroom door opened, along with a swirl of warm, damp air, and out strolled Clark. "What do you want for breakfast, eggs, toast, or a muffin?" she called out.

"Coffee and a muffin will be fine." He took a sip of the coffee and a bite of the muffin. "Your coffee is getting better. Thanks, sweet wife." He kissed her soundly.

"If that's my reward for fixing you a breakfast of sorts, I'll do it again tomorrow." She hugged him.

He pulled on his boots, wrapped the muffin in a napkin, and filled his travel mug with more coffee. "See you tonight." In a swirl of light snow, he stomped out the door and hurried into his car.

Ana Lea stood at the sink looking out her kitchen window, watching the snowfall increase. *Not another snowstorm. I know we need to build the snowpack for water storage and to have plenty of water use next spring, But the sky is so dreary.* She sighed. *I could go back to bed. No. You promised yourself that you would try and align your activities with Clark's schedule. Go get* ready for the day. You can drive down to the shelter school and see how the remodeling is coming along. She turned and headed for the shower.

The Christmas season came upon Ana Lea in a rush. While she was at her small office at the shelter school, she made shopping lists. First on the list: gifts for her family and Clark's father and sisters. Her plan was to get them in the mail ASAP. She thought about shopping for individual gifts but decided that gift cards were the best option.

The week flew by, and suddenly, it was the next Saturday before she approached Clark. She wanted him to go up in the attic and drag down the Christmas tree and the boxes of decorations.

"Can it wait until the Utah-UCLA game is over?' Clark grumped from his position on the sofa in the TV room.

"How long will that take?" She tried not to sound irritated, but she was unable to do so. Then she decided that *sugar* would work better than *vinegar*. She sat down close to him on the couch and pretended to be interested in the game. When there was a timeout, she asked, "What about halftime? Could you get those things down then?"

He turned and smiled. "I suppose I could get into the attic during the half. But you could stand at the bottom and take the boxes as I bring them down, OK?"

"Fine, I'll go make some lunch." She stomped off to the kitchen.

After the game, and the decorations were down and lined up in the hall, Clark found he was now expected to string lights across the front porch and on the large pine tree on the corner of the lot. *When was the last time I did this chore? Must have been when we lived in … before Boston at any rate. At least it isn't snowing.* She stood at the foot of the ladder and handed him up the lights, which helped.

Once the lights were draped in on their hooks on the roof, she came out with a mug of cider for him.

"Thanks, wife. Do you have some cookies to go with it?"

"Come in and see." She gave him that sidelong sexy glance that warmed him inside but left him wanting.

"Now, we need to put the lights on the tree," she said sweetly.

"What's my reward for that chore?"

She tilted her head and glanced over her shoulder as she walked into the house. "I'll think of something."

He caught up with her, whirled her around, and began a kissing assault that left her breathless, with color warming her cheeks.

She took a deep breath and pushed at his chest with her hands. "Hang on to your libido for a few more hours. At least until the tree is finished."

"What a man has to do to earn some loving from his wife," he grumbled but grinned.

After the tree was finished, he went for wood in the garage and built a fire in the fireplace. He was not disappointed, because when he came back, she met him wearing a silky caftan. "Come sit on the sofa."

She knelt and spread the blanket throw on the floor before the fire. "We can sit on the floor if you would prefer." She jumped up and came back with a bowl of popcorn and more cider.

He had to give her credit. She liked to set up a seduction scene, and he was eager to participate. "Absolutely, I think I'd like to do this on a regular basis." She stood with her back to the fire, the light etching her silhouette and her hair down around her shoulders. Was she also working to become a seductress along with also improving her cooking skills? He was a lucky man.

CHAPTER 27

The newlyweds were invited to spend Christmas Eve with Ray, Lorrie, and the Rossiter children. The large house was beautifully decorated, and festive aromas wafted through the front door as Ray invited them in. "Wow, where did you find such a large Christmas tree?" Ana Lea asked.

"I ordered it through a catalog. It comes in pieces, so it's not too difficult to put together. The boys are big enough to help me if Ray is not here, and, usually, he isn't. They all like to help with the decorating."

Candace Rossiter came into the room carrying a large red tray with cups and small plates on it. "Mom, where should I put this?"

"Set it on the coffee table. Thanks, girl." She turned to Clark and Lea. "Come have some predinner treats."

On the tray were cups of spiced hot tomato juice and crackers with dip and vegetables. Clark strolled over. "What have we here?" He fixed himself a generous plate of the snacks.

Ana Lea made a plate and picked up a cup. "This looks and smells marvelous."

A few minutes later, Lorrie called them into the dining room for dinner. Ana Lea was pleasantly surprised how cooperative the children were. They wore nice clothes and made conversation with the adults.

They all helped clear the table after the meal, and Jeremy brought in the dessert.

Sometime after dinner, the phone rang, and Candace brought it to Ray. Seconds later, Clark's beeper went off. "I wondered if we would get through a Christmas Eve without being called in." Ray gave a mirthless laugh.

Clark glanced over at him in surprise. "This happens often? I mean, you have been called in to the hospital on Christmas Eve?"

"More often than not. It seems some people find the need to celebrate the season by driving around on the snowy roads too fast. Or with some, it's too many belts of liquor with or without the Christmas turkey. It hasn't snowed today, but the roads are far from clear."

Ana Lea touched Clark's arm. "Do you want to take the car, or should I drive it home? Or perhaps wait for you here?"

"Go home when you choose, Lea. I'll drive us both up the hill and drop him off when we're finished." Ray patted her shoulder.

The Rossiter children were accustomed to seeing their father go to the hospital at odd hours, even on holidays. They waved good-bye and went back to their activities.

Lorrie put an arm around her guest. "Come on, girl, let's go have some cider and cookies and sit by the fire. This *is* Christmas Eve. We can celebrate it even if the two demigods are off doing their thing."

"Is that the way you view Ray, as a demigod?"

"Notice I said *demi*, half. No, they're human, very human. Although, at times, I have seen Ray's artistry and skill, and it makes me wonder if he was blessed on high. He's saved many lives. Someday, you could ask the boys to tell you about the day he took them skiing at Brighton. It was a Saturday last February."

Jason came into the room carrying a plate of cookies and a bottle of Coke. "Hey, Lea, I heard Mom talking about when Dad took us skiing. It was pretty awesome."

"Did it involve a rescue?"

"Yes, it did. One of my friends who is a player on the soccer team with us was up skiing one Saturday. We were at Brighten, and Gavin's mom was up there skiing too. She's a pretty good skier and went to get on the lift on the difficult side of the resort. Then there's this idiot kid, and he tried to beat her to the lift. He skied over the top of her skis. They both crashed, but she didn't get up.

"The lift operator saw what happened and kept this dumb kid there at the lift shack.

"He called for the ski patrol, but Dad saw it happen and skied over, and I followed him. He kicked off his skis and knelt down to check on this lady. She had a head injury. Dad jumped up and called for a helicopter from U Med. Then he talked to the ski patrol about the dumb kid who caused the accident.

"He turned to me and said, 'Find your brother and this woman's son. I'm going to go to the hospital in the chopper with her.'

"He handed me the car keys and said, 'Take Gavin home in our car. Tell him I'll call his dad later.'

"That was my first time driving the SUV down the canyon, but we got home just fine." Jason touched his chest and smiled.

"What happened to your friend's mom?" Ana Lea asked.

"Oh, she had a head injury, but Dad did a surgery, and she got better pretty fast.

"Gavin's dad was really grateful, and later, when Dad had some problems with selling a cabin in a national park, Gavin's dad, who is in real estate, helped us. Oh, and our team won the state division."

Lorrie picked up the story. "When I saw Jason drive my Lincoln Navigator into the garage, I nearly had a heart attack. The boys had just passed their driver's test. The poor kid, Gavin, was so upset. He went straight up to the hospital. So I went over to their house and brought the three other kids all over here and made dinner. Then Ray called and said she was doing fine. He had stopped the bleeding."

"I can see why you call him a demigod," Ana Lea said.

"He's like a battlefield surgeon, quick decisions. Luckily for me and the kids, he's too old to go in the military. Clark will be that good someday. Ray says he's gifted and will only get better."

"Now he has you to provide him with a sounding board and a safe haven to come home to. That's your job."

Ana Lea was suddenly struck with the awesome responsibility of being married to someone so vital to so many people. Her throat felt thick with tears, and she blinked them back, but she managed to smile. "Thanks for your hospitality and your wise advice. I think I'll drive home now before the temperature drops even more and the roads become more ice than snow."

On the drive home, rather than feeling sorry for herself because she was alone on Christmas Eve, she felt OK. She had a glimpse of what her future with Clark would be. She began to understand the role she had taken on. She had a new role, a new career—the wife of a gifted surgeon.

Ana Lea was in a deep sleep when an exhausted Clark crawled in beside her. Sometime in the early morning hours, she got up to go to the bathroom and get a drink of water. When she slid back into bed, she found her husband asleep beside her. Sometime later, the phone rang.

"Hello?" her voice low and hoarse.

"Ana Lea, dear, this is Mother. How was your Christmas?"

Ana Lea shoved some pillows against the headboard of the bed in an effort to sit up yet bury most her body back under the covers. It was a defense against a chilly room. "Christmas? Oh, fine, Mom."

Clark's head emerged from the covers; he yawned and gave her a questioning frown.

"Oh, that's nice to hear, dear. What did you think of the gift Walter and I sent you? If you would rather have something different, I'm sure I can exchange it." Doreen's voice took on a definite edge of disappointment, as if needing to exchange the gift would mortally wound her.

"The gift you sent? Hang on a minute." She clamped her hand over the receiver and turned to Clark. She whispered. "Mother wants to know how we like the gift my parents sent us. It's under the Christmas tree. Would you please go find it?" She gave him a sweet searching gaze. She watched as a naked Clark ran out of the bedroom, down the hall into the living room. Faintly, she heard rustling of wrapping paper.

"Yes, Mother." She was responding to her mother's monologue about a neighborhood Christmas party they had attended. "I'm sure you were a great help to the committee."

From the living room, she heard an audible curse coming from her husband. She tried unsuccessfully to stifle a giggle. She heard a loud "Why is it so damn cold in here?"

She clamped her hand over the phone. "If you had some pajamas on, you'd be warmer."

"What are you laughing at, dear?" came a rather stern comment from her mother.

"Oh, I'm sorry, Mom. Clark is running around the house, ah, barefoot. I think he stubbed his toe. "Clark, love," she called out in a saccharin voice, "you need to put some slippers on."

"That's the least of what I need," he growled, and he threw a large, rather heavy box on top of the bed, just missing Lea's foot. He exaggerated a limp and slid back into bed. "Well, open it!" he said in a stage whisper. His wife pointed to the phone in her hand, and he took it from her.

"Mother Andreasen, how was your Christmas?" His tone dripped syrup. Ana Lea went into another fit of giggles. He frowned at her and turned away, while she began the task of opening the gift as quietly as possible.

Soon, she tapped his shoulder and held up the unwrapped box.

"We really appreciate the copper tone grill. Both Lea and I prefer to eat low-fat foods. Thank you. This is a wonderful gift. Now I'll give the phone back to your daughter."

"Thanks so much, Mom. We really love this grill. It will get lots of use." "I knew you two were careful in your eating habits. It's quite obvious, because you're both so trim and athletic. I told my friend Sally just the other day what a fine-looking couple you two are. Oh, by the way, those wedding pictures you sent are really beautiful."

Lea pulled the phone away from her ear as her mother rambled on and on.

Finally, she heard her mom say, "Oh, that's the front door. I must go now.

Call us soon."

"Nice talking to you, Mom. Merry Christmas. Bye."

Ana Lea set down the phone. "Whew, that was a close call. I'm sorry you hurt your toe. Let me take a look at it."

He lifted his foot from under the blankets. "It hurts, but it's still attached to my foot. That's something, I suppose. Hey, why is it so bloody cold in this house?" he grumped.

"Hmmm, when I turned the heat down last night, maybe I dropped it a degree or two too low." She threw back the covers and bent over to search for her robe and slippers. She twisted back because he was holding on to the hem of her nightgown.

He grabbed her around the waist and pulled her back into bed. "The temperature is perfect in this bed. Stay here." He began to pull her nightgown up and over her head.

"Only for few minutes." She giggled and snuggled down beside him.

Later that evening, they sat in by the fire with the Christmas tree lights glowing and the firelight cutting through the darkness. "So far, it has been a very memorable Christmas," Clark said.

"Especially since your father called to wish us glad tidings," Ana Lea commented. "How do think his health is—in general, I mean?"

"Oh, for sixty-two, I suppose he is in pretty good shape. But who knows the toll of all that drinking he did when Mom died?"

"I noticed he liked drinking the wine at our wedding dinner, several glasses, in fact."

"You noticed my father taking in too much alcohol? That surprises me." Clark straightened up, his glance sharp.

"You must know I grew up in a family where no one used alcohol. I tend to notice when other people drink, and how much."

"You had a glass of wine, didn't you?" His voice was deceptively bland. "Yes, nonalcoholic. I've had a drink or two in the last few years, but it never interested me when I was a teenager. That was one of the things I liked about you when we were dating. You didn't seek out places to go out for a drink." She reached over and kissed him on the cheek.

"I suppose I usually avoid alcohol for several reasons. One, I watched my dad get stupid drunk too many times. Medically, I know overconsumption of alcohol was damaging. And … three, living here where half the population doesn't drink, I wanted to fit in. Drinking is not important to me."

CHAPTER 28

Ana Lea decided to change the subject. "Since this is our first Christmas together. What will you tell our children about it in, say, fifteen or twenty years?"

"That we were madly in love, and we didn't dream of our life getting any better." He sealed his words with a kiss.

Although the newly married Knowles were extremely busy with their own careers, they worked at making the time they did have together precious. They rented movies they both wanted to see and sat cuddled together on the sofa in the den watching the films and munching popcorn. Ana Lea tried to make gourmet meals and left her warm bed each morning to fix Clark a light breakfast and kiss him good-bye.

In mid-January, she traveled again, this time to a convention in Phoenix sponsored by the American Charitable Foundation Inc. Ana Lea, as manager of the Make It Wright Foundation, had resisted joining the organization, but Joanna encouraged her to attend and bring back a report.

While Ana Lea was away, Clark came home to an empty house except for the cat and found being alone was miserable. He missed his wife more than it seemed rational. He had been a bachelor for over thirty-four years, yet he was irritable and slept poorly.

The third night she was out of town, he decided to look for Emily's journal. He opened it to

September 1886

I believe that I am with child. It was a very warm day, and working in the barn, I fainted. Samuel was very concerned and carried me to our room, bathed my face with cool water, and brought me a cup of tea. I then suggested to him that I could be carrying a child. He was so pleased and later took me to a doctor.

He told Jerusha that I must have easier chores to perform. She mumbled under her breath that no one gave her easier chores when she carried little Anna. Yet she did as he asked, and in a few weeks, I began to feel better. I am still unusually sleepy, and some foods I used to enjoy I can no longer tolerate.

Christmas 1886

This is our second Christmas as a polygamous family. In the Sugar House area, we are accepted as a combined family, yet others denounce plural marriage. The federal government has sent a cruel governor to take charge of the valley and his men to seek out those living "the principle." I fear what will happen to me and my babe.

April 1887

I was delivered of a precious baby girl. My mother and a midwife came to help me. The pain of childbirth was terrible, yet I will do it again to give Samuel another child someday. We talk of naming her Erlina.

October 1887

Samuel is adding on to the house a second kitchen and living area for me and Erlina. He began working on it early in the summer. It will be modern, with a "cold" room and an underground earth cellar.

As Clark put the journal away, he mused about Emily and her daughter. Though she lived in perilous times and could lose her husband, she was happy to be what she was. He compared her at age twenty to Lea, at thirty-two. He hoped and prayed that he would soon hear the news of Lea carrying a child.

The flight from Phoenix was in its final descent into Salt Lake International. Ana Lea had a window seat on the right side of the plane and could see the twinkling lights of the city and snow-covered mountains beyond. The flight, mercifully, was short, and she hoped that Clark would be able to pick her up.

Clark must have heard the phone because he picked it up. "Hello?"

"Hi, love, the plane just landed. Come and get me. I'm still sitting on the plane, so it's going to be at least twenty minutes before I am ready to leave the terminal."

Just the sound of her voice gave him a jolt of desire, yet it was more. It was because of his love for her, and he had missed her so much.

He spotted her waiting for her luggage to come up on the carrel. He came up behind her and gave her a squeeze. She turned and gave him a slanted kiss.

"Oh, it's great to see you," she whispered in his ear. She ran her hand along the back of his neck, lifting his shirt and his parka.

He strolled over to the moving luggage. "This plaid one is yours, is it not?" He pointed to a large soft-sided case coming around.

"Yes, that's the only piece I checked," she answered.

He grabbed it up and strode toward the door, and she scrambled behind him, carrying her purse and her laptop.

Once they were in the car, she commented as she stared out the window, "Did we get more snow this week?"

"Yes, a midsize storm, Wednesday. The mountains are covered over. You know when I gaze at those lumps of granite, soil, and trees, I marvel at their beauty. Back east, you don't see the majesty of huge mountains from base to summit as you do here."

"I think we should get up into those mountains and enjoy them the best way I know how, skiing! You do own skis, I've seen them."

"Yes, but I've never skied here in Utah. I just haven't thought much about it, because both of us have been so busy."

"Well, the first day off you have, we're going skiing. We'll start out easy." She seemed to warm to the subject. "When I was a kid and learned to ski, my dad would always take us to Brighten the first time each season."

"Why Brighten?" He imagined them schussing down the broad runs at Park City or Deer Valley.

"Because it has easy, intermediate, and some more difficult ski runs. And it's cheaper than the larger resorts. It's just a friendly hometown destination." "What, are you going to test my skiing skills?" He realized that sounded somewhat sharp.

She gave him a sidelong glance. "I will if you think you need testing. I would imagine that you, being as adept at so many physical activities as you are, skiing would be just another of your well-developed talents," she teased.

"Hmm, are we speaking of indoor or outdoor activities?"

"Both. I know firsthand of one of your indoor talents. Of course, I have no experience to judge your surgical skills, but I suppose you could be a fair cook."

"So you are comparing my chef skills with, say, building a fire?" he asked. "Oh, you have other more practiced talents. However, you can demonstrate your fire building expertise when we arrive home."

"What would like to move onto after my skill at making a fire?"

"Oh, popcorn making, ice cream sundae building. Yes, I would love see those skills firsthand. And others." She gave him a resounding kiss on his cheek.

The early morning sun glinting on the newly fallen snow forced Clark to drop the sun visor across the windshield. As he drove up the winding road of Big Cottonwood Canyon, the sun nearly blinded him, but around the next curve, it disappeared into the shadows. Finally, he pulled off his ski goggles and grabbed his sunglasses from the side pocket of the car.

Ana Lea, sitting in the passenger seat, had less trouble with the sun and shadow. She gazed up at the bright blue sky. "It's going to be a beautiful day. Being a native to this area, it's easy to become a fair-weather skier. You can choose a ski day by the weather forecast."

"I'm going to be blind before we get there, and you'll be forced to tow me down the hill with a rope," he grumped. Suddenly, the road straightened and leveled out, and the next curve took them into a large, flat snow-covered parking lot. Clark followed the cars in front of him and managed to find a parking spot on the third row.

"Hey, I'm pleased you found a parking place near the ticket booth. We won't have to walk too far." Ana Lea jumped out of the car, went around, and opened the back door of Clark's station wagon. She began to haul skis, poles, and boots from the rear hatch.

"Boy, you're eager. Hang on a minute, and I'll help you." He stomped around and pulled out his longer skis and accessories.

Soon, they were clomping up a short hill to the Majestic lift. "These runs are intermediate, a good place to warm up." She adjusted her goggles as she climbed on the lift and rode up the mountain. "It's such a glorious day." She smiled and reached over to squeeze her husband's arm.

Clark followed her down the back run, and soon, he felt the muscle memory of skiing kick in. He began to find a rhythm to each turn. The run was easy, but just to work his legs in the precise manner of a christie turn felt familiar. When they reached the bottom and moved into the line for another ride up, Clark said, "Are there more challenging runs on this side of the mountain?"

"We can take one through the trees or cut down the face. What's your pleasure?" She tilted her head.

"Through the trees. Lead the way."

She turned and polled a tight parallel through a narrow path lined with trees. He just had time to admire her skill before he had to focus on the trail. *OK, you're good, girl. I now want to see you banging down the face.*

On this run, Ana Lea was more cautious. She was making tight pole plants. However, he found another spot and passed her as the trail opened up. When they reached the bottom, her cheeks had reddened, and she seemed breathless.

"I wondered when you would pour on the power." She smiled. "Once I catch my breath, I'll lead you over to the other side where there are the more challenging runs."

He adjusted his goggles and banged snow off the side of his boots. "I thought you'd want to go in for a hot drink and a little rest."

She took a deep breath. "Not this soon, I'm just getting warmed up. Let's go."

They skied until his stomach growled from lack of food. They took the cross trail back to the easier side and went into the Alpine Rose cafeteria for some lunch. Once they found a table and pulled off parkas, hats, and gloves, he offered to pick up their food.

He set a tray loaded with steaming bowls of soup and sandwiches on the table. "Have you noticed that this place is filled with women and girls and only a scattering of the male gender?"

"That's because Monday. Here at Brighten, it is ladies' day. Their lift tickets are half price."

"Is that why you suggested we come here today?"

"Not entirely. It was a good deal for us to ski here today, but it happens to be the day you managed to have off, correct?"

"Well, I'll keep that in mind for next time we can manage a ski day." He smiled and sat down to eat.

Through a mouthful of sandwich, she said, "Next time we ski, I'll choose a resort with runs that will really challenge your skills." She patted his hand.

CHAPTER 29

That evening, an exhausted Clark had showered and picked up a medical volume to read in bed.

"Planning a little bedtime reading already, I see." Clark's half-closed eyes flew open to see his beautiful wife wrapped in a large blue towel and her damp tresses wrapped in another. Her skin took on a golden sheen, and her face was flushed from a ski sunburn and a warm shower. She dropped the towels, and he watched as she took a nightgown from a drawer and pulled it over her head. It pleased him that she was comfortable stripping down in the bedroom.

Once she had put the towels in bathroom, she returned to the bed and slid in." My feet are cold, so I'll just warm them on yours."

He wrapped her in his arms but then sat up and rubbed her cool feet with his warm hands. "That's nice." She sighed. She shook out her pillow and lay back and closed her eyes.

Just as he planted a little kiss on her mouth, the phone rang. "I'll get it." She slipped out of bed and stuffed her feet into furry slippers.

He could hear voice from the den saying, "Hello?" "Hi, Nichole, What's up?"

"Good evening. I have two messages to deliver this evening. First, an update on Kitt. He is home from the hospital and now goes to therapy twice a week for his shoulder."

"He's out of the coma?" Ana Lea asked.

"Yes, but his memory is foggy about some events. He didn't remember I'd given birth to JJ. Melanie has taken a leave of absence to care for him for a while. It seems to be a good arrangement for both of them."

"I'm sorry the Aces didn't make it further into the playoffs."

"Yes, Josh is too, but he had a difficult time working with those two less experienced pass receivers. Anyway, can you get down here for a couple of days, say, come down Thursday and stay until Sunday morning?"

"I suppose I could. Why?" Ana Lea asked.

"We have another center opening up in Van Nye's. We need you to coordinate the little celebration, ribbon cutting. You know the drill. Some of Aces players sponsored this center."

"I'll call for a flight tomorrow and get back to you to tell you the time your personal taxi service needs to arrive." She laughed.

"Sounds good. Talk to you later. Bye." Nichole clicked off.

When Ana Lea walked into the bedroom, she found Clark asleep, the book open across his chest. She set the book on the floor and brushed a kiss across his mouth. "Poor tired doctor, good night." She turned off the bedside lamp and slid in next to him. Once she rested her head on the pillow, her own fatigue caught up with her, and she fell asleep.

Clark still felt a little uneasy about reading the pioneer journal when Ana Lea was home because she'd ask where he found it. He would need to tell her it was with Kitt's scrapbook. It was when she traveled that he then would remember to drag it out. The entry that intrigued him was dated late in the fall of 1888.

November 1888

> Samuel's brother came to ask for his help with his barn and repairs on the roof of his house. It was most advantageous that Samuel was away from our farm, because the next day, a U.S. marshal came to the door inquiring of him. Jerusha shut herself in her bedroom

and directed me to answer the door. I had little Erlina in my arms and told the man, his name was Mr. Miller, that my husband was gone to help with a barn raising (a little white lie). He asked where that would be, and I told him I could not direct him to the place because I had never been there (the truth). He left a legal summons for Samuel.

I was terrified but knew that I must be strong in the face of such danger.

Late November 1888

One very cold evening, there was a knock at my new kitchen door. When I opened it, there stood an Indian woman wrapped in a filthy blanket. "I need to be near the fire," she said. She was shivering and looked so bedraggled that I had sympathy and let her in. She sat by my warm hearth for some time. I made her a cup of tea and gave her a hunk of bread. She seemed starved. I asked her what her name was. She said something that sounded like Moki Roby. So I decided to call her Ruby. When she dropped the blanket, I found she was pregnant. She asked if she could stay until the sun was high in the sky. Samuel was spending the night with Jerusha, so I said she could. She mumbled something about going back to be no more with baby.

I told her she seemed to have at least three months before she delivered. "No," she shook her head, "Need to go back, and no more have baby inside." I asked her where she would go, and she said to where the earth turned before. I asked how, and she said to the split willow. I did not understand of what she spoke.

She slept on by the hearth all night, and in the morning, though it was cold, the sun shone brightly. I gave her oatmeal and milk. Then she set off walking through our orchard. I had chores, and Baby Erlina needed to be nursed.

Jerusha came in that morning and scolded me for allowing that "filthy savage" in our house.

Samuel listened to Jerusha's angry words and turned on her. "The woman came to Emily's room, and she saw fit to help her. There was no harm in her actions. Enough!"

Later on, when the sun was high and bright in the sky, I walked the orchard searching for Ruby, but she had vanished.

The phone rang, and Clark picked it up. "Hello? Hi, Ray, do we have a new patient?"

"More than one. I need you to scrub in. Get up here, quick."

"I'll be there in twenty minutes." He put a bookmark in the journal and closed it. He slid it back into the new bookcase on his way out the basement door.

All through the month of February, Clark and Ana Lea tried, but only managed, to get up the mountain for one ski day. Their combined professions did not allow them to spend more than one ski day together. So Ana Lea was overjoyed when an invitation arrived in the mail. The Hospital Association of Utah was having a gala at the Marriott Hotel in Park City, and Mr. and Mrs. Clark Knowles were invited to attend. It was black tie.

The first thing Ana Lea did was to go to her closet in search of a winter formal dress. She found a beaded black sheath, but the skirt was narrow, and at the gala, there was to be dancing. She went shopping but found nothing that was within her budget. Then she remembered a friend telling her about a woman who designed and sewed formal gowns. She went to her sewing box and pulled out all her dressy patterns and narrowed it down to two.

That evening, she discussed their formal clothing needs with Clark. "I already have a tux," he announced with a pleased smile.

"You do? Where is it?"

"I rented it Monday at lunch. Some of the other doctors were wondering where they would find formal clothes, and a hospital administrator named Hughes suggested a formal wear place that did the wedding for his son. So Paul Landis and I went down there and lined up suits."

"Well, I wish my formal dress needs could be that easily solved. I think I'll have a dress made, but I haven't yet searched for the fabric. Let me show you some patterns I picked out," Ana Lea said.

"You want me to check out dress patterns?" he asked.

She jumped up for the table and ran to the den for a folder containing the patterns. She had picked out two of them, and she passed them to Clark.

"Please, just a look at them," she begged.

He studied them but, with a grin, handed her one back. "Make this one, and try to find cloth in a gold, tan, or brown color."

She looked at him with surprise. "Not black or red?"

"You have beautiful light brown eyes and dark brown hair with that lighter streak in your hair. Find fabric that looks good with your hair." He stroked her cheek and then leaned over and kissed it. "This dress has a nice line and a fuller skirt." He held up a pattern. "Have her make this one, and we'll dance." Then she remembered a golden-beige fringed shawl she had purchased years before while in Hawaii. She would search for it after she cleaned up dinner. She didn't want Clark to see it yet. She hoped it would work well with the dress.

The next day, she called the dressmaker and made an appointment. After her input, she would go shopping for the fabric.

Saturday, Clark came home jubilant. He barreled into the den, where Ana Lea was working. "Guess what? Ray and Lorrie have invited us to stay with them at their condo in Park City the weekend of the gala." He picked her up out the swivel chair and gave her a hug.

"They have a condo in Park City? Wow! Where is it?" she asked.

"It's in an older group of units just inside the Deer Valley area. They own it with two other doctors. One guy is from Las Vegas, and the other one here in Salt Lake. Each family gets to use it at least one week each month. So we can go up Friday evening, and Saturday, we can ski. I'm scheduled to work Sunday afternoon, but we can stay up until Sunday morning." He fairly danced around the room. "What do you think?"

"I think it sounds … wonderful, a great getaway. And both of us can be in the condo at the same time?" She laced her hands around the back of his neck and kissed him. She looked at her watch. "I've two hours before this particular fabric store closes. I'm going shopping."

After spending nearly an hour at the store, Ana Lea left with a package of sheer wool knit, the color of mink brown. She dropped it off at the dressmaker's on her way home. She also had the shawl with her. The seamstress, Myra Gates, nodded with approval.

"Yes, this is going to be a lovely, if not an unusual party gown. We'll design the back of the dress in a deep oval and make the front a draped neckline. All you'll need is a pair of dramatic gold earrings."

Ana Lea smiled. "I already have those. I was wearing them the night I met Clark."

It was close to midnight when Ray drove his Audi into the single garage of their condo. The garage was in the bottom level of the Rossiters' three-bedroom vacation residence. The four of them, Lorrie, Ray, Clark, and Ana Lea, exited the auto and climbed up the stairs.

"What's over here?" Clark asked, tilting his head at double white-painted doors.

"That's the hot tub." Ray opened the door and revealed the tub; warm moist air emanated from the small room. Clark stepped in and had a look.

"You two should take a dip in there. It's especially nice after a vigorous day on the slopes," Lorrie said. She turned and picked her way up a set of stairs leading to the main level of the place. She picked up the hem of her formal gown, and her high heels clicked on the wooden stairway. Ana Lea followed her.

"Would any of you like a cup of tea or something stronger?" Lorrie smiled and moved into the U-shaped kitchen. She filled the teakettle with water and set it on the burner of the gas range.

"Tea's fine with me," Clark said and dropped unto the beige tweed sofa.

"I guess it's four for tea," Ray said.

"That was a pleasant yet elegant dinner-dance. The food was good and the speeches short," Clark commented.

Ana Lea moved in the kitchen to help Lorrie and set a box of tea bags, sugar, and tray of mugs on the coffee table.

CHAPTER 30

"Watch out, I'm bringing hot water." Lorrie carried in the teakettle and filled each mug. "Turn on the fireplace, Ray. It makes it more cheerful in here."

"How long have you two owned a share in this condo?" Clark asked.

"About nine years. The four couples bought it from a guy who lived in California. The interesting thing—three of the four owners met him and each of the other two owners while skiing at Brian Head one spring. This condo group was constructed about fifteen years ago. Back then, the prices weren't too steep. And it is large enough to accommodate the family."

"The problem with this place is it's so generic, beige sofas, beige carpet, beige and cream flooring. I'd like to perk it up, but among three women, nobody can agree on any major changes." Lorrie frowned. "Are the other two bedrooms upstairs?" Ana Lea asked.

"Yes, the master and another one with bunk beds. It's about the same size as the one you and Clark are sharing," Lorrie answered.

With a yawn, Ray stood up and set his mug on the counter where three barstools stood. "If we're going skiing tomorrow, we'd better hit the sack."

"Good thinking," Clark said. "We'll see you in the morning. What time?" Clark turned and walked into the bedroom near the living room. "Ana Lea, you coming?"

"I'll help Lorrie clean up and be there in a minute."

"Not much to clean, just pop the mugs into the dishwasher." Ray had already gone up the stairs to the third level. Lorrie snapped off the kitchen light. "Night, you two. Breakfast will be at eight."

After a hearty breakfast, they drove to the Canyons Ski resort about five miles outside Park City. The resort had been bought and sold, and now a group of owners with deep pockets was building a semicircle of four- and five-star hotels, and large groups of condos had been and more were being constructed along the edge of the mountain behind the hotels.

"Wow, I haven't been up here in several years, I wouldn't recognize the place!" Ana Lea exclaimed. "They've really made this resort a destination." "What I want to know is how's the skiing?" Clark asked as he ogled the large hotels.

"Well, we're here to find out." Ray parked his Audi station wagon, and they all readied for the slopes and found they were close to a lift. "Meet you two back here for lunch, say, one o'clock?"

"Good. We'll see you then," Clark called out.

The sun was shining, and the sky looked like a deep blue bowl. A light dusting of new snow was light and dry and was known as world famous, nature's concoction at Utah ski resorts. It was called "the greatest snow on earth," and Clark and Ana Lea had one of the best ski days ever.

Soon, it was time to meet Ray and Lorrie at the buffet in the Canyon's Sunset Hotel.

Ray signaled the two of them by waving his hat. "How has your day been so far?"

"Now I fully understand why I moved here." Clark dropped his ski jacket on one of the chairs by the table. "I've never skied better. When we're on the ski lift, it's breathtakingly beautiful to look down at the runs."

"I believe he might decide to stay here." Ana Lea laughed.

Lorrie returned to the table. "The restroom's pretty nice too. I'm starving, so let's go get some lunch."

They stayed in the restaurant for nearly an hour. Ana Lea was pleasantly full and slightly tired, but when Ray suggested they meet at the car when the lifts shut down, she was game for another two hours of skiing.

When they reached the car, Ray was pacing, waiting for them. "I need to drop you two off at the condo. It seems that I have a patient waiting for me at the emergency room down at the clinic. He's had a ski accident."

"What about you, Lorrie? Are you going to stay here or go down with Ray?" Ana Lea asked.

"Oh, I probably need to go home to see what our kids are doing. But you two stay up until tomorrow morning. There are plenty of restaurants and fast-food places where you two can pick up some dinner. Enjoy the condo, and give the key to Ray when you see him at the hospital tomorrow. I wouldn't mind if you to pull your car into the garage for tonight. It will be pretty cold up here in the wee hours of the morning."

"OK, if you're all right for us to stay up tonight," Clark said.

"Tomorrow morning, just pull the sheets off your bed and gather up the towels. Put them downstairs in the laundry alcove," Lorrie said.

"No problem," responded Ana Lea.

Ray dropped them off, and Ana Lea took a look around the kitchen. She opened the fridge and found the remains of a vegetable tray. "Before you change out of your ski clothes, Clark, why don't you go get us a pizza?"

"I'll do that if you promise to get into the hot tub with me when I get back." He wiggled his eyebrows and tilted his head in a lascivious grin.

"You're on." She laughed.

"Not yet, but I will be." Clark scooped up his car keys and ran down the stairs and to the garage.

Ana Lea went upstairs and snooped while Clark was gone. She checked out the master bedroom and the second one with the four bunk beds in it. The condo could use some colorful decorative touches, but, basically, it was a great vacation place.

Back in the kitchen, she found some sodas and a bowl of grapes. By the time Clark bustled up the stairs, carrying a medium pizza, she had the table set.

To her surprise, she was hungry and noticed Clark eating with gusto. Together, they consumed most of the food. "Oh, I ate too much." She flopped on the smaller sofa and rubbed her stomach.

"I helped make that food disappear. Now I have to rest to let everything digest." Clark found the TV remote and turned it on. He flipped through the channels until he found a Jazz basketball game.

For a while, she watched the big men run up and down the court but grew bored with the game and Clark yelling at the screen. She retreated to their bedroom and dug out a new Karen Robards novel. Settling on the bed, she began the book, but after ten pages or so, her eyes grew heavy, and she fell asleep.

A while later, she woke and glanced at the clock. It was after nine. Ana Lea flipped on the TV in the bedroom and checked on the basketball game; she found it was halftime, She went down to the living room and found Clark had fallen asleep. Then she thought, *Hey, the hot tub.* And they hadn't tried it yet. Images of the two of them enjoying the hot bubbling water brought a flash of longing, and the stiffness in her legs needed its therapeutic offerings. How could she entice Clark to forego the TV and join her downstairs?

Ana Lea stood and stared at the clothes she had brought for the weekend. She reached for the bikini, but then something else caught her eye. The crème and gold shawl would do nicely as a wrap over her with or without a swimsuit.

Clark felt something tickle his nose, and he sat up with a start. He blinked because Ana Lea was standing near him swinging the fringe of her shawl across his face. "What the ... ?" He straightened and looked at his wife in the soft lamplight. She was wrapped in the silky fabric, her hair tied up in a scarf. *And she was beautiful.*

He felt his face widen into a broad smile. "That shawl has more potential than I first thought. Where's your swimsuit?" He stood and took a large step toward her.

"Actually, this shawl has versatility. It covers me." Her voice was low, and she wiggled a finger at him. She dropped a corner of the silky fabric on the carpet and walked toward the stairs. She took a step down.

"Wait." He touched her shoulder. "Where are ... ? Oh, the hot tub." "And you're overdressed." She giggled and descended the stairs. He made a dash into the bedroom and finally found his swim trunks.

He pulled off his sweater and threw it onto the bed. He changed in record time.

As he walked in, the warmth and humidity of the small area seemed to envelope him. Ana Lea stood waiting, draped the shawl carefully over a chair, and climbed the two stairs to the rim of the tub. She gave him a teasing smile. He dropped into the chair, pulled off his socks, and followed her in.

He leaned back against the side of tub and let the swirling water relax sore his muscles, but one muscle was becoming quite rigid.

"Isn't this great? Do you think we could dig up a place in the backyard and put one of these in?" She purred.

The swim trunks floated to the top of the tub, and Clark grabbed them and threw them over the side. "Come here, wife." He growled. "I'm about to ravish you."

"You can't do that. I promise to cooperate." She came close and kissed him everywhere her mouth would reach. Holding on to the side of the tub, she wrapped her legs around him and slid down until she could take him into her body.

"Wife, you are full of surprises." His whole focus was on her and what she was doing to him. Their coupling was swift, wild, and deeply satisfying to both.

She lolled her head against his shoulder and closed her eyes. A few minutes later, she looked over at Clark; his eyes were closed and he had fallen asleep and was sinking into the water. She reached for him, and he struggled to stand. "I think we should move this activity to the bedroom so you can sleep without taking in water."

With supreme effort, he climbed from the tub and pulled her up along with him. "Come, let's go upstairs."

After Clark had gone into the hospital the next afternoon, Ana Lea found that her focus was not on work. She lay down on their bed and thought about their weekend. It had been near *perfect*. She thought about becoming pregnant. Could she work through a pregnancy and still travel? But for how long? How would this affect her job? They needed her income for at least the next few years. Up until now, the thought of starting a family was just that, thoughts and dreams. Maybe she would have trouble getting pregnant, or perhaps she was pregnant already?

Clark had been urging her to come up to U Med and have a physical exam.

She decided to do that soon.

She finally made an appointment with a female ob-gyn, a doctor named Judith Jolley. The lady was very busy, and she had an opening three weeks later. On her way to her appointment, Ana Lea wondered if the woman would live up to her name—Dr. Jolley.

It was a routine physical, blood drawn, urine donation. She liked her choice of a doctor immediately. The lady was in her forties, a little too round, and she had a long ponytail of streaked blond hair.

"Well, you seem to be in excellent health, muscle tone is good, weight is right on. Whatever you're doing, eating, keep on with your lifestyle. So far, I can't see why you would have any trouble conceiving. I've met your husband, and he's a real cute guy. From your application, it says that you travel for you career. Flying is not dangerous to a pregnancy, unless you go into labor on a flight. But we'll worry about that later. I'll send you your test results in a few days."

Ana Lea was scheduled to fly back to Detroit on Friday afternoon. The day was clear and unusually warm for the third week in April. She kissed Clark good-bye that morning, but he phoned and said he was coming home and bringing her some lunch and a surprise. She waited until well after one o'clock, but he never came, and she was forced to leave for the airport.

CHAPTER 31

Clark parked in the long driveway and noticed Ana Lea's car parked in front of the house. He carried two boxes of lunch, and the surprise was in his coat pocket, the results from Ana Lea's tests. She was pregnant!

He hurried to the basement door and pulled the key out of his pocket. Just as he swung open the door, he looked up into the sky; it was exactly 1:00 p.m., mountain daylight time. The sun was at its zenith. It was a beautiful early spring day.

The heavy door swung closed, and the basement was nearly dark. Clark reached for the light switch, but his hand seemed to slide down without moving it. He tried again, but no light came on. *Maybe the power is out.* Moving across the family room to the stairs suddenly became a challenge. The lunch boxes had disappeared from his hands. He couldn't make his legs work to take a step and then another. He lunged forward, and his feet came off the floor, and he found that he was floating.

This is crazy. What's wrong with me? He turned back toward the basement door. *I have to get out of here, back into the sunshine.* He reached for the knob, but it would not turn, or he couldn't make it open. In frustration, he launched himself at the door and found that he had slipped right through it.

Suddenly, he was outside, but the sunshine had disappeared. A cold rain poured down. Clark looked down at his clothes. He no longer wore his jacket and dark slacks but was dressed in his ski clothes, dirty and stained. The left sleeve was torn as well as the right leg of his pants. He examined the stains. *Blood!*

He watched the rain fall, not on him but through him. *I'd better go back inside.* He mentally directed himself in and again found he was in the basement. Moving became easier because he found he could mentally direct his body across the room and up the stairs. The main floor door was closed, and he tried to turn the knob. No success; his hand bumped the door and then went through it, and he followed his arm unto the landing.

Once into the kitchen, his attention turned to a new calendar on the bulletin board. April 18 was a Saturday, and it read one year ahead. He was standing in his kitchen, but one year ahead of what it had been a few minutes before. What had happened? Where was he? What had he become?

Clark's thoughts moved him into the front entrance hall. There, Ana Lea had placed a small table for mail, keys, and other small items. Above it was a mirror. He caught his reflection in the glass, or an outline of his reflection. He could see through it to the planter behind and the door of the coat closet. He studied his visage for several seconds and more carefully examined the clothes he was wearing. The ski clothing was torn, dirty, and had bloodstains on it. He put his hands against the mirror and dropped his head. A cold fear enveloped him. The reflection in the mirror was an apparition, a ghost of his former self. Somehow, while walking into the basement, he had died?

At the south end of the living room was the dining area. On the table were the makings of a scrapbook. He drifted nearer and studied the open pages. It showed a newspaper article, and he found he could read it.

Doctor Sacrifices Life to Rescue Skiers

Dr. Clark Knowles, while driving down Little Cottonwood Canyon, stopped his car when he saw a sports Jeep roll down the canyon. Tom Jamison had lost control of his vehicle and rolled it down into the streambed about three miles down the canyon from Snowbird at the top of a place the skiers call Seven Sisters.

Dr. Knowles managed to pull Bret free, and his companion also managed to free himself from the car. The car rested against a tree, and when Bret came free, a tree limb broke. The car then rolled on Knowles, crushing him. He was DOA on arrival at University Hospital. Knowles is survived by his wife, Ana Lea, and an infant son.

So he *was* dead. How could that be? He glanced back at another article. It talked about his blossoming career as a surgeon. The newspaper was dated January 22. What was today's date?

Clark moved back to kitchen and studied the calendar more carefully. Ana Lea would write dates and messages on it. There were notes up to April 18 on the calendar, dated one year in the future. Somehow, he had died in the future, and now he was in future time. Had he been dead for three months and just now having a memory of it?

Of all the movies he had seen of vampires, other paranormal events came to mind. He decided he was now a ghost.

He was getting better at moving his ethereal body around, and he drifted down the hall to the den, which he found now to be a nursery. The walls were painted a pale yellow with a bright motif of little boys at top of the walls near the ceiling. The room held a light oak crib, a matching dresser, a change table, and a rocking chair, along with other accessories needed to clothe, diaper, and sooth an infant. Where were the computer, TV, and bookshelves? They must be downstairs.

The master bedroom seemed familiar. It looked much as he had left it this morning. Wasn't it just this morning? He realized he had no sense of the passing of time. Was it because he had no beating heart and no sense of the turning of the earth?

The smaller closet door was open. His clothes were missing. What had Ana Lea done with them? He drifted back to the dining area. There were other articles lying out to read. It was just like her to build a scrapbook in his honor. Hadn't she done that years before for Carlson Kittredge?

As he bent over to read, the french door opened. Lea loaded down with a baby carrier came in. She set it down in the kitchen and went back outside and brought in a diaper bag and her purse. She slammed the door shut against a rising wind and shrugged out of her coat. She picked up the carrier and moved to the nursery.

Clark followed her for a chance peek at the baby. The sleeping child wore a blue sweater and cap and was wrapped in a blanket. She carefully took off the outer clothes from the baby and laid him in his crib. She exited the room quietly and nearly walked through Clark. She moved to the kitchen, set the teakettle to heat, and took the makings of a cup of tea from the pantry. He felt great sadness for that was a habit of hers, a cup of tea in the afternoon. Now watching her do this was so endearing to him.

He watched as she changed out of her business clothes and into jeans and a sweatshirt. *Now I understand what it is to be dead. I can watch my shapely, sexy wife take off most of her clothes and feel nothing but appreciation for her beauty.*

She walked back to the whistling teakettle and poured water into her mug.

She sat down at the table and went through her purse for her checkbook. Next, she went out the front door and picked up the mail, found a bill among the stack and sat down to pay it, and sipped her tea.

Soon, though, she sat back and closed her eyes. Abruptly, she stood and walked into the bedroom, lay down, and pulled up the quilt. She looked so drawn and fatigued. She had dark circles under her eyes that he could not ever remember seeing. She fell asleep quickly.

He knelt close to her. "Oh, Lea, I so wish I could be *alive* to hold you near, to love you again, both physically and intellectually. There must be some way back to you, to be alive again. I must return to the past, my living past." He could still feel his love for her. Love really did transcend death, as so many pastors and other religious leaders had preached, as the

Bible told. If ghosts could shed tears, he certainly would now be crying. His love for her was as sure as the setting of the sun and of the turning of the earth.

Clark drifted downstairs, looking, searching for some clue to what had happened to him. He found that Ana Lea had made a newly constructed family room. In this year he missed, they must have had Jonas finish off the rest of the basement.

There, he found the sofa he had slept on, the desk, the computer setup. On the desktop, he found a stack of papers and, in plain sight, the journal. Inside that red leather book must be the answer to his dilemma. There must be some clue mentioning the house and the bazaar situation he was in.

He drifted to the heavy door he had walked through not long ago.

When he had seen the warning "Never Open" on the wall, he should have heeded it. He was beginning to understand the door. Somehow, walking through that door put him one year into the future. And in the future, Clark Knowles had *died!*

Another aspect—how long would he be allowed to wander the confines of this house as a ghost? Wouldn't he be whisked off to some otherworldly existence?

He sat, or at least hovered, on the bottom stair and tried to think through his predicament. He could hear Lea walking around upstairs. At least he could hear and see. He also heard the soft vocalizations of the baby. He shot up and nearly went through baby Clark's swing near the kitchen wall. Lea had put the infant into it, and he hung contented, chewing on his fist, while Lea made some supper. The amount of food she prepared was much less than half of what she would have eaten when they dined together.

She was thin; her soft curves were nearly lost in the oversized sweat outfit she wore. He knew about the needs of a breastfeeding mother. She had lost too much weight.

She turned on the TV he had mounted on the corner of the kitchen wall, watching it while she ate dutifully and did not seem to be enjoying her dinner.

The baby began to fuss. Lea immediately picked him up and walked into the nursery and changed him. After washing her hands, she sat down in the rocker and fed him. All Clark could see was his little head covered with soft light brown curls. At that moment, she set him on her shoulder to rub his back. His eyes opened, and his ghostly father looked into eyes nearly the same color as his own.

Back to his feeding, the child soon fell asleep. Gently, Lea laid him in his crib and dressed him in little pajamas with green frogs on the fabric. She covered him with a small blue blanket.

As she walked into the kitchen, she began to talk. "Oh, Clark, you would be so proud of him." Though her words were audible, they did not seem to be directed at the ghostly Clark. "He's such a fine child, bright and good-natured. You would be pleased to be his father."

If a ghostly father's heart could break, Clark's just did. He watched her clean up the kitchen and then go downstairs to work on some files for a time. The skies outside darkened, and the drizzle outside turned to snow.

She gave up working and went back upstairs, flopped on her bed, and picked up the TV remote. She spiraled through channels, searching for something that would catch her interest.

Suddenly, the doorbell rang. She glanced at the bedside clock; 8:32 p.m. "Now who could that be?" An impatient second ring brought her to her feet, and she pulled the band from her long, dark hair and straightened her loose-fitting shirt. She glanced at the sidelight on the door but then opened it.

CHAPTER 32

There stood Carlson Kittredge, impatiently jiggling his car keys. Clark could see the heavy snowfall outside.

"Kitt!"

"Hello, Lea. May I come in? Because I need to talk to you."

"For heaven's sake, why do you need to talk to me? I appreciated the card and the check for baby Clark's college fund, but … why now?"

Kitt had already opened the security door and stepped into the entrance. "Forget the manners, Lea, I need some information."

She sighed and ran her hand through her hair. "All right, come in and sit down. She led him into the living room. All six feet five inches of him picked out the largest chair, Clark's favorite. Clark hovered near and found, even in his between-worlds state, he could become irritated. *What in the hell is he doing here?*

"Lea, my wife's pregnant, by in vitro. We did it at U Med," Kitt said.

"That's wonderful news. But how does that affect me?" Lea said, and Clark could see her discomfort.

"I understand that's the way you became pregnant."

"What?" Her voice's tone told Clark she was getting mighty irritated. "I'm happy for you, Kitt. I know that you and Melanie have wanted a child for years. How is she doing?"

"She's fine," he said dismissively. "You didn't answer my question. What I want to know is ... is your child really Clark's?"

"What! Are you out of your mind? Of course, he's Clark's child." Lea's eyes darkened in anger, and Clark could see the tension in her body.

"I had a phone call from a tech saying that your husband swapped our sperm samples, or at least tampered with them."

That' right. One night, when I was on for the graveyard shift, I went to the infertility clinic, and because I was an MD, I could take a look at their records. I had donated sperm, as most young medics are asked to do. I wondered if any of the vials had been used. The attendant told me I would need to have authorization to peruse the records any further.

"That's ridiculous. Where in the world ... ?" She stopped; her eyes narrowed. "For one thing, I know how well those samples are protected. They are numbered, not listed by name. The only people that have access to those samples are the fertility specialists and the lab technicians. And those people are bonded. Besides, when would he have time to go over to the fertility wing from the surgical wing? And why would he bother with *your* samples, if he knew they were actually there?" She crossed her arms and tapped her foot in front of him.

He was silent momentarily, and his anger seemed to diminish. "Why would someone call and tell me ... about Clark?"

She slumped into a chair. "Why would they? OK, you're a celebrity of sorts. Think about what a human interest story these lies could be used. Most likely on the Internet. Also, Clark is deceased and cannot defend himself. Oh, and one more thing, we never used the sperm bank."

"You didn't?" He blinked and sat back. "So you and Clark ... just a normal night in the sack?"

She looked away but smiled. "Not in the 'sack'—a hot tub, after a glorious day of skiing in Park City." As if on cue, Clark Junior began to fuss. She stood. "Excuse me." She went quickly to the nursery and returned with the baby on her shoulder. He opened his huge blue eyes and stared at Kitt.

Kitt came over and gently touched little Clark's head. "Hi, little guy." He wiggled his fingers at the infant and was rewarded with a toothless grin and a milky burp.

The ghostly Clark drifted over to get a closer look at his namesake. *Yes, he is a fine child.* Clark felt a smile crease his ghostly visage, and the baby looked directly at him and grinned. *I wonder, is it possible he can actually see me?*

"I can see he's Clark's." Kitt seemed to grow smaller in the chair. "I'm sorry I made you angry, but I just want the baby Melanie's carrying to be mine. I mean, with Melanie's height, the child could be a great athlete."

"Men! You guys are so ownership oriented. What if the baby turned out to be a highly intelligent bookworm? You need to focus on Melanie and her needs right now and be happy for any healthy baby. Let me be the devil's advocate. Let's say that child of yours inherits some of Clark's DNA. What you may have is a brilliant quarterback."

Yeah, the ghostly Clark thought. *You tell him, Lea.*

Kitt sighed. "I suppose I never thought about a child that wouldn't be like me. It might be a girl."

Kitt stood and moved toward the door. "I'm sorry to have bothered you. Are you doing OK?"

"I have more-than-enough financial help from Josh and Jake. I'm very fortunate to have such good friends." Little Clark let out a fussy cry. "It's time for his nightly feeding." She walked toward the door and opened it to allow the big man to step outside. "Go home and be good to your wife. It's snowing. You'd better run for your car."

"Thanks for seeing me," he called out and jumped into his car.

Lea waved and closed the door with a thud, locking it securely.

She kissed the baby on his cheek. "Time for bed, babe of mine. Time for some sleep for your mommy."

Though she closed her eyes, she couldn't sleep. Thoughts of what Kitt had said swirled in her brain. She tried different positions but could not relax. *Clark, I need you. I need the comfort of your warm body. Ugh! I need some loving. After we'd had sex, I could always sleep.*

She tried to relax with the TV again. Finally, she found a late-night mystery series she enjoyed. During one of the commercials, she felt as if a butterfly had brushed against her neck. She sat up straight with a start. "Clark, are you visiting me? Or is it the other ghost you talked of. Is he touching me and living in the house?" She slumped back down into the pillows. "I need the real, living, breathing Clark, not your ghost."

Sometime in the early morning hours, Clark Junior began to fuss, which quickly turned into an earsplitting howl. Clark hovered over him anxiously, watching the baby punch the air with his fists and scream with his eyes closed. Lea dragged out of bed and picked him up.

"What's all this fussing about?" she said softly. "Oh, you're all wet and became chilled, I'll bet. Better change you first." Soon, the now dry baby was wrapped in a blanket, being rocked and fed. "Well, little one, you made it nearly six hours between feedings. That's pretty good." She looked up. "If you're up there watching down on us, Clark, you can see we're doing pretty well. Not as good if you were here with us, but OK.

It's not OK. I miss you so much, your wide smile and hairy chest to nestle against." She sighed and dropped her head and moved the baby to the other breast. "I'm glad you went out a hero, but it's not fair being a widow at age thirty-three."

Clark watched as she hummed and rocked. If ghosts could cry, he would be shedding buckets of tears right now. Little Clark fell asleep and was tucked back into his crib. Lea went back to bed and closed her eyes but sat up a few minutes later. "Damn, I hate it when I can't get back to sleep," she mumbled.

She stomped into the kitchen and put on the teakettle. Soon, she had a packet of hot chocolate stirred into a mug of hot water. She went downstairs and stood examining the paperback books in the bookcase Jonas had made for them. Clark followed her downstairs and hovered near. "The journal, I need to read it. Please go find the journal. I'll read over your shoulder. I know the secret to the basement door is in there." She stood barefoot, hopping from one foot to the other and plucking one paperback after another and reading the pitch on the back. There were dozens in that bookcase. He had no idea she had that many novels.

She sighed, walked into the basement den, and stood there for a moment, and then snapped on the light. "Look, Lea, the journal. It's right here on the desk."

"Oh, for heaven sake, here's the old pioneer journal that Clark liked to read." She grabbed it and scurried up the stairs. With her hot chocolate in one hand and the journal in the other, she walked back to bed, fluffed up her pillows, put some socks on her chilled feet, and opened the journal where Clark had put in a marker. She sipped the hot beverage and began to read. Actually, they both read, because Clark sat on the back of headboard behind her back.

March 1889

> Jerusha now complains to Samuel that if he had never married me, the marshals would not be searching for him. When she has the chance, she yells at me, that I should take my daughter and go back to my father's farm. I cannot leave my new house addition and Samuel. He is my husband, and I love him.
>
> He brought me a new cookstove for my new kitchen. It is shiny black and has metal trim and warming oven. It easily heats the kitchen.
>
> One night, the Indian girl Ruby came to visit and, of course, to beg for food. She was grateful and promised Samuel to show him how to get away from the marshals. He went with her the next day into the orchard. He did not come back until the next early afternoon. He was smiling and spoke of an escape for all of us close in our orchard.

Lea shook her head. "I suppose being a polygamous wife is almost as difficult as being a widow, but not quite." She sighed and finished her hot chocolate.

"Please, Lea, read on. Now I understand our house now sits on an ancient vortex. But I must learn precisely how to use it to get back to you," Clark said.

July 1889

> Samuel has gone into hiding. He left with a bedroll and some food and promised to return when it was safe. I know his hiding has something to do with the split

willow deep in the orchard. When he returns, I will ask him to show me. I am trying to be brave, but it is difficult. Already, the marshals have arrested not only the husbands but also some of the sister-wives. Some of the children have been sent to a special school in another county.

August 1889

The marshals finally caught Samuel and took him to the prison in the Sugar House jail. I visited him once, and he told me not to come back. Jerusha and I can keep the orchard going, but I am so frightened. We do have help from Samuel's brothers.

September 1890

Ruby came last night and wanted food, but she stayed and helped me milk the cow. She told me she has a great secret to show me, because she promised Samuel she would.

We go to the split willow and wait. She stands and studies the sky for such a long time. I feel she is in a trance. But then she grabs my hand, and I carry little Erlina through the willow split.

We walk through to the west, and the sky looks wavy, like water, but we stop, and the sky has changed.

It is now cool, and great clouds hide the mountains. We carefully walk back to the house, but it is quiet. I unlock the door, and it is dusty, and cobwebs hang from the candelabra in the kitchen.

Ruby goes to milk the cow, but it is gone. I build a small fire and make bread. The flour bin is nearly empty, but the chickens have eggs, and we will have something for supper. It seems as if no one has been in the house for a very long time.

CHAPTER 33

We sleep in the barn that night, Then the next day, we go back to the split willow. Again, we wait until the sun is at its highest in the sky and walk through to the east. We walked back to our house, and the chickens are in the barn, along with the cow, and my house was the way I had left it two days before.

"Wait a sec—is she describing a time vortex?" Ana Lea set the journal down. "Clark, if you're around here with me, and tonight I feel you so close, you'd enjoy this entry." She smiled and closed the book, as well as her eyes.

If ghosts could do handstands, Clark would be walking on his hands all over the house. *Now I know I must walk through the door at the zenith of the sun at precisely 1:00 p.m.*

He knelt by Ana Lea and gave her a ghostly kiss and watched her brush her hand across her face. "We're so close right now. I hope I can remember this feeling when I'm alive again."

Clark loses any sense of time. He seems to have gone into a dead zone. Slowly, he becomes aware of movement, of the baby crying. Ana Lea gets out of bed too and goes to the nursery. He is next aware of music playing in the kitchen and baby sounds, squeals, sounding almost like laughter. He rouses himself and drifts around to find the noise. It comes from the bathroom. She is bathing the baby. The bathroom is quite warm, and that warmth seemed to invigorate Clark's ethereal body. He finds he can move better. In the kitchen, she is feeding the little one cereal, and he seems to like it. His father watches with sadness yet pride in his little son.

Clark knows he must go through the door at high noon, which is 1:00 p.m., daylight time. He watches the clock in the kitchen, He hears Ana Lea take Clark Junior and leave. He sees that it is raining. Suddenly, the clock reads 11:43, so he goes downstairs. The clock in the small den reads 11:47. Which one is correct?

He moves through the ceiling and finds that there actually is two minutes' difference between the two clocks. The one in the master bedroom reads two minutes later than the large round one on the kitchen wall. He has over an hour to wait, so he slides through the front door and hovers near the porch railing. It has been snowing, but it has stopped. The clouds still hang heavily, and he realizes he must rely on clocks, not the sun.

He floats around the downstairs family room. Ghostly anxiety overwhelms him. It is difficult to keep track of time, something that seems to be natural to a living human with a beating heart.

He checks the clock on the wall in the family room; 12:59. He waits for it to strike 1:00 p.m. Slowly, he moves to the door, hesitates, but then thrusts his right hand through it. Someone or something grabs his hand and pulls him through, and he lands in a heap on the concrete stairs. His first breath of cold air stings his lungs. The weight of his living body seems nearly impossible to move. However, he looks up, and hovering over him is another apparition, a man dressed in woolen trousers, a blue shirt, and suspenders. A wool cap covers his head. He smiles at Clark and doffs his hat to reveal gray hair.

"Samuel?" Clark croaks. His mouth is so dry he can barely form the word. The ghost nods and then goes right through Clark and disappears back into the house. With great effort, Clark climbs the three stairs and stands on wobbly legs. He reaches in his pocket and pulls out his set of keys.

He turns his head and sees his car in the driveway. Finding the key that fits the south french door, he manages to open it. The warmth of the kitchen overwhelms him.

As he moves to the kitchen sink for water, he slams his hip into the corner of the counter.

"Ouch!" He rubs his painful hip but grins. He's definitely alive again because he feels physical pain. His throat feels as if he has been in the desert the whole twenty-four hours without a canteen. After two large glasses of water, he decides to take a shower.

Suddenly, under the pounding water, he feels so hungry he almost bites the washcloth.

Once out of the shower and wrapped in a towel, he opened the fridge and, from the carton, drank the remains of Ana Lea's skim milk. He fried eggs and ate them from the pan and made toast but ate it without butter or jam. As he swallowed the last bite of toast, he sat down with such fatigue that he could barely walk to the bedroom and collapse on the bed.

He had no idea how long he slept. The insistent ringing of the phone woke him. "Hello?"

"Dr. Knowles, this is Nelly Parsons. My father's stitches have ruptured, and there is puss and blood dripping out of the bandage. Can you meet us at the hospital? Please?"

"Right away. Meet me in half an hour at the emergency entrance." After throwing on some clothes, he hurried out the south door and jumped into his car. The wind had picked up, and it looked like some clouds would drop some rain later on in the evening.

Two days before, Robert Parsons, age seventy-eight, had undergone hip replacement. Clark had put in drainage tubes, and as he drove to the hospital, he wondered why the bleeding had become serious.

As he entered the emergency entrance, it was filled to overflowing; typical for a Friday evening. Breathing in the chilly air, feeling his heartbeat, and being able to put one foot in front of the other is a small miracle. It was so good to be alive.

He found Robert Parsons to be in an emergency partition, number five. A nurse had already taken information from the man and his somewhat overwrought daughter. "Good evening, Robert. Let me take a look at the incision." Clark checked it over carefully. "Have you been taking your pain prescription, Robert?"

"Well, no, not exactly. I read the bottle, and it said hydrocodone, 15 mg. They worked pretty well for the first day, but isn't that the medicine the one people get hooked on? And I don't want no addiction, so I took some aspirin every once in a while instead."

Clark caught the attending nurse's eye roll and couldn't stop his mouth from twitching. He tried for a calm, reassuring voice. "OK … two things I want you to do. First, don't take any more aspirin. It thins your blood and causes this seepage. Please go back to your prescription and take it as directed. Besides, hydrocodone slows metabolism, and you won't become addicted in a week or two on it. Second, please empty the drain often enough that the blood being drained doesn't soil your bed or clothing."

The old man pointed to his daughter. "She's supposed to do that for me, and I guess she forgot."

Clark glanced at Nelly Parsons, age over fifty, single, and the look on her face bordered on terror. "Come here, Nelly, I'll show you exactly how to empty this drain and clean it. It's a very quick and easy task for an intelligent girl like you." He demonstrated and even took her hand and showed her how to tape it back to her father's leg.

"I guess I can do that, doctor." The words from Nelly came out shaky, while she twisted a small cross hanging around her neck.

"Good. You know where to call if you have any more trouble with that drain." He patted Nelly's narrow back and shook hands with Robert. "Excuse me, I'm needed upstairs." He moved to the elevator and went up to check on his other patients.

When he walked to the first door of one of his patients, the night charge nurse came bustling down the hall to him. She planted a white orthopedic shoe in his path. "Dr. Knowles, when a small emergency arose, we couldn't reach you last night. What happened to you and your pager?"

He slid a hand through his short dark hair. "I was unavoidably detained where there was no phone service. I only returned early this afternoon." His little smile lasted only a second.

"Well, unless you're caught in an avalanche in the mountains or adrift at sea, you'd better call in." She put her hands at her ample waist, whirled around, and stomped back to the nurse's station.

"Believe me, next time, I'll be much more careful."

When he arrived home, it was dark, and he was hungry again. He searched and found another frozen casserole Ana Lea had left for him, and he began to prepare some dinner. He also made up a green salad and found the heel of french bread.

After his first bite, the phone rang. It was Lea. "Hi, lover, I just wanted to tell you that I'm coming home Sunday. Do you think you could pick me up around seven in the evening? I'm missing you already."

He cleared his throat. "Sure, do you want to go out for dinner or pick something up on the way home?"

"Let's find food on the way home. I don't want to spend hours in a restaurant. I'd rather spend our evening closer to you." She moved away from the phone but then came back. "I called and left a message last night because you didn't answer your cell or the home line. Did you have to work?"

"No. My whereabouts last night are rather complicated. I'll try to explain them when I see you again. When I think about it, I can hardly fathom it myself."

"Sound intriguing. Can't wait to hear your story. Love you. Bye."

How am I going to explain to Lea where I actually was? And what a story it was going to be, he thought and continued to eat his dinner.

Clark picked up Ana Lea Sunday evening. She settled into his car and kissed him. "I'm so glad to be home." She turned to him. "So how was your weekend?"

He began by telling her about Robert Parsons and his emergency trip to the hospital. She listened quietly. He mentioned other patients he had and another surgery he assisted.

She sat silent for a moment. "Now why don't you tell me about where you were Thursday evening? That night I called and called and you didn't answer, you weren't home?"

He hunched forward, seemingly concentrating on the road. "No, I wasn't home, not exactly at least."

"How can you 'not exactly' not be home? You're either home or out."
"You could say I was *out*. Can I wait to explain to you what happened to me, because there is something I must show you first?"

She took a deep breath and tried to hide her irritation. *What is he talking about?* "OK, I can wait until we make it home."

Until Clark drove the car into the rear driveway close to the side porch, there was a cold silence in the car. Before she could even climb from the car, he was out, had the rear hatch open, and had carried her luggage to the porch. Once inside, she followed him and went into the bedroom and kicked off her high-heeled shoes and found her gray fuzzy slippers. He came in and set her suitcase on the bed.

"You're upset, and I'm sorry" His kiss was sweet but brief. "The only way I can explain this experience of mine is to find Emily's journal."

"That little red book? I saw it in the bookcase in the den. Have you been reading it?" She turned and filled the teakettle with water. Would you like some tea?"

He nodded and left the room. He returned, sat down, and began thumbing through the book.

CHAPTER 34

"Oh, good, you found it. You know I believe it belonged to my great-great-grandmother."

"First of all, I must tell you how I found this book." He went on to tell her about climbing up in the attic and finding it. He tilted his head, and a slight smile curved his mouth. "Come to think about it, I believe the ghost helped me find it. He wanted us to know about the dangers of the basement door."

"*Ghost,* what ghost? We have an otherworldly resident in our house? Why is the basement door dangerous other than someone may fall down the outside stairs?" She rolled her eyes at her own joke.

"The only way to tell you about what happened to me is for me to read to you the critical passages in the journal. You haven't read this?" He patted the book and began to look for the entry dated September 1890. His hands shook as he turned to the page.

As he read, her eyes widened, and she stopped him and asked, "You walked through the place where the split willow was? And that's our door? Did you go a year ahead or a year back?"

"I walked through the door. Apparently, this house was built on the exact place where the tree once stood. The builders must have taken the roots out, but the vortex remains," he explained.

"How in the world did the vortex get into the split willow tree in the first place?" she asked.

"I believe we'll find the answer to that by reading more of the journal. But, first, I must tell you what happened to me." He then told her in detail of what happened to him when he came into the house.

"Wait, you actually think you were dead. How? Why?" She felt her face tighten, and tears blinded her for a moment. She sat forward and stared at him.

"You were in the process of making a scrapbook about me. All the articles from the newspaper were there—actually, here on the table, along with cards and letters from friends and strangers alike. Soon, though, you came home carrying the baby."

"Baby? We had a child? What was it, and how old?" This time, the tears ran down her face, and she dabbed at her cheeks with a tissue.

"He was probably three to four months old. You were very proud of him, and he was beautiful."

"Of course, I would be, because he was our son. Did he have blue eyes?" "Yes, big, and he looked right at me and smiled."

"OK, now you're wandering around the house dead. How did you get back to the present time? Oh my gosh, that sounds so bazaar." She gave a shaky laugh.

"I walked back through the door at exactly the time of the zenith of the sun. But I had help. Samuel helped me through."

"Samuel, Emily's husband? He's the ghost?"

Clark could only nod. He cleared his throat. "My problem is how do I keep from dying next January 22?"

She was silent for a long moment, turning over these amazing revelations about Clark's fate and this house they were living in. "If you're supposed to die coming down Little Cottonwood Canyon, just don't go up there."

"What if my death on that day is inevitable?" He blinked and shook his head.

She went over to him and put her arms around him. "We won't let that happen. In the meantime, we board up the door and live each day as if it is our last."

"That's an interesting philosophical way to live our lives, but I guess I'm afraid."

"Of course, you're afraid. I'm afraid, but we have nearly a year not let anything happen to you. And if you're correct and I'm pregnant, we have a wonderful year ahead of us." She drew him over to the sofa, and they sat down. "We have many plans to make."

She felt tears burn down her cheeks, but she couldn't stop them. "What can we ... you do? Somehow, we must change our future history."

He seemed to breathe easier. "Of course, we can. I'm not planning on dying again or anytime soon. I didn't care for that otherworldly state at all."

Ana Lea awoke early the next morning. The light was on in the kitchen, and she could smell coffee. She shuffled in and found Clark at the table reading the journal. "Couldn't you sleep?"

"I kept thinking about why Samuel is here in this house trying to keep us from becoming victims of the vortex. So I found more entries toward the back of the book." He began to read.

March 1891

> Samuel has found uses for moving through the split willow. He goes ahead a year to check on the weather in the orchard, and once, he went back on a day when we had freezing temperatures. He put barrels of smoke near the most vulnerable trees and saved our crop when others in the area lost theirs.
>
> But tragedy has struck. Little David followed him to the tree but went forward rather than back. Samuel, Jerusha, and I all searched for him for hours, but he could not be found. Samuel went forward the next day and brought home his lifeless little body. It was early March, and he had died of the cold. Samuel found him outside the barn door, but he was too small to open it.
>
> We buried him two days later. He was not yet three years old.

"Poor family, to lose a little boy that way. Do you think that is why Samuel haunts this place?" Lea asked.

"Most likely, but the boy, David, is not the only death directly caused by the vortex. I've been sitting here thinking about your cousin, your uncle Dennis's daughter."

"Yes, of course. They found her dead at a rest stop in California. She may have walked through the door and found herself to be eight or so months pregnant. It would have been a year later, and so she panicked and took her mother's car. She drove to California, but why there?"

"Possibly she thought of someone she intended to go to for help? That's what I've been thinking. She goes into labor, stops at the rest stop, goes into the restroom, and delivers."

"So the baby was kidnapped by someone who just happened along, or perhaps followed her, possibly to help, finds her dead and takes the child and doesn't want to get involved with police. Wow, the history of this vortex goes on and on." Ana Lea shook her head.

"Is there an entry as to how it all came about?" Lea poured a mug of coffee and sat down. She watched as Clark turned pages in the journal. "This entry is dated January 1892."

January 1892

> Ruby came again with a small child named White Cloud. He was quite sick, and she wanted me to help heal him. I had a number of herbs, and so I made a poultice and put it on his chest. His breathing was labored, but I had him sip weak tea and wrapped him up tight.
>
> He was filthy, so I suggested to Ruby she wash him. This she did with my direction. Once the child's breathing eased, we sat by the fire and talked. I asked her about the split willow and how it came to have such power.

This is what she told me. Once many suns ago, a great storm came up, and strong winds came with it. One wind came down and lifted up a shelter and blew it away, killing many in the tribe. The chief medicine man prayed for a great magic so that when the winds came again, the people could escape. A great bolt of lightning hit the willow and split it. The medicine man discovered its magic, and the people used it.

"Sounds like a tornado. I suppose this 'magic' was only used from time to time. Perhaps the ancient people abused it rather than using it to save lives." She sipped her coffee. "Think of what would happen if some scientist discovered the vortex."

"We can't let that happen. We must cement it up and forget it even exists." Clark scowled at the book. "Let me read you this last entry.

April 1892

> Jerusha is with child again and very ill. She stays in bed most of the day, but when she has Samuel's ear, she nags him about moving away from the orchard to another farm. She wants to get away from the evils of the split willow.
> How can she want to move away from her fine house and a very prosperous fruit farm? Anna loves her school, and little sister is now old enough to attend. The area is building up with families, and they are good customers for our fruit.
>
> Samuel has chopped down the split willow to quiet Jerusha. He burned it in our fireplaces and planted another tree in its place, but it does not grow, only withers and dies. I fear that burning the willow has not killed its evil magic.

"There are no more entries? What happened to Emily, and how did the journal get into this house?" Lea jumped up and stood behind Clark's shoulder.

"It looks like some pages were torn out." Clark frowned at the little book. "I'd like to know what happened to Samuel and his wives."

"Maybe someone in the family has come upon the missing pages. I'll ask around. In the meantime, I have another appointment with Dr. Jolley." She patted her flat stomach. "I'll go check on baby Clark. But in the meantime,"—she looked at the clock—"what time do you have to be at the hospital?"

"Seven thirty." He checked the big clock on the kitchen wall and grinned. "Are you thinking what I'm thinking?"

"Yes, I am." She walked back to the bedroom, took off her robe, and dropped it at the end of the bed.

Afterward, he held her as she slept. With each breath he took, he thanked God to be alive.

CHAPTER 35

Spring came gently; some days warm and sunny, others windy and wet. As the season progressed to warmer days, so did Ana Lea's pregnancy. She had bouts of nausea, which sometimes led to losing the contents of her stomach. Other days, she was hungry all the time.

By the middle of June, she felt well enough to begin planning more charity functions and traveling to those places. She also wanted to go to Columbus to see Joanna's new baby girl.

She arrived on the usual afternoon flight, but this time, it was the nanny, Mrs. Jacobson, who picked her up.

"Yoo-hoo! Mrs. Knowles!" the older woman called out and scurried toward her. She waved a picture of Ana Lea taken the summer before at Jake and Joanna's house. She came up breathing hard and coughing. "They gave me this picture, and it looks like you, but now you're a little rounder." She laughed.

"Oh, you must be Mrs. Jacobson. Jake told me that you'd pick me up." Ana Lea smiled at the woman.

"I didn't think Joanna should drive a car just yet. The sweet baby is only a week old. Come, I parked my car out in front." She tried to take Lea's bag, but the younger woman shook her head. "I can still manage it. Just point me to your car."

Once they were moving out of the airport area, Mrs. Jacobson began to give Ana Lea a history of her service to the Wright family. "You know, I've worked for Jacob Wright and his family for years. I became the nanny when the first Mrs. Wright, Jackie, became ill. Little Callie was only two then. It was such a sad thing when Jackie passed on. The boys seemed to manage fairly well without their mother, but little Callie, well, she just slipped into babyhood again."

"I didn't think you were here when Jackie died," Ana Lea commented.

"No, I wasn't actually. My daughter Jennie had a baby, and she lives in Idaho. I went to take care of her for a while. So that brother of Mr. Wright, Joshua, came and took care of Mrs. Wright. He told me that he was through playing football for the season, so he could come and help. He's the one who found her collapsed in the shower and sent for an ambulance. She didn't last the night."

Ana Lea was silent as the fear of losing Clark stalked her nearly all the time and grabbed at her heart. Would Clark soon die as the future foretold, or could they somehow change it?

The older woman noticed Ana Lea's silence. "I'm sorry, dear. Did my talking about Jackie's death upset you? I know you are such a good friend to Joanna."

"I've heard the story of Jackie's death and how Jake met and married Joanna within a year. I'm a good friend to both of them and only wish them the best with this new addition to their family. Joanna has done a wonderful job as stepmother to those children. When I'm here visiting, I see the positive results of her love and influence on those young ones."

The older woman cleared her throat. "Of course, the new Mrs. Wright is a fine mother, I can't say anything less."

Lea swallowed her irritation with the woman and gave her a conciliatory pat on the arm. "I believe their street is the next one coming up on the right. Good, soon we'll be there."

Clark asked about Joanna's new baby as he drove his wife home from Salt Lake International.

"Oh, as beautiful as a new baby can be! Right now, her eyes are a cloudy blue, and it looks like her hair will be light in color." She hugged her husband's arm as he drove. "I'm getting excited to see and hold our own little guy. I only have six months to go." *I know Clark will still be alive for the birth, but will he survive the month of January?*

Clark seldom spoke about his strange experience with death. Yet the thought of him dying the next January 22 hung in the air like a dark cloud.

Ana Lea went on with her usual schedule, and Clark had even more responsibilities, helping the new crop of residents as they took on their medical assignments. Clark did something else. To him, it just seemed a natural precaution to protect his wife and coming baby. He bought a large term insurance policy.

Ana Lea traveled until about the end of October. Her last assignment was hosting a charity ball in Oakland, California. It had the support of both the NFL team and the NBA basketball team. Joshua came to be the guest speaker and brought his wife, Nichole. The function had a Halloween theme. So Ana Lea dressed for the occasion. She sewed a black chiffon dress of many layers of soft, deep ruffles. They began as a collar around her shoulders and ended at the floor. She walked to the podium carrying a witch's hat covered with fabric that sparkled. She wore her long, dark hair in a braid, and after she introduced the program, she popped the hat on her head.

"My plans are to disappear after tonight. So if any of you see a puff of smoke, you'll know I have returned to my Rocky Mountain hideaway. If I can't get my disappearing act to work, I may have to fly home on my broom." She produced a glitter-covered broom from the side of the stage." The audience clapped and whistled in delight.

Nichole followed her out on stage. She lifted a layer of ruffle from Ana Lea's dress. "Don't let her fool you. She's hiding a baby bump under this dress. I don't think that broom will fly high enough with the extra weight." She turned a hugged her friend. "She'll have to depend on Delta to get her home."

"Nichole will be my substitute manager while I am learning to be a mommy. As you all can see, she's spent time in the gym getting slim and ready for the challenge now that baby JJ will soon be a year old."

The Oakland charity ball was the most financially successful of any that Ana Lea had planned.

The evenings when Clark was home alone, he managed but realized more and more how he missed and worried about his wife. One evening, he took out the journal and reread the last few entries. He so wanted to find out what happened to Emily. He also called Jonas, the contractor, and made plans to cement up the basement door. The young man questioned why Clark would want to have a door removed when it had only been installed a little over the year before.

"Why do you want to take it out?" Jonas asked.

"We didn't find it that useful. Instead, I plan to hang my flat-screen TV in the place where the door is. The door takes up too much room."

"We'll need to replace the outside siding and perhaps some brick trim." "OK, it's your house and your dollar." Jonas hung up.

The last two months before Ana Lea's due date went along quite normally, at least on the surface. Yet there was always the unspoken fear that the future could not be changed—that Clark would die the third week of the coming January.

They decorated the outside of the house with the Christmas lights as they had done the year before. Clark brought down the Christmas tree, and they decorated it. Ana Lea shopped and sent gifts to her two bosses and their families, her parents, and Clark's father and sisters.

They were again invited to the Rossiters' for Christmas Eve dinner. This time, both doctors made it through the evening without being called into the hospital.

The Knowles were up much earlier this Christmas Day than last year, exchanged their gifts, and called their families. Clark was called into the hospital that afternoon. During the time he was at the hospital, Ana Lea took a nap. She awoke to a wet bed. Her water had broken, and she soon began to have contractions.

Clark was in helping with a code blue when his pager went off. The patient was an older man who had had a four bypass surgery two days before. His cardiologist was quickly called.

Once Clark was free, he ran to the phone. "Ana Lea! What is it?'

"While I was taking a nap, my water broke." She gave an exasperated sigh. "Now I have to change the whole bed."

"Are you in labor?" He became aware of anxiety in his voice. "I've had a few contractions, yes, but nothing earthshaking."

"How far apart?" He found some control and tried to sound professional. "About four or five minutes." She stopped talking. "I'm having another one."

He glanced at this watch and began timing. "Tell me when it eases." "It's pretty well gone." She took a deep breath. "How long was it?" "Eighteen seconds. That's pretty good for early contractions. I'm coming home for you, so get your things together." "OK. I will, as soon as I change the bed."

"Forget the bed." He was irritated but wanted to keep her on track. Someone touched Clark's shoulder, and he whirled around, glancing, and saw Ray's face.

Clark, still talking to his wife, watched as Ray pulled out his cell phone. "We'll be down to get you, so be ready—oh, and rest."

He heard the last of Ray's conversation. He was talking to Lorrie. Ray looked up and grinned. "Lorrie's going to pick up Lea. Now call her OB, and I need to you to come with me. I've got a lap chole, and I need you to scrub in. It shouldn't take too long."

Clark felt as if he were being pulled apart into two big chunks, one toward Ana Lea and the other toward his profession, but he followed Ray.

Lorrie brought the laboring mother in about a half hour later. Clark and Ray finished up the cholecystectomy a few minutes after. The maternity nurses had her in bed and as comfortable as was possible.

"Your wife is in bed, and Mrs. Rossiter is in there with her. She's dilated to two centimeters. I spoke with Dr. Jolley, and she wants me to wait until she reaches four," Marge Foster, the attending nurse, said.

"Did Dr. Jolley say when she was coming in?" Though he shouldn't be, Clark was concerned.

"She's on her way, but she's coming from South Jordan. So it's going to take her at least a half an hour."

"Good." Clark motioned to the labor room. "I'd better get in there." He forced a smile at Marge and opened the door.

Lorrie moved away from the bed, allowing Clark to come close. "How you doing, lady?" he asked and picked up Ana Lea's hand and gave it a squeeze. He turned. "Hi, Lorrie, thanks for bringing her in."

Lorrie laughed, her blond hair swinging as she sat down. "I'll tell you, though, it's hard watching her have those pains. I'd rather be lying in that bed than standing here cringing."

"If you want to know, I'm getting miserable. It's boring and it's frustrating to finish up one contraction, and just when you think you can relax, here comes another one. Can we put this whole thing off until later in the week?" Ana Lea tried to smile.

"You're doing great. A few more contractions, and you'll be ready for an epidural, and it will go much easier after they thread that baby in," Lorrie said.

CHAPTER 36

"Thread! They're going to put needles in my back?" Ana Lea blanched as her hand gripped Clark's.

"You won't feel it. They wait until you have a contraction."

"Here, I thought modern childbirth was a breeze." She reached over and grabbed a chip of ice.

A few minutes later, the nurse came in for another check. "Could you two step outside for a minute or two?"

The nurse came out. "She's ready for the epidural. Come on, Dad, you have to hold her up while the tech threads it in."

While Clark held Lea, he felt no better than the average expectant father. They had to do it correctly, because two lives most important to him in the world were entering perilous waters. Even though women had been giving birth to babies for eons, *This is my wife and my baby they are working on.*

Now he understood how Joshua Wright felt when Nichole had baby JJ. Now being a brand-new father, the combination of concern for his wife and his son soon to be born overwhelmed his medical training. He felt so helpless.

Dr. Jolley arrived and checked Lea. She came out to speak with Clark. "She's making progress, but as first babies are, it's slow." She checked her watch. "It's ten thirty now. I doubt that the little guy will be able to celebrate his birthday on December 25. I suggest that you go in there and see her, but you'll have time to grab a sandwich before the delivery."

"Lea, how are you doing?" He brushed a kiss across her cheek. She was curled up in a ball, facing the window.

"When I get through this and start to feel normal again, I'm going to send a big box of chocolates to the guy who invented the epidural. I'm just glad I don't believe in natural childbirth."

"Is that your way of saying you're more comfortable?" He laughed and brushed her hair away from her face. He took a chair by the bed and sat down.

She glanced over her shoulder. "It's not that I'm being rude, but lying on my side and not moving much is best. Besides, I love looking out the window —the city is so beautiful with all the Christmas lights." She was quiet for a few minutes. "It's fascinating. I feel my body tighten, but there is little or no pain."

"So we thank the Lord for epidurals. Yes, we do." Clark folded his arms across his chest and closed his eyes. He was so tired. Sometime later, he felt a tug on his pant leg.

"Clark, go get some coffee and something to eat. You're falling asleep." She had rolled over and managed to reach his slacks.

He jerked awake." Do you mind? I won't be gone long." He stood, blinked, rubbed his face, and left.

Clark went down into the hospital cafeteria and found it nearly empty. The sandwiches were refrigerated in glass-enclosed shelves. He chose a turkey and Swiss. The coffee maker produced a hot, strong brew. A nurse— nameplate read "Bevins"—from the men's surgical wing came down for two cups of coffee and some cookies.

She stopped by his table. "I hear your wife is up in maternity. Has she delivered yet?"

He smiled and shook his head. "No, she's had an epidural, and she sent me down here to wake up for the critical time later. I'm no ob-gyn, but I think she has a few hours to go."

"Well, we wish you two—excuse me, three the best." She laughed, picked up her tray, and left.

Clark ate and drank without really tasting the food. He felt at such loose ends. Other times when a patient came in, he could do something positive, act in favor of the patient's benefit. Now, all he could do was wait.

He finished and went back to Ana Lea's room. He walked in just as the attending nurse came out. "How's she doing? How close is delivery?"

"She's up to eight centimeters. It may be up to two more hours until she reaches ten, or she could go faster. Best thing you can do is go rub her back and talk sweet words. First babies show up when they are ready, not before." "Hi, lady, and why are you lying around in that bed, doing nothing, when the rest of the world is up and progressing?" He came over and kissed her cheek.

"Oh, you're cute," she said with a snap to her voice. "You want to trade places? Come on, you can morph into my pain-wracked swollen body." She stopped and sucked in a large breath. "Oh, that hurts."

"Let me check your pain connection." He felt her whole lower body tighten in a huge contraction. He rubbed her back and shoulders. "Here." He lifted her. "You were lying on the drip line." He slid her over, and she settled down.

"That's better." She took a large breath and blew out. "I can feel when they come on and how long they last."

"Have you timed them?" he asked and continued to rub her back.

"Thirty, some as long as forty-five seconds. I'm getting close, aren't I? I'm so tired of this. I've been here since six, and now it's 1:10." She squeezed her eyes shut, and tears filled the corners and trickled down her face.

"The average first labor is about thirteen hours."

"Great, now all I get from you is medical statistics. How about you get me some more ice chips?"

"Absolutely." He grabbed up the plastic cup and practically ran from the room. He went to the little kitchen near the nurses' station and found the ice machine. Marge Foster came into the room for a drink.

"How's Ana Lea?"

"She doing great, and I want to run screaming into a snowdrift."

"I know. It's tough being the observer, especially when you want to *do something* to move things along. But her body and that fetus are in charge. I'll go give her a check. Dr. Jolley is in finishing up a C-section. She should be out in a few minutes."

Marge came out of Ana Lea's room with a big smile on her face. "I think we're ready for the arrival."

Clark walked his newborn son to the nursery. He had watched Dr. Jolley ease little Clark away from Ana Lea's body and lay him on her chest. The assisting intern cleaned out his nose and mouth of mucus and gently tilted him feet up. His father watched and listened to baby's first intake of air, and then the release was a high-pitched cry, very much like being dead and then coming to life again. Tears filled the father's eyes, but he could smile through the mist.

"Hi, little one, nice to finally meet you." Ana Lea breathed. She cradled him on her chest and stroked his back. He quieted with a cough and tiny sigh. He was readied for the hospital nursery, while the new mother was taken to recovery.

As he entered the neonatal area of the nursery, he was met by a fairly tall, attractive girl. Her name tag read "T. Johansson."

"Hi, aren't you Dr. Knowles? This little guy is yours? Congratulations. Bring him over."

Clark wheeled the crib over and put it next to the examining table. Ms. Johansson tore a new sheet of paper down and lifted baby boy Knowles onto the soft paper. She weighed and measured him, listened to his heart, and watched him flail his arms and legs. She spoke softly in the infant's right ear and watched him turn in that direction. Then she did the same on his other side. She checked his arms, legs, and groin, and then wrapped him up in a soft blanket. He opened his eyes and stared at her.

Ms. Johansson smiled and tucked him into his tiny crib. "OK." She typed into her computer. "Seven pounds, fifteen ounces, twenty-two inches height. Seems to hear and see. Good reflexes."

She glanced up at Clark. "He's A-OK. I'll print out the stats. You may pick them up tomorrow."

When Clark walked into the curtained recovery area, he found Ana Lea dozing. He touched her hand, and she smiled.

He brushed a kiss across her mouth. "How are you feeling?"

"Quite happy to have that child out of me." She closed her eyes for a long moment and struggled to open them. "And very tired."

"You did just great, and I'm so proud of you." He felt his chest actually hurt, as if his heart would burst out.

Her eyes fluttered closed, and she yawned. "Yes, and I love you too. Now go home and get some sleep and come back tomorrow, when I can stay awake." She rolled onto her side and pulled the cotton blanket up to her shoulder.

A young nurse came in to take Ana Lea to her room. "She's ready to go, Dr. Knowles. Do you want to follow us?"

"No. I'll come back tomorrow morning." He turned to the elevator, whistling.

The next three weeks seemed to fly by. They brought Clark Junior home two days after he was born, the usual time of a maternity stay. Ana Lea was determined to work the baby into a schedule. Most of the time, her efforts seemed to work, unless the infant decided to eat more often or stay awake half the night.

Clark could usually sleep anytime, anywhere, until, of course, he had to listen to his son fussing. Yet he had to meet his schedule at the hospital and stay awake for most of it. When he thought about his possible impending death, he decided to treat January 22 like any other day. He would go to work and then come home. It fell on a Saturday, which meant a busier-than-usual emergency room.

At two fifteen, his pager went off. The call had an Alta prefix. Clark dialed it.

"Hello? This is Dr. Knowles. Who's calling, please?"

"This is Edith Griffith, and I am a friend of your father, Patrick."

"I see. What is the nature of your call?" Clark felt tension in his shoulders, which made his voice sharp.

"I'm calling about Patrick. He is not feeling well. Actually, he's ill. We're up here at the Cliff Lodge at Snowbird. I'm afraid it has something to do with his heart. He wanted me to make sure that I reached you."

"My father is at Snowbird? What in the world . . . ?"

She answered quickly. "We have become friends, your father and I, and came here to learn to ski. He fell yesterday, and now he's in a lot of pain."

"Pain, so you think it's his heart? Did you call the clinic at the lodge?"

"We did, but the medic is out checking on a ski accident. At any rate, Patrick is so proud of you because of your medical skills. Now he's complaining of chest pain. Is it possible for you to come up and check on him?"

Clark had no choice. He had to go help his father. He called Lea, but the call went to voice mail. Next, he made arrangements for another doctor to cover the last hour of his shift.

CHAPTER 37

While driving up Little Cottonwood Canyon, he worried about his dad. After all, he was sixty-three and had not taken the best care of his health. Halfway up, it began to snow, and the wind picked up. This was exactly the weather described in the article he read in Ana Lea's scrapbook.

Well, if he was going to die driving down the canyon, he would have had a good reason to have been there rather than a day of skiing, as the article had said.

Thousands of years ago, when the Rockies were in a geological uplift, the canyon had been glacier cut, even though it does have some twists and turns, basically a straight ascending drive, very different from the wraparound curves of Big Cotton Canyon.

A stream runs through Little Cottonwood Canyon, sourced by melting snow. In the winter, it was merely a trickle; come spring, a roaring torrent. The stream cut across the resort, with most of the ski runs on north-facing mountains. January was particularly good for skiing, because there was some freezing at night but little melting in the daytime.

Clark parked his old station wagon and trudged back through blowing snow to the Cliff Lodge. He soon found room number 530 and knocked. The woman, Edith, answered, "Come in, Dr. Knowles. My goodness, of course, you are. I can see the resemblance to Patrick."

Clark glanced around. The room was typical for two or more people. Large bathroom, with jetted tub, two queen beds, a desk, with Wi-Fi, a flat-screen TV resting on a large dresser, with a small refrigerator tucked in next to drawers. A small sofa hugged the wall next to the window. The room was simple luxury, common in a five-star hotel. The top two floors of the twelve-story building had been turned into luxury condos.

Patrick lay in the bed closer to the wall of windows. Every room had sliding glass doors out to a small patio, with a view of the mountains. He seemed to be asleep, propped up on a several pillows. Clark touched his hand. "Dad?"

Without opening his eyes, Patrick shifted and brought his right hand around and patted his son's hand. "Thanks for coming, son," he whispered and then coughed.

Even though he had not even begun a cursory exam of his father, Clark was weak with relief. Driving up the canyon, Clark had imagined his father struggling to breath, suffering a major heart attack. "Dad, is it your heart?"

"At first, I thought it was. When I tried to get out of bed this morning, my chest, arms, and shoulders hurt like the dickens. I fell back into bed. Edith went for some aspirin, and I took it. Since then, I slept some."

Clark had his stethoscope out, opened his father's pajama top, and listened to his heart. Clark heard a heart with a steady beat, although somewhat slow. He then began examining his shoulder and left arm. "I don't think it's your heart, Dad."

"I just ache all over, especially my ribs. Then Edith reminded me that I fell yesterday while I was skiing."

"You went skiing? When did you take up that sport?" Clark was incredulous.

"Edith and I decided we could learn to ski if we took it easy. It's because we found this ad in the newspaper about a package deal at Snowbird. We came out day before yesterday—no, two days ago—had a lesson in the morning, and skied awhile in the afternoon, and yesterday, we tried for a longer time. I was doing fine until I missed getting off the ski lift. Here I am lying in the snow, and the darn thing came around and smacked me in the side."

Clark turned around and stared at Edith sitting on the other bed. She nodded. "I have a friend who works for Northwest Airlines. She found us a real good package, three days skiing and four nights lodging. We planned to call you and your cute wife because we wanted to come and see the baby."

She stood and nervously slid her hand down her rose-colored wool tunic. "I'll let you check your dad, while I go fetch us some lunch. You would like to eat with us, wouldn't you, Dr. Knowles?"

"I've had lunch, but I wouldn't mind some coffee."

"Good, I'll be back shortly." She picked up her handbag from the desk and left.

Clark went on with his examination. Finally, he said. "Dad, do you think you can stand up?"

"Yes, if you help me. I still hurt lots of places." With his son's help, he stood.

"Now take a deep breath and blow it out slowly." Clark began feeling his father's sides and chest. He also noticed bruises on his shoulder and hip.

"Ow! Oh, that hurts" was Patrick's response to the squeezing of his rib cage.

"Without an X ray, I'm guessing you've cracked some ribs. We'll find out more when we get you to the hospital."

"Who's we?"

"Me and the hospital staff, why?"

"I'm not going to any hospital," the older man grumped.

Clark growled with irritation. "Dad, I can't give you a definitive diagnosis until I order some tests."

"Look, *Dr. Knowles,*"—Patrick spat out the words with emphasis—"tape me up so I can be comfortable and ski tomorrow."

Clark ran his hands through his hair in frustration. "Dad, you can't ski with broken ribs and whatever else you have broken or bruised."

"Humph. Well, at least you can tape me up. Isn't that what you did for some of those soldiers you doctored in Iraq?"

"At times, but they were young and in very good shape physically." He stood and stared at the old man for a long moment and shook his head. *What do you do with a stubborn old man?* "OK, Dad, I'll go get some tape."

When he returned, his father and Edith were sitting at the table eating the food Edith had brought. For the first time, he really perused Edith. She was tall and fairly slim, with curly dark gray hair and bright blue eyes. "Here, Dr. Knowles, sit down on the small sofa. Eat something." She handed him a white paper carton and a paper mug of coffee. Inside the box, he found a wrapped sandwich and a small carton of potato salad.

After a sip of the brew, he was surprised that his stomach growled in response to the food. He took a few bites and then looked up at his father. "How are you feeling, Dad?"

"I'm surprised that I'm not in so much pain. Maybe moving around has helped, and eating too." He touched Edith's hand and gave her a wink.

After eating, Clark taped his father's ribs. He suggested some ibuprofen. But just to make sure, he listened to his father's heart again. "I talked to the tech at the clinic. You can go down for X-rays tomorrow morning. She said she would fax me copies of the pictures."

Patrick shook his head, but Edith touched his arm. "Yes, Pat, you will have those X-rays taken."

She smiled at Clark. "Thank you for your personal, medical service. We both really appreciate you coming up here. I hope you can drive safely down the canyon in this storm. It looks nasty out there."

So do I. Dear God, so do I. Clark shook hands with her, gently hugged his father, and went out into the storm.

It took Clark several minutes to brush inches of snow from his car. After starting the older vehicle, it took more time to clear the windshield so he could drive up to the main road. The ski lifts had closed at both Alta and Snowbird, so the traffic was bumper to bumper down the canyon. He eased his station wagon down the hill, and so far, the going was crowded, but he was making progress. Yet his anxiety grew and escalated.

In the lower end of Snowbird parking, two teenage boys started up a Jeep Wrangler and began the drive out of the lower parking lot, up the hill to Snowbird Entrance One. Just before Bret turned to ease unto the main road, two other boys waved them out of the line of traffic. These teenage boys waved with thumbs up, wanting a ride down the canyon.

"Hey, Bret, I think I know one of them," Trent said. "Pull over." The teens ran to the vehicle. Trent rolled down the window. "Hi, Tom, how was your day?"

"Awesome. Man, do you have room to take us down the canyon?" Tom asked.

"Why, did you guys have a breakdown?" Bret asked.

"Nah, we rode the bus up from Seventieth South, and we just missed it. There won't be another one for, I don't know how long. If this storm keeps up, they may close the canyon."

Bret checked out the two boys. "OK, bring your boards, and we'll strap them down with ours."

It took several minutes to clear the snow off the roof of the Jeep and tie down the boards, but, finally, the four of them shook off the heavily falling snow and climbed back into the Wrangler.

Bret eased the vehicle into the down traffic, and they began their descent on down.

Driving down the canyon, Clark thought long and hard about what he was doing. The only change from the future prediction he had read in Ana Lea's scrapbook was that instead of making a house call to his father, he had been skiing. The storm was as fierce as predicted, and his fear of dying was off the charts.

He reached the top of the seven sisters, the spot where the canyon drops off on the upside of the canyon and opened to the streambed a hundred plus feet below. The road narrowed but was open on that side for seven curves down until it widened and had land on both sides. It was a tricky area to drive in good weather and had been nicknamed the Seven Sisters by skiers. Many accidents and roll-offs happened along this stretch of road down the canyon.

In his nervousness, he slowed down too much, and an impatient driver passed him, too close, and sideswiped his Volvo wagon. Clark overcorrected, banged his Volvo into the upside near the rocks, and lost his traction, and his car slid across the road. Front tires dropped over the lip of the shoulder, and the car slipped over into the ravine.

Crashing into bare scrub oak branches pounded the windshield, and the car dropped and slid. Further down, the trees became larger, which caused the car to angle nose first. Despite the seat belt, Clark's head banged into the side window, stunning him. His foot automatically stomped on the brake. It seemed to him as if he was sliding down for hours. The car finally slammed into a large boulder, and a searing pain shot through his lower leg. He had the presence of mind to turn off the engine and release the locks on the doors.

He felt down and knew his leg was broken just above his snow boots. Clark grimaced with each move, but he searched his pockets for his cell phone, but he could not locate it. Well, here he was in a ravine, near the streambed, but he was the one to have an accident, not the two boys.

CHAPTER 38

The car that had sideswiped Clark's station wagon stopped several yards down and called 911. Three other cars passed, but along came the four boys in the Jeep Wrangler. "Dude!" Tom yelled. "Did you see that car go off the road?"

Bret slowed and brought the Jeep to a stop near the rocky face on the upside of the road, just above the first curve. "Hey, dudes, we gotta check this out." The four boys scrambled out of their ride and began crossing the road. The traffic had slowed to a crawl, so it was easy for them to run across to the edge of the drop.

"There's the car. The headlights are still on." Trent waved them on, and he began easing down the hill. He followed the path of the broken tree limbs and tire tracks cutting through the snow.

When Bret reached Clark's Volvo, he banged on the passenger side of the car. "Hey, man, you OK?" He could see the guy inside trying to roll down the window. "Turn on your ignition."

He nodded. The car's engine sparked to life, and the window came down. "I think I've broken my leg, the right one."

By now, all four boys were close to the car. "The car is listing toward the stream. Let's find some rocks to stop it from rolling!" Tom yelled. He turned and found a large rock, freed it, and rolled it toward the left front tire.

"That's going to take too long." Bret knocked on Clark's window. "Does your seat recline?"

"Yes, and the backseats do too." Trent lifted up the rear hatch and found the seat lever, and soon, Clark lay nearly flat, except for his legs.

"OK, guys, Trent, you and Tom get into the car on the right side, and I'll climb in and grab this dude by the shoulders. That should stabilize the weight long enough for Chris and me to drag him out."

The pain in Clark's leg was so severe he had to bite down on his glove to keep from screaming. He felt them pull him further back until his head rested on the rear of the trunk area.

"Now, help me drag him out." The two boys bounced him out but slowly pulled him up the hill away from his car. They managed to drag him about ten feet away, but when the other two boys got out of his old station wagon, it rocked, slid sideways, and slowly rolled over and came to rest on the driver's side.

Trent came over and put Clark's medical bag near him and wrapped him in the blanket Clark always kept in the car. The boy knelt close to him. "Did that other car sideswipe you?"

"Yes, I guess that's what happened." Now, Clark was cold, so cold he was shivering uncontrollably, and his teeth were chattering. He knew he was going into shock. Would the rescue effort of the four boys rescue the one who may die from shock?

Ana Lea paced through the kitchen to the living room window, to the dining area, and back. *Where was he?* He had called and left a cryptic message. He said he was driving up to Snowbird to make a call on a patient. Why had he gone up there *today?* The phone message had gone to her voice mail. That was her fault for not answering her cell phone soon enough.

She had gone down the shelter school to do their taxes. Baby Clark had been cooperative and slept most of the time she was there, but now it was 6:30 p.m. and no husband. The latent fear of him going up to Snowbird on this particular day had risen up like a ten-foot ghost. The weather had turned from a normal January snowstorm to a whiteout. Because of slick roads and a blinding storm, she barely made it home safely. Luckily, it was Saturday, and the traffic was not as heavy as it would have been on a weekday.

She was afraid to turn on the TV, because she did not want to hear of Clark's death. Thankfully, she had the baby to occupy her time. He fussed, and she knew he needed to be changed and fed. She paced to kitchen window and stared out at the snowy scene in the backyard. There was at least six inches of new snow since this afternoon, covering everything in sight. The barbecue was a shapeless white mound.

Automatically, she put on the teakettle and searched the pantry for a tea bag. Her one comfort in a storm, she thought. Before she sat down to nurse baby Clark, she would call Ray. Perhaps he would know where to find her husband. "Ray, this is Ana Lea. Do you know where Clark is? He hasn't come home from the hospital."

She could hear Ray ask around the floor. Then he came back on. "He supposedly went up to Snowbird to check on a patient. We are getting a trickle of accidents in from both canyons. Maybe he's up helping someone who's had a crash."

"That's what I was afraid of. Thanks." She put down the telephone.

One of the boys called out. "Hey, we could use this blanket like a litter. We'll put this guy on it and drag him up the hill."

"My name is Clark. And what's yours?" He touched the boy's sleeve closest to him. His voice shook as he spoke.

"I'm Trent. We're going to use this blanket kind of like a litter of sorts." He pulled the blanket from Clark's chest, shook it out, and lay it on the hill close to where they had dragged him. "Tom, come help me." They dragged Clark onto the blanket, and with a boy at each side, they grabbed a corner and then hauled him up the hill littered with broken limbs of trees, and thankfully, the new snowfall covered them. Yet they still dug into his back and legs.

Through the snow, they could hear a siren from up the road rather than down. Bret stomped up to the top and waited for the emergency vehicle to stop. It wasn't an ambulance; rather, a truck with "Canyon Transport" printed on the side. A big, heavily built man got out and walked over to Bret.

"We got a call about a car off the road." He walked to the edge of the road and looked down." Wow, clear to the streambed!"

"We managed to get him out. He's down there on a blanket we're using as a litter."

"Just one individual?" the big man asked.

Bret nodded. The big man turned and waved at another man in the truck. "Bring the stretcher."

The two big men stomped down the hill. They were dressed for the weather and took little time to reach the three boys standing around Clark. The driver turned to Tom and put out his hand. "I'm Hank. You four guys pulled him out?"

Tom smiled. "Yes, sir. We decided we could do it, but it took all four of us. He thinks he's broken his leg. There is also blood on his head."

"Good work. Now, two of you help me position the stretcher, and we'll lift him."

Clark felt himself being lifted, tied to a stretcher, and sometimes carried, but also dragged up to the top of the ravine. A large hand shook his shoulder. "Hey, buddy, talk to me."

He knew he was in shock and had trouble answering. "Hi ... Clark, ah ... Knowles, and a doctor." The words came out slow and low.

"OK, Clark, we're taking you to University Hospital in our truck. The canyon is closed to up traffic, but we can still go down. We're not equipped for critical emergency, but I don't think you qualify."

They carried him up and lifted him into the back of the truck. He closed his eyes and wiped his face of the snow that had fallen. That one act seemed to take what little strength he had. He felt a heavy quilt tucked around him, and the second man got into the back to ride with him.

The driver was out talking to his rescuers. "Look, you guys are heroes, but because of the snowstorm, I want you all to go home. If you want, you can call the hospital tomorrow and check on him." He took out a card and handed it to Bret. "Call me tomorrow and give me all the details. Snowbird has a newsletter, and this will make a great story."

Clark heard the engine of the truck rev up as well as the tailgate slam shut and then the downward motion of vehicle. The man who had crawled in beside him patted his shoulder. "I'm Juan Chavez. Tell me your name again?"

Clark knew what he was doing, trying to keep his patient awake on the ride to the hospital. His foggy brain wanted to sleep, but he fought to answer Juan's questions. He tried breathing more deeply, concentrating on inhaling and exhaling, answering questions. It was a fight, but he knew it was critical if he were to live.

The teakettle whistled a signal that the water had boiled. Ana Lea laid down the baby and poured the steaming water into the mug she had set on the counter. Immediately, baby Clark screamed his displeasure of being interrupted during a feeding. She went back into the nursery and again offered him a breast.

She didn't feel like singing, as she sometimes did when she nursed her babe, but she rocked and sang her words to him. "I hope we can soon hear from your daddy, because you and I don't do well without him," she said in a singsong voice.

Just as she finished up feeding Clark, or CJ, the lights blinked once and then went out. "Great, now the power has gone out." She looked out the front window. All the houses across the street were also dark. She knew what had happened, too much snow weighing down old power lines. With the freezing temperatures outside, the house would cool off quickly. She doubted the power company would be out to find and fix the problem this evening.

Meanwhile, she would build a fire in the fireplace.

She tucked a blanket around CJ and carried him into the living room. She searched for a flashlight in the kitchen drawer and found that Clark had already laid a fire ready to light. He was like that, dear, loving man, taking care of his family, because he put flashlights, matches, candles, and batteries in a special place in the kitchen. Once the fire caught and she began feeding it small pieces of wood, Clark always brought in a piece of coal when the fire was hot enough. She knew it would burn much longer. She sipped her now cool tea and began to prepare for an extended power outage.

Just as she was about to go out to the porch for a chunk of coal, her cell phone rang. She ran to it, but when she saw Ray's number, she was so frightened; her heart seemed to block her breathing. Yet she had to know about Clark.

"Hello?"

"Good, I reached you, Ana Lea. They just brought Clark in."

"Who brought him in?" She took a deep breath and blurted out her question. "Is he all right? What happened?" She tried to tramp down her fear and clear the anxiety from her voice.

"His leg is broken. I'm guessing a compound fracture to the tibia. Plus he may have a slight concussion, but he's awake and talking. I'm sending him to radiology. Oh, Canyon Transport brought him in. He drove his car down into the ravine at the top of Seven Sisters."

"He had the accident, not the boys? What about the boys?"

"How do you know about the boys' involvement?" Ray turned away from the phone as someone asked him a question. "No, those four kids saved him. It's going to be quite a story. He wanted me to call you. Look, I think he's going to need surgery on that leg."

"OK, Ray, tell I love him, and our power is out, but CJ and I are doing fine.

Can I speak to him?" She knew she was rambling.

"He's had a sedative, and he was in slight shock when they brought him.

Your power is out? Do you have a fireplace?" he asked.

"Yes, and I already have a fire going. I was just going out for some coal when you called."

"Coal, huh? Good idea. Stay warm, and I'll call you later." He clicked off.

CHAPTER 39

Ana Lea held the phone for a long time, as if it were a direct line to Clark. She was weak with relief, and for a moment, she forgot what she was about to do. *Oh, yes, coal.*

She went to the side door to where he had covered a bag of coal with canvas. She brushed off the snow and grabbed a chunk. When she came back in, the baby was making noises, as if he were talking to the fire. You never knew what would entertain a month-old child.

The phone woke Ana Lea out of sound sleep. She glanced at her wristwatch and read eleven fifteen. "Hi, Lea. Clark came out of the surgery just fine, but he's going to be on crutches for at least a month. He said for you to wait until the weather clears before you try to come up to the hospital. Another message—his father, Patrick Knowles, called the hospital to see if he had driven down the canyon OK. He's the individual whom Clark went to see."

"Patrick is at Snowbird?"

"Yep. Anyway, he said he'll try and call you tomorrow. That's all I have to report. I've had a rough night, and I'm going home. Talk to you tomorrow. Bye."

Clark's strange trip to Snowbird was now making sense. She understood. When it came to family, Clark would have done anything to help his father. Suddenly, she was starving. What could she find in the refrigerator to fill the empty void in her middle?

She took out the fairly cool milk and grabbed a box of cereal and a banana. The food helped the hunger pangs to ease. This time, when she went out for coal, she brought in two chunks. The heavy snowfall had become flurries, and it was bitter cold. The frigid temperature made her hurry back into the relative warmth of the living room. The coal helped keep the temperature in the living room a stable fifty-eight degrees. She had removed the mattress for CJ's crib and set his infant carrier on that. He slept wrapped up in blankets, with a cap on his head. She had put on sweats and heavy socks, and lying on the sofa wrapped in two blankets, she was comfortable.

About the time the kitchen lost its darkness, she awoke to the approaching dawn. She snuggled back under the blankets, but later, the sound of the forced air from the furnace woke her. Soon, the baby also woke and needed to be changed and nursed. A while later, it was warm enough to put the baby's mattress back in his crib, as well as the child.

Before she dressed for snow shoveling, she decided to climb up into the attic. Once up there, she searched for the box that had held the journal. Examining its contents, she was shocked to find the old scrapbook she had made years before. It was about Kitt. *Oh my gosh, did Clark read this scrapbook? Did he think I was in love with Kitt?* She'd worry about that later.

Just as she was about to put the lid back on the box, she found the reason for her search. Stuck in the top of the lid were several pages that seemed to be part of Emily's journal. Snatching them up, she put everything back and hurried down from the attic. If she was going to visit Clark, she would first have to shovel out the driveway.

Clark had had better nights. His head ached, and he was already miserable, because his leg was in traction. At seven, the night nurse checked up on him before going off duty. She showed him how to use the morphine pump and helped him drink some water. She adjusted his IV and told him that he would be brought a clear diet that morning.

About midmorning, Ray came in to check on him. "Well, doctor, now you're on the other side of the bed, so to speak." He gave him a cursory exam. "I had to put a pin in your tibia, because the fracture needed stabilizing. You'll be able to prognosticate the weather for a year or so, but the bone should meld with it nicely."

"Thanks for the head's-up, Ray. I'm just happy my injuries weren't more extensive. I'll try to enjoy my misery." *Anything is better than being dead, again.*

"I spoke with Lea and your father at the Cliff Lodge. I would imagine she'll be visiting you sometime today. Maybe he'll come down too."

"Hey, Ray, thank you for being here when I really needed you, and for being such a good friend."

"No problem. I know you'd do the same for me." Ray smacked his shoulder and patted his cast and walked out of Clark's temporary prison.

When Ana Lea walked in carrying Clark Junior, she found Clark's room was filled with medical people.

"Move, guys, let the wife in." A nurse shoved a group of young doctors back to make way for her. Clark looked up.

"Hey, lady," he said. "Come over here."

She went directly to the bed, setting the baby carrier down and hugged him. He looked past her. "Thanks for coming in to check on me." He waved at the group.

"I think he wants us to leave," a tall red-headed guy said. "OK, but we'll be back later, for some more of your wisdom." He laughed and pushed the people out the door.

She bent over him and kissed his cheek, chin, and, finally, his mouth. "I was so worried, so scared. I'm so glad to see you alive and kicking." She glanced at his elevated leg and giggled nervously. "Alive anyway."

He wrapped his arm around her waist. "I am too. The alternative is not what I want for another fifty years. Well, look at that, a waistline I can wrap my hands around." He laughed.

"When can you come home?" she asked and bent to snuggle his shoulder. "Ray and a technician are deciding if I can have a walking cast or if I must use crutches for a while. I guess it's going to be two or three days until they release me. You can do without me for that long, can't you?" Clark frowned. "It will be a struggle, but we'll manage. I have something to show you." She went to the diaper bag she now carried along with the baby. She withdrew a large manila envelope. "I went up into the attic this morning and searched the box where you said you

found the journal. Jammed in the lid I found these pages. They seem to be the same paper, and they belong in
Emily's little red book."

"Can you move the food tray? I want to take a look at them too."

She put another pillow behind his head, so he could sit up a little more. After moving the tray to a side table, she sat down and set the pages on her lap. She shuffled through them and chose what seemed to her to be the first entry of the group.

January 1896

Utah has officially become the forty-sixth state in the Union. There have been celebrations all over Salt Lake City as well as other cities in the state.

I now understand why it was imperative that we as a state abandon the practice of polygamy. We must conform to the rest of the nation. Other states have their own problems, such as thinly veiled slavery, but I am not privy to all their sins. I just comment on the inequities in various states.

We now have the telegraph, which gives us the news from across the country. There are also a few telephones in the city. Because of the railroad across the whole country, we have goods coming in from all over the world, and shopping is now much more of an adventure. We are truly looking at great progress now and in the future.

Since I was "put away" from Samuel, I pursued my second dream, that of becoming a secretary. Part of my pursuit of the position came when Erlina and I were forced to live in the Alta house for a time. While we were there, there also were several other families of women torn away from their husbands, with nothing but charity to support them.

Now I work for a Mr. William Brennan, an attorney. I file and fetch items for him, as well as take dictation. I have learned to use the big black machine called a typewriter. I love the work.

I have rented a small house on First Avenue, and my only child, Erlina, is now nine and can attend school. My younger sister, Charlotte, has come to live with me. At the present time, she is not interested in marriage. She works at a mercantile store called the ZCMI. She loves the new fashions and wants to design some professional clothing for women who work in the offices.

I still greatly miss Samuel, but the three of us are happy.

March 1896

My parents visited with our little family and brought us food and the latest news. It seems that Jerusha, Samuel's legal wife, has a wasting disease and is no longer able to do much. I have great sorrow for Samuel and the three children in his care.

June 1896

Samuel came to visit us and brought Erlina a lovely gift. It is a dress of the finest spun wool in a shade of light blue. I asked after his family, and he said that his brother Daniel has moved into the part of the house that was mine and is helping around the orchard. Daniel asked if I was interested in marriage. I told Samuel that I was happy with my position at the law firm.

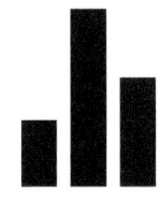

CHAPTER 40

"What do you know? The first career woman in the family," Clark commented. "Good for her. But we still don't know how the journal came to be in your—I mean, our attic?" Clark yawned.

"I think you need to rest now." And as if on cue, baby Knowles began to fuss. Ana Lea bent and kissed her husband. "I'm going home now. I received a call about your car down near the steam in Little Cottonwood Canyon. I need to make arrangements to have it towed out." She stood. "I'll come back tomorrow."

"Leave the pages, but when you come, bring the whole journal, OK?" he asked.

"I can do that. See you tomorrow. I believe the insurance adjuster will 'total' your car. What do you think?"

"I think I'm glad I married to a business-savvy lady who can wade through all that paperwork. I'll bet you must have inherited that talent from Emily." He laughed.

"I'll do what I can. Good-bye, love. See ya later."

Clark woke up in the early hours of that Monday morning. He was alert, and the pain had subsided. He brought up the backlight behind his bed, struggled, but reached for the journal pages in the nightstand drawer. He began reading the next entry.

September 1896

I received word that Jerusha had passed on. The funeral is the day after tomorrow. Because of the heat, they must bury her soon. After work, the day of the funeral and interment, Charlotte, Erlina, and I rode the streetcar to the mortuary. We paid our respects to the family, and specifically to Samuel. He was pleased to see me and mentioned that he wondered if I would come. He spoke of her poor treatment of me. And I told him I had forgiven her. Daniel had a young lady with him. I believe they soon will be betrothed.

November 1896

Samuel came to visit Erlina and me and brought us a pumpkin and roasting chicken. He shyly asked if he could court me. I told him I was not sure if I wanted to marry again. However, I told him I would tell him of my decision at Christmas. I am soon twenty-nine years old. Some days, I feel much older, although the years have been kind to me. I still have a trim figure, and my hair is long and full. Mr. Brennan says that he would court me if he were twenty years younger.

Clark's eyes became heavy, and he set the pages aside and fell asleep.

The next morning, after Ray had come in to check on his leg, he received a more substantial breakfast. He waited anxiously for Ana Lea to arrive. Now that he was feeling better, he found being a patient to be boring. He wanted to be up and doing something productive. Patients must learn patience, he surmised.

Ana Lea breezed in about noon, without baby Clark. After she kissed him, he asked, "Where's the baby?"

"Your father and his friend Edith are our first babysitters." She raised her eyebrows and quirked a smile. "They offered, and so I took them up on it." From her large purse, she took the red leather journal. "How far have you read?"

"I stopped here." He took out the pages and placed them on his tray table.

December 1896

I have allowed Samuel to court me. He says that we should pretend that we have only met a short time ago. Erlina wants to move back to the orchard farm and be with her father. I finally told him I would legally marry him on two conditions. One, that he builds me a new house, because Daniel has married and is now living in the part of the old one. And, two, I will not marry him in the temple.

Perhaps, someday, I will soften my anger against the church for its support of polygamy and then so easily abandoning it. The pain it has caused so many women and children is unfathomable.

June 1897

Samuel and I were married on June 25. My new home is nearly complete. It has a large kitchen with a black stove and a cold room. We have a spacious bedroom with a brass bed, a parlor, and a dining room. Then there is a space for a bathroom and a big white tub. Erlina has a large room that she will share with Samuel's older daughters. Next to that is a smaller room for Samuel's little boy. These are close to the kitchen, so they will be warmer in the winter. We also have a loft. I am excited to live in such a modern house.

We do not want anyone to be a victim of the split willow's evil power. We have purchased more land to the east of the original orchard and will put in new trees when the land is cleared. I believe I will be content with Samuel, his children, and mine because I do love him.

Clark looked up from the pages and saw tears running down Ana Lea's face. "At least we have the vortex under control, for as long as we live in the little house on Victor Street. I called my mother and told her we had found Emily's journal. She decided that Grandmother must have inherited it from her mother, and she, my grandma, had boxed it up in the attic."

Ana Lea walked over and sat on his bed and hugged him. "As far as the vortex is concerned, we control it, and you and I are aware of its dangers, but what will the future bring? Who can say?"

"I can think of a partial solution. We can write and leave a journal of our own." He took her hand in his. "We'll write it together."

THE END

www.ingramcontent.com/pod-product-compliance
Lightning Source LLC
LaVergne TN
LVHW040140080526
838202LV00042B/2969